"W-What are you doing?" Hannah gasped.

As she'd reached for her mascara, Nick had pulled off his T-shirt. Now she stared, openmouthed, at his bare-chested reflection in the bathroom mirror.

Nick's expression was carefully blank. "We don't have much time before we meet your mother. I was going to shower so we wouldn't be late. Unless, of course, I'm bothering you."

Hannah forced herself to concentrate on darkening her eyelashes. If her hired husband didn't mind getting naked in front of her, she refused to mind watching. "Be my guest."

She calmly reminded herself that she knew what the male form looked like.

Which didn't stop her from nearly poking herself in the eye when Nick dropped his briefs.

Heat rippled through her belly, making her thighs quake.

Dressed, Nick Archer was handsome enough to take her breath away.

Naked...he was borderline illegal!

D0047825

Dear Reader,

May is a time of roses, romance...and Silhouette Special Edition! Spring is in full bloom, and love is in the air for all to enjoy. And our lineup for this month reflects the wonder of spring. Our THAT SPECIAL WOMAN! title, *Husband by the Hour,* is a delightful spin-off of Susan Mallery's HOMETOWN HEARTBREAKERS series. It's the story of a lady cop finding her family... as well as discovering true love! And Joan Elliott Pickart continues her FAMILY MEN series this month with the frolicking *Texas Dawn*—the tale of a spirited career girl and a traditional Texas cowboy.

Not to be missed is Tracy Sinclair's warm and tender *Please Take Care of Willie.* This book is the conclusion to Tracy's CUPID'S LITTLE HELPERS series about matchmaking kids. And speaking of kids... *The Lady and the Sheriff* is Sharon De Vita's latest heartwarming installment of her SILVER CREEK COUNTY miniseries. This story features Louie, the kid who won readers' hearts!

May is also the month that celebrates Mother's Day. Cheryl Reavis has written a story that is sure to delight readers. Her FAMILY BLESSINGS series continues with *Mother To Be.* This story is about what happens when an irresistible force meets an immovable object...and deep, abiding love results.

Finally, we round off the month by welcoming historical author Barbara Benedict to Silhouette Special Edition. She makes her contemporary debut with the lighthearted *Rings, Roses...and Romance.*

I hope you have a wonderful month of May!

Sincerely,

Tara Gavin,
Senior Editor

Please address questions and book requests to:
Silhouette Reader Service
U.S.: 3010 Walden Ave., P.O. Box 1325, Buffalo, NY 14269
Canadian: P.O. Box 609, Fort Erie, Ont. L2A 5X3

SUSAN MALLERY

HUSBAND BY THE HOUR

SPECIAL EDITION®

Published by Silhouette Books
America's Publisher of Contemporary Romance

To my readers—with heartfelt thanks
for the wonderful support

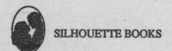

SILHOUETTE BOOKS

ISBN 0-373-24099-6

HUSBAND BY THE HOUR

Copyright © 1997 by Susan W. Macias

SUSAN MALLERY

lives in Southern California where the eccentricities of a writer are considered fairly normal. Her books are reader favorites and bestsellers, with recent titles appearing on the Waldenbooks bestseller list and the *USA Today* bestseller list. Her 1995 Special Edition title, *Marriage on Demand*, was awarded "Best Special Edition" by *Romantic Times* magazine. Susan shares her life with her charming husband and her two beautiful-but-not-bright cats. Susan enjoys hearing from readers. You may write to her directly at P.O. Box 4188, Costa Mesa, CA 92626.

Chapter One

"You need to get out of town," Captain Rodriguez said.

Nick Archer leaned back in his chair and rubbed his temple. "You think I don't know that? Easier said than done."

He was lying. Leaving wasn't so hard. He'd done it a million times. He just left. What held him back this time was the fact that he couldn't think of a single place to go. Hell of a situation for a man to find himself in.

Rodriguez turned toward his computer terminal and touched a few buttons. "They're getting closer, Nick. If they blow your cover, you're dead in less than four hours. Southport Beach is too small to keep you safe. Leave the city. Leave Southern California."

"Yeah, I will." Just as soon as he figured out where he was going. May was a nice month just about anywhere. Maybe Vegas. He could get real lost there and not surface for days. "I'll let you know when I get there," he continued. "And I'll make sure I'm close to a phone."

"Good idea," the captain said. Concern drew his mouth straight. "You've risked it all for this assignment, Nick. Just give it a few more days. A couple of weeks at most. By then the Feds will have what they need and we can issue the arrest warrants. By the end of the month, you'll be back at the Santa Barbara Police Department."

"Great."

Nick had been undercover for over a year. It was difficult to imagine returning to Santa Barbara and picking up the threads of his life. After a year, how much of a life would he have to pick up?

He stood and walked to the door. When he pulled it open, the captain frowned and said in a voice loud enough to carry, "If you want Pentleman out of jail, you're going to have to spring for bail. This time, we're not cutting a deal."

Pentleman was a small-time crook picked up for robbery earlier this morning. He was one of Nick's "employees" and had given him an excuse to come to the station and talk to Rodriguez. Only his captain back in Santa Barbara, Rodriguez here in Southport Beach and the FBI agent coordinating the sting knew Nick's real identity. The rest of the world considered him a successful criminal.

Nick gave the captain a mock salute and headed for the front desk. He would make Pentleman's bail, then leave town. The issue of where to go nagged at him until he saw Hannah Pace coming off her shift. She spoke to the young officer taking her place at the communications console. As she turned to step into the corridor, she spotted Nick. Her eyes narrowed in annoyance.

Nick jogged the last couple of steps to catch up with her. She was tall, nearly five-ten, with long legs and an awkward grace that made him think about foals loping through pastures. At six foot four, he could easily match her stride, which he did. She ignored him. It was a ritual between them. One he enjoyed more than he wanted to admit.

"Hey, beautiful, you off work?"

"Obviously." The single word was clipped.

She didn't look at him, not even when he put his arm around her shoulders and hugged her close. She simply grabbed his wrist and let it fall behind her. Nick took advantage of the position to pat her curvy rear. That earned him a quick glare.

"I'm armed," she said, heading for the side door and the officers' parking lot. "And I'm not afraid to use it on low-life scum like you."

"Hannah, you've got me all wrong. I respect you."

"Yeah, right. What does that mean? You don't expect to pay for sex with me?"

He winced audibly and pressed a hand to his chest. "I'm deeply wounded."

She pulled open the door and stepped outside. Warm air, smelling of sea and sunshine, enveloped them. The sky was clear and California blue. If he'd bothered glancing out at the ocean, he would have been able to see all the way to Catalina. But he doubted any view was lovelier than the woman in front of him.

Hannah paused, inhaled deeply and stared up at him. Her eyes were big and brown, the color of milk chocolate. He'd always had a thing for chocolate. Apparently, he also had a thing for women in uniform, although he hadn't realized that until he'd seen Hannah in hers. There was something about a sensibly cut garment hugging the female form that got his blood hot and his body bothered. Only it wasn't just any female form; it was very specifically Hannah's.

"What do you want, Nick?"

The defensiveness was gone. She sounded tired. He looked closer and saw shadows under her eyes. Thick, shiny, dark hair had been pulled back into a prim bun. Not even one tendril escaped to taunt him. Yet the thought of releasing her heavy hair, of running his fingers through the loose strands, made his fingers itch.

"Let me buy you a drink," he said and gave her his best grin. It usually worked. He'd used it on countless women before and had been successful enough to make his friends grumble. The only person who seemed immune was Hannah. For a year she'd ignored his teasing, his compliments, his lines and his invitations. He suspected she viewed him as a life-form only slightly higher than a cockroach.

She stared at him a long time. "You don't give up, do you?"

His grin turned wicked. "On you? Never."

"Why? What is so appealing about me?"

Her question caught him off guard. Normally she just rolled her eyes and kept on walking.

"I like how you keep your desk organized. All those piles are always tidy."

She shook her head. "Just as I thought. You're nothing more than a schoolboy defying authority."

Before she could leave, he placed his hand on her forearm. Her uniform had short sleeves, and he could feel the warmth of her skin and the slight tremor that rippled through her.

"It's more than that, Hannah." He leaned close and, with his free hand, touched his index finger to the corner of her mouth. "I like how your lips always turn up a little, even when you're mad. Like now."

She stepped back and pulled her arm free of his touch. "I'm not mad, I'm impatient."

"Impatient?" He raised an eyebrow. "I like that. Impatient. Could a little of that impatience be because you're tempted?"

"Oh, grow up," she said and headed toward the parking lot.

"I've been a man a long time, Hannah Pace. Don't tell me you haven't noticed, because I've caught you looking."

That made her stumble. She spun toward him. "I've never looked."

He moved closer and lowered his voice. "Sure you have. Lots of times. You think I'm a good-looking charmer."

"I think you're a thief and a swindler and Lord knows what else."

He stared down at her flashing dark eyes. "I knew you'd been thinking about me."

"Damn," she muttered, then drew in a long breath. "How do you always win?"

"Because you think I'm teasing, but I'm telling the truth."

Amazingly enough, he was. He meant every word he said to her. He *did* think she was beautiful and funny and smart and all the other lines he'd spoken over the past year. Hannah would never believe him, which made them safe to say. Sometimes, though, he wondered what the cool, self-contained lady would think if she knew his attraction was surprisingly genuine.

She blinked at him uncomprehendingly. He took advantage of her confusion and placed his arm around her shoulders again. "The thing is," he told her, "you've never given me a chance. I'm not nearly as bad as you think I am. Or maybe I am and that's what tempts you the most. One drink. What would it hurt?"

As he spoke, he led her toward his midnight blue Mercedes convertible. It was one of the perks of his assignment. Of course, a flashy car wasn't going to be much good to him if he ended up dead. A couple more weeks and the job would be finished. Then he could go back to his regular life and Nick Archer would be no more.

He paused in front of the passenger side and pulled out his keys from his pants pocket.

Hannah stared at the car. "Is it stolen?"

"If I say no, will you say yes?"

"Is it?"

He grinned. "I've got the title in the glove box. Want to check it out?"

He opened the door and motioned to the pale gray leather seat. He fully expected Hannah to slap him across the face, call him several obscene names and stalk back to her sensible sedan parked on the other side of the lot. He even stiffened in anticipation of the blow.

The blow came in a completely different form.

Shock. Mind-numbing shock when she muttered, "I'm insane," and slipped inside his car.

Nick carefully closed the passenger door and swore under his breath. Just his luck. The ice queen decided to thaw the day he had to get out of town.

Hannah touched her tongue to the rim of her glass and let the salt dissolve in her mouth. With a quick prayer that she wouldn't choke—or worse—she picked up the shot of tequila sitting next to her margarita glass and downed it in one long, burning swallow.

Fire ripped through her. She gasped out loud but didn't cough, then blinked back the tears that sprang to her eyes. Better, she thought, relieved as the fire turned to an almost comfortable heat.

"You all right?" Nick asked, frowning faintly.

"Fine," she managed to reply, her voice only slightly raspy from the alcohol.

He leaned back against the red booth seat. "You win this round, Hannah. I never guessed you did shooters."

She shrugged as if to say there was a lot about her he didn't know. Actually, he didn't know anything about her, but he *had* been right about the shooters. She'd never had one before tonight. And probably wouldn't again, she reflected as a wave of alcohol rushed to her brain and made the room tilt slightly. Normally she limited herself to a single drink. White wine, or maybe a spritzer. If it was a special occasion, she might indulge in a glass of champagne. Not today. She was on her second margarita and had ordered extra shots with both.

What was the phrase? Dutch courage? She needed her share of that, plus as much as she could get from any other source that offered it. If she did what she was thinking, it was going to take every ounce of bravery she'd ever had. If she didn't, she was going to break an old woman's heart. Talk about being between a rock and a hard place. Sometimes life wasn't fair.

The cocktail waitress strolled by. "Can I get you two something else?"

She asked the question of both of them, but her attention clearly focused on Nick. Hannah couldn't blame the woman. She often had trouble noticing anyone else when he was around. It was as if the whole world was dark and Nick was the only light. The fact that the waitress noticed, too, only meant the other woman had good taste.

Hannah resisted the urge to drop her head to her hands and moan. She was more drunk than she realized if she'd started thinking positive things about Nick Archer. He was nothing more than a common criminal. Oh, he hadn't been arrested for anything…at least, none of the charges had stuck. He had a clean record. But she knew the type. He was smooth. Too smooth for someone like her.

"Hannah?" Nick motioned to her half-empty glass.

She waved him off and he dismissed the waitress. The busty blonde gave him a quick smile. Funny, he didn't seem to notice.

"But she's beautiful," Hannah blurted out, then covered her mouth too late to hold in the words.

Nick frowned. That was twice in as many minutes. She liked how his eyebrows drew so close together. His forehead got all wrinkly, then when he relaxed, it smoothed out again.

"Who's beautiful?" he asked.

She'd almost forgotten her statement, so it took her a second to figure out what he was asking. "The waitress."

He didn't even look over toward the bar to find the woman in question. "If you say so."

"You didn't think she was pretty?"

"I didn't notice."

"Sure."

Boy, next he would be telling her about some oceanfront property he had in Arizona. All he needed was the Big One to push California into the ocean. Only California wouldn't fall into the ocean during an earthquake. The tectonic plates were pushing north. Eventually, Los Angeles and San Francisco would be within commuting distance. It would only take a couple million years to accomplish.

"I liked geography," she said. "So you can keep your oceanfront property."

"Excuse me?"

He looked puzzled. Genuinely flummoxed. Hannah smiled. At least, it felt like she was smiling. It was hard to tell. Her lips were numb. Flummoxed. She repeated the word in her mind. It was a good word with a nice sound. She should try to work it into a sentence more often.

"Hannah?"

She glanced at Nick. He was staring at her. "What?"

"What do you mean 'what?' Why are you talking about geography?"

"I'm not."

"But you said..." He shook his head. "You're drunk. I can't believe it. On a margarita and a half. Talk about a lightweight."

"I had shooters," she reminded him, then wondered if she should protest his statement that she was drunk. Of course she was. And there was that pesky numb feeling creeping from her lips to her cheeks. "It's your fault," she muttered.

"Mine? Why?"

"You're always there." She took another sip of her drink. "Talking to me. Asking me out. Why'd you have to do that?"

"Maybe I like you."

"Oh, sure." He liked her. Yeah, right. No doubt. Average-looking female police officers were every man's fantasy. She must get a hundred offers a day.

"You don't believe me." It wasn't a question.

"Why should I?"

His mouth curved into a slow smile. She felt the impact all the way down to her toes. He was sinfully handsome with big eyes the color of midnight blue. Thick lashes, sort of a medium brown and tipped with gold. Gold blond hair, layered and just to the top of his collar. Broad shoulders, great body, at least what she'd been able to see of it under his expensive suits. Despite being a criminal, Nick dressed like a corporate executive. He was funny, although she always tried hard not to laugh at his jokes. He was a smooth talker, charming and way out of her league. She knew better than to believe anything he might try to tell her.

He leaned forward and touched the back of her hand. It

was just one finger barely stroking her skin. Her cheeks were completely numb, she couldn't feel her legs at all, yet that single touch burned through her like a laser through steel.

She told herself to pull away, or at least to slap him real hard. She did nothing but stare at his finger, at his hand, at their hands so close together. Then her chest got tight and she had to remind herself to breathe.

"What's wrong, Hannah?"

"Nothing."

"Bull. I know you, and something's wrong."

The assurance in his voice made her nervous. She withdrew her hand to her lap and took another sip of the margarita. Then she glanced around the room and tried to see if anyone she knew was in the bar. It wasn't likely. The cops at the station had their own hangout and it wasn't this trendy beachfront establishment. She and Nick were in a back corner booth with a view of the ocean to her right. The sun was just setting, sending shards of yellow and gold light across the calm sea. It was a picture-perfect moment, complete with the handsome, albeit slightly blurry escort.

"You don't know me at all," she said.

"I know that you don't trust me, so why'd you accept my invitation for a drink?"

"Maybe your charm won me over."

He laughed out loud. The pleasant sound brought a smile to her lips. "Try again," he said.

He wasn't the only thing that was blurry, she realized. The edges of the room were starting to fold in on themselves. When was the last time she'd been this drunk? Once, at a friend's wedding, she recalled hazily, trying to remember exactly when. Maybe five years ago.

Why had she come out with Nick? She ignored the shifting room and thought about his question. Because he'd asked her out about twice a week for a year and every single time she'd wanted to say yes.

It was dumb for a woman like her to be attracted to a man like him. It wasn't just that he was so much better-looking, or even that he was a criminal and she was a cop. It was that Nick lived life on a completely different level than she did. He got into the moment while she walked around with her head down. He was spontaneous laughter, spontaneous fun, spontaneous sex—oops, where had that thought come from?—while she planned everything out. He joked and teased while she kept the world at bay.

"I needed a break," she said at last, mostly because it was true.

"Something tells me that's just an excuse. You're using me to put off something you don't want to do."

Her head snapped up. Big mistake. The slight blurring became a wild spinning. Even her seat seemed to be moving. Then she sucked in some air and it all slowed to a manageable level.

"Maybe," she admitted.

Her hands were once again on the table. He reached across and grabbed one. His thumb brushed against the back of her fingers. It felt nice.

"I need a husband," she blurted out.

To his credit, Nick didn't withdraw, or even stiffen. His thumb kept moving back and forth, back and forth. A lethargic heat crept up her arm. His gaze continued to hold hers, the half smile still hovering at the corners of his mouth. Maybe he hadn't heard her. Maybe she hadn't actually said it out loud.

"A husband?" he asked calmly. "The usual reason?"

"Usual reason? What's that?" She thought for a second. "Oh. Oh! Ah, no, not that. I mean, I'm not pregnant."

Embarrassment flooded her and she gulped the rest of

her drink. She thought about flagging down the waitress for another, then decided she was going to be sick enough in the morning as it was. Besides, Nick was still on his first beer and he'd barely touched it at all.

"Good."

She blinked. What were they talking about? "Good what?"

"I'm glad you're not pregnant."

"Me, too. Oh, the husband thing." She waved her free hand. "I have some family business. It requires me to be married for a few days. I don't know. Maybe not. Maybe I should just come clean. But she's so old. What if the shock kills her?" She stared at him earnestly. "I really wouldn't want that to happen. I haven't actually even met her, but I want to. Do you think she'll understand?"

"Yes."

She had a brief moment of clarity. "You don't have a clue as to what I'm talking about, do you?"

"Nope. But I like the sound of your voice, so just keep talking."

She realized he was still stroking her fingers with his thumb. Regretfully, she pulled free of the seductive contact. If only it was true. If only Nick Archer really *did* think she was a hot babe.

Hannah giggled. She was athletic, strong, and she wore a pistol when she went to work. Somehow she didn't think she fitted the definition of the word *babe*.

He toyed with her because it amused him and probably because she hadn't fallen at his feet the first time she'd seen him. She would have fallen, but she'd already been sitting down, so it had been easy to pretend to be calm.

"You could hire a husband," he said. "If it's only temporary."

"Oh, it is. Just for a few days. Believe me, I've thought

about it and I could phone..." She glared at him. "You're laughing at me."

"Only a little. So what kind of guy would you ask for, Hannah? Who's your ideal man?"

The numbness spread up her face, although strangely enough, she could actually feel her eyelashes.

Him. He was perfect, at least physically. But she wasn't about to say that. She would have to be a whole lot drunker than this to confess that little secret to Nick.

"Someone who follows the rules," she said.

He winced as if she'd slapped him. "That one hurt. Are you implying I'm not a rule follower?"

"You're a common criminal."

"I might be a criminal, but I've never been common." He leaned back in the booth. "How long do you need the guy for?"

"Three or four days. Just to drive north, meet my family, then come back."

"Sounds simple enough. What does it pay?"

"Why do you ask?"

He held out both hands, palms up. "You could never phone an escort service to hire someone and we both know it. Call the interest a friendly gesture on my part."

"But we're not friends," she muttered, then cleared her throat. Nick? A temporary husband? She shuddered. It would never work.

"How much?" he asked. When she stared at him blankly, he asked, "How much are you willing to pay?"

"I'm not sure. I haven't thought about money." What was the going hourly rate for fake husbands these days? "It doesn't matter. You're not right for this. I'm sorry I mentioned it."

She started to slide out of the booth, but it was harder to move than she thought it would be. Then he placed his hand over hers and that darn heat started up again, and she didn't want to move.

"I'm happy to help," he said. "I need to get out of town for a few days anyway."

"Oh, I'll just bet you do. What is it this time? A real-estate deal gone wrong? Or maybe the husband of one of your women decided to take matters into his own hands."

Nick stared at her for a long time. Something flickered in his gaze, something dark and secretive. Then he blinked and it was gone. "You wouldn't believe me if I told you," he said lightly. "Face it, Hannah. Where else are you going to find a man willing to pretend to be your husband on such short notice?"

He was right. She certainly didn't have the skills to seduce a man into doing it, nor was there a man around. Except for Nick. Not that she was interested in seducing Nick.

She hunched over, half expecting lightning to strike. When it didn't, she straightened. She could do worse. At least he was gorgeous. And he thought on his feet. If anyone started asking questions, Nick would be able to ward them off. It was only for a couple of days and it wasn't as if she was overflowing with other options.

"I'll pay two hundred dollars and the travel expenses," she said, then nearly bit her tongue in her haste to call the words back. But it was too late.

He raised his eyebrows. "I was thinking more of a trade. One weekend of husbanding for one night of—"

She raised her hand. "Don't say it."

"Passionate lovemaking," he finished.

She winced. "Four hundred, in cash. No touching."

"Let's spend the weekend negotiating. When do you want to leave?"

Was there really a choice? Despite all her talk, she would

never have been able to call an escort service. Wasn't bringing Nick along better than breaking an old woman's heart? "In the morning. I want to be there on Saturday."

"Where is there?"

"Northern California."

He held out his hand. "Do we have a deal?"

She wished she had another shot to give her courage. She wished she'd never mentioned it in the first place. She wished she'd never gotten in his car.

But wishing didn't change anything and he was her best bet. That's probably why she was here, having a drink with him. The power of the subconscious mind at work.

She slipped her hand in his and they shook. The contact was electric. She expected to see smoke and fire, but there was only Nick smiling at her. Enjoying her predicament and having power over her at last.

And he did have power. Comparing his power to the power of the subconscious mind was like comparing an eighteen-wheeler to a toy truck. She had a bad feeling she had just stepped in front of headlights and was about to be mowed down.

Chapter Two

Hannah stared at the front door. She didn't want to open it. Not only because her head hurt and the thought of sunlight was enough to bring tears to her eyes, but also because she didn't want to face the man on the other side.

Insanity. There was no other explanation. Maybe it ran in her family. She'd been adopted, so there was no way to tell. Or maybe her blood sugar had dipped below the normal range and she'd had a brief blackout episode. Whatever the explanation, she didn't have the guts to face him and accept what they'd agreed to do.

He knocked again. "Hannah? Are you awake?"

"Yes," she whispered even though she knew he couldn't hear her. She cleared her throat and spoke more loudly. "I'm right here. Hold on."

She turned the key in the dead-bolt lock and pulled open the door. Nick stood on the front step of her town house. The sunlight made her blink, as did Nick. It wasn't fair.

Even in her weakened condition—with her head pounding and her stomach rolling—he looked good. Better than good. He looked tempting.

She was used to being impressed by his sheer male beauty. He was a California cliché with his blond hair, blue eyes and loose, easy stride. The well-made suits he wore only enhanced his assets. If he had any physical flaws, she'd never noticed. She'd gotten used to ignoring his good looks, his tailored clothing, his bright smile. They were meaningless trappings that merely concealed the flaws in his character. She was immune.

Well, unless she had a hangover. She stood in the doorway and reminded herself to breathe. In and out, in and out until the involuntary function kicked back in on its own. He wasn't wearing a suit, or handmade shoes, or even a tie. Instead, he'd dressed in jeans and a plain white shirt with sleeves rolled up to the elbows. His boots looked worn. But the smile was just as devastating as it always had been. Thank the Lord she could blame her weak knees on her hangover.

"You look awful," he said cheerfully and pushed past her into the town house. "Hangover?"

"No," she murmured between clenched teeth. The volume of his voice made her head ache. "I feel fine."

"Uh-huh." He moved in front of her, shoved his hands into his pockets and rocked back on his heels. "I can tell. Are you packed?"

"Yes."

It wasn't only the effects of the alcohol that were slowing her down. It was also lack of sleep. At four in the morning, her eyes had popped open. Despite how awful she felt, or perhaps because of it, she hadn't been able to get back to sleep. She'd stared at the ceiling alternately praying that her memories about their evening together had been a dream, then hoping they were real.

"Did you take anything?" he asked. "Aspirin?"

She nodded, then wished she hadn't actually moved her head.

His smile was sympathetic. "You're such a straitlaced person, I doubt I could talk you into trying the hair of the dog, right?"

She stared at his face, at the wide blue eyes, the straight nose that should have been broken countless times but obviously hadn't been. At the strong mouth, stubborn chin, the freshly shaved, tanned skin. He was gorgeous. It wasn't fair.

His being nice to her only made it worse, she thought miserably as her stomach churned again. She hated when people tried to take care of her. She knew what was going on. They wanted to lull her into trusting them, then they would leave. She wasn't about to play that game again.

"I'm fine," she snapped and took a step back. "And I'm ready to go."

"Great."

She sucked in a deep breath, grabbing hold of the front door when dizziness threatened. "Where's my car?"

"In the carport."

That's what she'd been afraid of. Her recollections of the end of the evening were fuzzy at best. She did remember Nick telling her she was way too drunk to drive and her agreeing with him about that. So instead of taking her back to the police station to collect her car, he'd brought her home. She vaguely recalled he'd promised to have her car delivered to her town house carport. Simple enough...except for one small problem.

She reached up toward the keys hanging from the lock

in the front door. She found her car key and tugged on it gently. "You didn't have a car key," she said.

His sympathetic smile broadened and she nearly lost her balance. "I know. I asked one of my associates to take care of it. You probably don't want to ask too many questions."

She squeezed her eyes shut. Nick was right. Questions— or rather, answers—would only make her uncomfortable. She didn't want to think about the ramifications of someone breaking into and then hot-wiring her car, all while it sat in a police department parking lot.

"Do I have to worry about this person joyriding in my car?" she asked, opening her eyes and looking at him. "It wasn't used in a drive-by shooting or anything, was it?"

He touched his hand to his chest. "I'm wounded. You talk as if I'm a thug. Hannah, I'm in real estate. I'm willing to admit a few of my employees are a little..." He paused.

"Creative in their dealings with the law?" she offered.

"Exactly. But my record is clean. You've seen that for yourself."

"Right."

She'd also seen him in the station bailing his associates out of jail. Only a madwoman would take Nick Archer to meet her mother. A really desperate madwoman.

"You're not having second thoughts, are you?" he asked.

"Oh, no." That was true. She was up to fifth or sixth thoughts. She opened her mouth to tell him that and to let him know that this was never going to work, but instead, she motioned to her luggage. "I'm packed."

In her weakened condition, she was willing to admit she wanted to spend a few hours in his company and discover the man behind the smooth facade. Crazy, certainly. He was a criminal and she was cop. She should loathe and despise him. And she did. Sort of. She also had to admit—if only to herself—that Nick's charm was hard as hell to resist. The way he made her laugh felt nice.

He moved toward her luggage. *I'm doing this for you, Mom,* she thought and hoped it was the right thing to do. A dying old woman expected Hannah to have a husband. Was it so very wrong to allow her to think one really existed?

Nick grabbed two of the suitcases. "This is a lot for a weekend."

"I'm not going for a weekend."

"You said a couple of days."

"That's right. You're staying with me for a couple of days, but I'll be staying for two weeks."

He raised his eyebrows and managed a hurt expression. "You're going on vacation and didn't tell me? Hannah, that's so insensitive."

She wanted to laugh, but he looked amazingly sincere. Yet he couldn't be. This was a game of some kind. She was too befuddled to figure it out right now, but when her hangover wore off, she was sure everything would make sense.

"Nice place," he said, nodding toward the living room on his left.

She glanced at the floral-print sofa, the white brick fireplace and the pale pine coffee table. What did her place look like to him? Everything was tidy. The colors were bright, definitely feminine. He probably sensed a man had never spent the night under her roof. The thought embarrassed her, although she wasn't sure why. It was none of his business. So what if she chose not to sleep around? In this day and age, anything but caution was foolish.

He headed out the front door. She picked up the remaining suitcase and followed him. After carefully turning off the lights and securing the lock, she moved down the two steps to his Mercedes parked at the curb.

Thankfully, the convertible top was up. She wouldn't have been able to face all that fresh air. Just the thought made her head ache more. Intellectually, she knew the car had been paid for with illegally obtained funds. It might even have been stolen, although Nick was probably smarter than that. It was more than she could ever afford and it was stunning. Even knowing where it had come from, she couldn't help admiring the beautiful lines.

She remembered the interior smelled of fine leather and the seats were a luxurious combination of softness and sup-port. The car was going to make the nine-hour drive seem like four.

She set her suitcase on the sidewalk beside the open trunk. Nick moved his garment bag to make room for the last piece of luggage. She watched to make sure everything was stowed in the car, then moved to the passenger door. It was locked and she had to wait for him to open it.

He did so, then paused. "You look pale."

"Gee, thanks." Her headache had increased until the throbbing sounded like drums beating in time with her heart.

"It was that second shot. You would have been fine if you hadn't had it."

She wanted to yell at him that it was all his fault. If he hadn't made her order the drink... But she couldn't. He hadn't made her do anything. She'd been nervous and had acted stupidly all on her own. Still, it would have been satisfying to get all huffy at Nick.

When she slid into the seat, he crouched beside her and made sure she was comfortable, with the seat belt adjusted correctly. She bore his attention for about twenty seconds, then slapped his hands away. "I'm not an invalid. I can do this on my own."

He was close enough that she could inhale the masculine scent of his aftershave and see the clean, smooth line of his jaw. Damn him for looking so good and damn herself for being so nasty for no good reason.

"I know you're not an invalid," he said quietly. "You don't feel well. I'm trying to make you comfortable. It's going to be a long drive."

Hannah prided herself on her control. She was a cop and she knew how to act in a crisis. Unfortunately, her hard-won skills seemed to have deserted her for the moment. She opened her mouth, couldn't think of anything to say, then clamped her lips together as a blush crawled up her cheeks.

She ducked her head and stared at her lap. "Sorry. I'm not myself this morning."

"Then who are you?"

His teasing made her smile. She glanced at him. He was staring at her as if he'd never seen her before. She rubbed her cheek, trying to brush off a smudge, then checked for loose strands floating free of her braid. Everything was in place.

"What's wrong?" she asked.

"Nothing. I was just thinking."

But he never said what he was thinking. Right there, with her sitting in the passenger seat of his car and him crouched next to her, in front of whichever of her neighbors might be home and watching, in front of God and the whole world, he kissed her.

He leaned forward and pressed his mouth against hers. Shock kept her in place for the first three seconds. She couldn't think, she couldn't move. She could only let her eyes flutter closed as she absorbed the heat and scent of him.

His lips were warm and firm, yielding, yet strong. He didn't try to move much, or deepen the kiss. They touched nowhere else, at least not at first.

Then she felt his fingers on the back of her hand. A sweet, gentle stroking that sent fire racing up her arm. The pounding of her headache receded, as did the rest of the world.

He released her, raising his head slightly. She nearly moaned in disappointment. She told herself to get all upset and complain, to unfasten the seat belt, slide out of the car and slap him until his head bobbed like one of those toy dogs in the back of cars. She told herself a lot of things, all the while waiting for him to kiss her again, or worse, to mock her.

What he did was even more devastating. He cupped her cheek with his free hand and murmured, ''Sweet Hannah.'' As if she really meant something to him. As if this wasn't a joke.

He leaned forward. She held her breath in anticipation. He covered her mouth with his and this time he moved. Back and forth, slow and sweet. As if they had all the time in the world. As if his legs weren't cramping, which she knew they had to be. As if she was a delicate and precious person in his life.

Maybe it was the unexpected tenderness, or the hangover, or some weird placement of the moon and the planet Pluto. She didn't have an explanation for her reaction, or for the fact that she leaned into the kiss and parted her mouth slightly in response.

Instead of deepening the kiss, he placed his hands on her shoulders and squeezed. For the first time in her life, she felt small and fragile. Delicate. Feminine.

Then the heat overwhelmed her, and all she could think about was how she wanted to keep kissing him forever. She could die happy right this moment.

At last he straightened. Hannah stared at him dumbfounded. Questions formed, everything from why had he kissed her to had he liked it as much as she had. But she didn't ask any of them. Instead, she swallowed hard and tried to summon up some fury. Barring that, she wouldn't mind going with a little righteous indignation. If Nick started teasing her, she would need something for protection. Right now, she felt very exposed.

He started to close the passenger door, then paused and leaned toward her again.

"Ten bucks," he said.

"Huh?"

He winked. "The kiss. It was worth ten bucks."

"I don't understand." He wanted money for kissing her?

"We agreed on four hundred dollars for the weekend. The kiss was worth ten bucks to me, so now you only owe me three hundred and ninety." He started to close the door, then paused again. "In cash...or trade."

Before she could say anything, he slammed the door shut and came around to the driver's side. Hannah couldn't bring herself to look at him. She stared straight ahead and wondered what on earth she'd gotten herself into.

Nick didn't say anything as he started the engine. He selected a classical station on the radio, then pulled out and headed for the freeway.

She leaned back in the seat. Her lips still tingled. Ten bucks. The kiss was worth that and more. Originally, Nick had wanted a night of hot sex in exchange for helping her out. She'd been the one to insist on cash. Maybe, just maybe, she'd been a bit hasty in her decision.

* * *

By nine, they'd reached the northern outskirts of Los Angeles County. Nick pulled off Interstate 5 in the bedroom community of Valencia and they got coffee at a drive-through fast-food place. When they returned to the freeway, Hannah sipped the steaming hot liquid and wondered for the four thousandth time what on earth she'd been thinking. Was she crazy?

To make matters worse, Nick could read her mind. Just as she was starting up another litany berating herself, he asked, "Why are you doing this? What's so important that you have to pretend to be married?"

She took another sip and pondered the question. Easy enough—except she didn't really want to have to tell him the truth.

He glanced at her and quirked up one eyebrow. "You probably think I'm just being nosy, but the truth is I need some background information so I can get into my role. I'm more of a method actor. You know, feel the part and all that."

Despite her apprehension, she smiled. "That makes sense. Okay, I'll fill you in, but I have to warn you. It's a long, boring story."

"No problem. This is a long, boring drive."

He'd always had a good sense of humor. That's one of the things she liked about him. Not that she really liked him or anything. Oh, yeah, she thought, wondering if lightning would strike the sleek car. She didn't like him and she wasn't attracted to him. That's why she'd invited him to be a part of her life for the next three days and why she'd kissed him back.

At the station, he'd been a lot easier to ignore, but now no one else was around to see. She could lighten up a little. It wasn't as if she was getting involved with Nick. She knew exactly who and what he was. No matter how charming and funny, he still lived on the wrong side of the law.

"My birth mother gave me up for adoption," she said and glanced out at the low mountains around them. They were climbing out of the Santa Clarita Valley, heading north toward Glenwood. "A few months ago, I received a letter from her."

"Your real mom?"

"Yeah."

He glanced at her. "Without warning? That must have kicked up your heart rate."

"I'll admit I walked around in a fog for days. I couldn't believe it. She'd hired a private detective to find me."

"Are you angry about it?"

Hannah was surprised at his perception. She shrugged. "I don't know. Sometimes. I seem to go through stages of curiosity, longing and rage. Right now I'm curious. I want answers. I guess most children who are given up for adoption have a lot of questions. What were the circumstances in my biological mother's life? Did she give me up right away, or did she keep me around for a while? Did she..." Did she love me?

Hannah didn't voice that, although it was always deep in her mind. That was the one question that plagued her the most. Had her birth mother cared about her at all? Had this been a callous gesture, the quick and easy way to get rid of a problem? Or had there been overriding forces at work, ripping an innocent child from her caring mother?

"Did she have second thoughts?" she said, completing the statement so Nick wouldn't get any ideas. She already regretted confiding in him.

"Had you tried to get in touch with her yourself?" he asked.

"No. I thought about it from time to time, but I never

knew what I was going to say if I found her. I figured if she'd wanted me in the first place, she would have kept me around."

"What do your adoptive folks say about this?"

"They died a long time ago." Hannah clutched the foam coffee cup in her hands. Twenty-three years ago. She'd been so young, she barely remembered them. She did remember being happy, though. Not just the occasional glad moment, but happy all the time.

"Any other family?" he asked.

"That's really none of your business."

"Right. I'm just the husband. Sorry, I forgot."

"It's not necessary for you to know every detail about my private life. I'm not trying to be difficult. I would simply prefer that you didn't pry."

"I'm sort of surprised you can walk as well as you do," he said.

She stared at him. "What do you mean?"

"It must be difficult, what with that giant chip on your shoulder. Most people would have to drag a leg behind them or something, just to keep balanced."

She didn't know whether to burst out laughing or slap him. "I do not have a chip on my shoulder."

"Yeah, right. You also don't keep the rest of the world away by pretending not to need anyone, either. Go on. You got this letter from your real mother. Then what happened?"

She was openmouthed at his assessment of her character. She wanted to protest that she didn't keep the world at bay. At least, not on purpose. It just sort of happened. She hadn't grown up the way everyone else had. After her adoptive parents had died, she'd never been a part of a family for any length of time. She'd been bounced around foster homes. She didn't know how to have several close friends, share pieces of her life, or even tell jokes. Socially, she was definitely at the dull-normal end of the range.

"Hannah? The letter?"

"Oh. Well, she found me by using a private detective. Apparently, all the records got messed up at the adoption agency. Plus, because I wasn't searching for her, they wouldn't give out any information they still had. Not that it would have helped, what with my parents dying."

"What does this have to do with me?" he asked. "Why do you need a husband?"

"Because when the detective located me, I was still married."

He turned his head and glared at her. "Married?" The outrage in his voice made her smile.

"Yes, married."

"Married?"

"Nick, watch the road. I want to get to Glenwood in one piece."

He returned his attention to the road and swore under his breath. "Dammit, Hannah, you didn't tell me you were married."

"Why are you acting like it matters?"

"Because it does."

"That's crazy. We don't even know each other."

"That's something a man likes to know before he pretends to be somebody's husband."

"Sorry. I'll remember that for next time."

He shook his head. "Married."

Her amusement turned to irritation. "I know it's hard for you to imagine this, but there are actually men who find me attractive. Amazingly, I did trap one into a committed relationship, at least for a short period of time."

She hadn't trapped Shawn, although the relationship had been a mistake from the beginning. They'd only been married five days. Even thinking about it made her embarrassed. It was a foolish episode from her past.

"How long have you been divorced?" he asked.

"About two months."

"Two months? You mean all this past year you were living with your *husband*?"

She sighed. "Why are you taking this so hard? You're acting like I've cheated on you. No, I wasn't living with my husband. We've been separated about four years. I just never bothered filing for divorce and neither did he. Until recently."

"What happened?"

"Nothing I want to discuss with you. The important point is that when the detective found me, I was still married. The letter from Louise—that's my biological mother—mentioned that she wanted to meet my husband."

"Why didn't you tell her the truth when you talked to her on the phone?"

The car glided over the paved highway. Hannah turned to her right and pretended interest in the billboards. "Well, one reason was that she said that she wanted us to get together while there was still time. I'm afraid she's very ill. I didn't want to upset her. She's an old woman. That's why I hired you. We show up together. I'm the long-lost daughter, you're my husband. We act pleasant. In a couple of days you get a business call and return to Southport Beach. When I'm sure she can handle it, I'll tell her the truth."

"Sounds pretty flaky to me."

"I don't recall asking your opinion."

"Hey, don't worry, babe. I'm not going to charge you extra for it. I've run plenty of scams in my time."

"I'm sure you have."

He winked. "Some of them have been legitimate."

"Want to give me a percentage?"

"Not really. The trick is to keep them as close to real as possible. You should have brought the ex with you. It would have been a lot easier."

"He wasn't available right now."

"Traveling on business?"

She wondered what Nick would say if she told him about Shawn. She could already hear the teasing remarks. Better to walk on broken glass and eat poisoned dung beetles for breakfast.

"You might say that."

"I might. What would you say?"

She sucked in a breath. "Shawn is working right now."

"Oh. Shawn. Let me guess. Some Ivy League type with three numbers after his name and a pedigree longer than the grand champion at a dog show."

She bit on her lower lip to keep from laughing. Please, God, never let Nick find out the truth. "Sort of."

Nick stewed over that for a while. She watched the mile markers zip by. Ten minutes later, he said, "You never finished answering my question. Why didn't you tell your mother the truth when you talked to her on the phone?"

She crossed her legs and folded her arms over her chest. "I haven't actually spoken with her on the phone. We've been writing letters."

"Why? Wouldn't it be easier to pick up the phone and call?"

"No, it wouldn't."

She half turned in the seat, facing away from him as much as the seat belt would allow. He couldn't understand her mixed emotions about what was happening. His life was so different from hers. Nick was one of those people who was blessed. He had good looks, charm, wit, a sharp mind. It was unfortunate he'd chosen to use his talents the way he had. If he'd been honest, he could have gone far.

It was different for her. She had to worry about things. She wasn't gifted. People thought she was so calm and composed, but she felt like a poster she'd once seen of a swan. Above the surface, the bird seemed to be gliding along, but underneath the water, where no one could see, its feet were working like crazy to keep up the facade.

From the time she'd lost her parents and been dumped in her first foster home, she realized that no one wanted her around. She couldn't remember the number of times she'd been told the state wasn't paying enough for the family to keep her for long. She'd lost track of the number of houses, apartments, schools she'd been in.

For a while, she'd wanted to fit in, to belong. She'd really tried. But her attempts hadn't been enough, or she'd done it the wrong way, because no one had noticed. Eventually, she stopped trying. Sometimes the people were nice enough, but she learned early on not to depend on anyone but herself. It was better not to care. Nothing ever lasted. Even when it seemed things were working out, she was always sent somewhere else.

She felt his hand on top of hers. She pushed him away.

"Hannah, honey, I know you're scared. But it's going to be okay."

"I'm not scared and you don't know it's going to be okay."

"Sure I do. I'm here. I'm going to make it work. You'll see."

She sniffed and ignored him. Cheap talk from someone used to buying whatever he wanted. Actually, she didn't know that about Nick; she was only assuming. But it was probably true.

Instead of taking the broad hint, he once again put his

hand on top of hers and squeezed gently. The comfort meant a lot to her, even though she didn't want to tell him. It would be too much like giving in. She was convinced that if she gave in—even a little—she would suffer for the rest of her life. So she held back. Resisted. Didn't say anything. She didn't trust Nick. She wasn't even sure she liked him.

But when he nudged her, she turned her hand over and let him lace his fingers through hers.

Chapter Three

Nick checked the rearview mirror. There was no one behind them but truckers and no one was going the speed limit. He touched a button on the cruise control panel, then glanced at Hannah. She was leaning against the passenger door, her head resting on the window. She'd been asleep for most of the morning.

He slipped a tape of classical music into the cassette player and kept the sound low. She didn't stir. He was glad. She obviously needed her rest. The shadows under her eyes weren't all from her hangover. No doubt the stress and worry about meeting her birth mother for the first time had kept her up nights.

Her color was better now, her breathing steady. Of course, her color wasn't quite as high as it had been when he'd kissed her.

He grinned at the memory. Kissing Hannah Pace was something he should have done a long time ago. Not only for the pleasure it had given him, but because it had left her speechless.

Oh, he'd thought about it. He couldn't be around Hannah for more than five minutes without thinking about kissing her and touching her. She was the kind of woman who lent herself to wicked thoughts—at least in his mind.

He'd wondered if she would resist the kiss and the heat it generated. Passion could be disconcerting if one was used to constantly being in control. He suspected Hannah prided herself on being in control. But she hadn't resisted or pretended not to respond. Even if he hadn't felt the clinging sweetness of her mouth, her fire-filled eyes and uneven breathing had given her away. Yup, kissing Hannah had been a great idea. He'd imagined it would be terrific, and the real thing had been better than any fantasy. He couldn't wait to do it a second time.

He checked on her again, but she was silent and still asleep. Was she dreaming? Was she worrying about what was going to happen? Did she regret her confession?

Hannah had been married. He thought he'd figured her out, but that piece of information had stunned him. Married. He swore under his breath. Why hadn't he known?

"Why does it matter?" he asked himself softly, then decided he didn't want to know the answer.

Married. To whom? Not a cop. She wouldn't have been able to keep that quiet. He would have heard about it— some kind of hint would have surfaced in the past year. He knew all about gossip at a police station. Everyone knew everyone else's business.

Who would Hannah have married and then divorced? A successful businessman with shady dealings? He grimaced. Hannah wasn't the type to get involved with a criminal. That's one of the things he liked best about her—her principles. Of course, those high standards meant she wasn't likely to give him the time of day.

He thought about the assignment he'd been working on. All the hours being alone, the danger, the tension. It was about to end. Just a few more days, maybe a couple of weeks.

He wondered what Hannah would say if he told her the truth. Would she like him more? Respect him? It didn't matter. Until the assignment was over, until the bad guys were in jail, he wasn't telling anyone anything. He wasn't going to risk all that time and effort. He wanted those guys caught.

So Hannah would continue to think he was a criminal and he would let her. Probably best for both of them.

An airline pilot with a girlfriend at every stop? Nick shook his head. He didn't like that scenario, either. He didn't want her ex-husband to have abused her, or cheated on her, or done anything illegal. But if the ex was so perfect, why had they divorced?

His stomach rumbled, reminding him it had been a long time since breakfast. He glanced at the billboards on either side of the multilane freeway, then took the next exit to a fast-food restaurant. He pulled in behind a battered pickup truck with two live caged chickens and a goat tied in the back. He glanced at Hannah. She stirred and blinked sleepily.

She had the best-behaved hair of anyone he knew. At the station she wore it in a bun at the back of her head. No matter what time he went by, whether it was the first five minutes of her shift or the last, every hair was in place. He'd never seen a strand sneak out to drift against her cheek or her neck.

Today she wore a thick braid down her back. Despite fighting a hangover and sleeping for the better part of four hours, she was perfectly groomed. He couldn't help wondering what she would look like all mussed up. Preferably naked, with her hair loose and her eyes heavy with passion.

The stirring in his groin made him shift uncomfortably. Think about something else, he ordered himself.

"Are you hungry?" he asked.

She glanced around. "No, but I should probably eat. Just a hamburger and soda, please."

"Sure." He pulled up to the microphone and placed their order.

"I've been asleep," she said. "You should have woken me."

"Why?"

"So I could spell you on the driving."

"I like to drive."

She leaned back in her seat. "Not surprising. It's a control thing. Men like to drive because it makes them feel in control."

"You learn that in Psych 101?"

"Are you denying it's true?"

"Nope. Just wondering where you got so smart."

One corner of her pretty mouth turned up slightly. "I figured it out all by myself."

"You can drive this afternoon." He wouldn't mind driving the whole way north, but as they got closer to Glenwood, she would get nervous. Driving would help distract her.

They collected their food and headed back on the road. Hannah handed him his burger and drink as he asked for it. He'd eaten in the car before, without help, but he liked her being attentive to him. Male vanity, he thought, grinning. She would probably slug him if she ever discovered what he was thinking.

They passed a sign showing the distances to San Jose,

Sacramento and the state line. He reached for his burger. She snatched it back.

"How fast have you been driving?" she demanded. "Were you speeding?"

"A little."

"More than a little. How fast were you going?"

"I'm not going to tell you." His voice was teasing. "Besides, this car was built for the open road. How could I resist?"

"You didn't even try."

"I try all the time with you, honey, and it doesn't do me a damn bit of good."

Her eyes widened, but she didn't speak. When he reached for his hamburger, she handed it to him, then faced front as if determined to ignore his presence.

He liked teasing her. He figured if he kept at it long enough, she would eventually lighten up. She had to. No one could be so uptight all the time. She might even find out he wasn't such a bad guy.

Perversely, he wanted her to like him for himself. He laughed silently. What a load of bull. If Hannah, or any woman, actually started to care about him, he would run so fast in the opposite direction, he would get road burn on his feet. Even if the thought of settling down tempted him on occasion, he preferred to travel light. If he was honest with himself, part of Hannah's appeal was that she was unreachable. She would never see him as anything but low-life scum.

He finished his burger and took another drink of soda. "Tell me more about your life," he said.

She collected their trash, transferring it all to one bag, then wiped her hands on a napkin. "It's really none of your business."

"You have to give me some personal information. I *am* going to be pretending to be your husband."

"You already know enough."

She made him work for every point. God, he adored her. "I know about the divorce, but that's not information you want spread around, right?"

She rolled her eyes. "Be serious, Nick. You're supposed to be my first and only husband. You know I was adopted, that I'm a cop. What else is there?"

"How about some information about your childhood? Your adoptive parents. Anything about them?"

She stared out the window. "I was too young to remember much. I don't want to talk about them."

"Okay. School. Your favorite subject."

"I don't remember. I don't think I had one. When I was moved around to different foster homes, I also had to change schools. I don't think this is necessary. It's not as if Louise is going to have a quiz after dinner and want you to recite details from my past."

He knew some of her crankiness came from nerves, but the rest of it was because they were treading close to dangerous territory. He knew all about the child welfare system. Some kids got lucky. Others, like Hannah, got passed around from place to place. He knew about growing up lonely and scared, too. He'd had one parent at home—his father. At times, he thought it would have been better if the old man had just kicked him out and let him make his own way.

Hannah twisted her hands together. Nick wanted to reach out to her, but sensed she wasn't in any mood to accept comfort. She was prickly, but the shell had to be hard to protect a soft heart. While the thought of her actually caring about him was terrifying, he could easily be concerned about *her*. It was safe because there wasn't a chance of it becoming real.

"You grew up in Los Angeles?" he asked.

"Orange County."

"College?"

"Yes, I went."

He smiled. "What did you major in?"

"Nick, none of this is important." She crossed and uncrossed her legs.

With a flash of insight, Nick figured it out. Hannah regretted confessing as much as she had to him. She wasn't used to sharing her life with anyone, let alone a man like him. She was afraid he would use the information against her. He wished he could reassure her, but doubted she would believe him. Besides, what was he supposed to say?

"I'm twenty-seven," she said. "A communications officer with the Southport Beach Police Department. I have brown hair and brown eyes. I think that's more than enough personal stuff, don't you?"

"Yeah. And I want to thank you for that revealing glance into your private life. We're going to be a completely believable couple."

She stared at him, wide-eyed. "Of course we will be. All you have to do is follow my lead. I'm a trained police officer. I know how to handle difficult situations. You're a professional con artist, used to thinking on your feet. This is going to be simple. The easiest scam you've ever pulled."

He knew what he was pretending to be. Her assumptions about him proved that his cover had been successful. Still, the remarks stung. As he concentrated on the road, he told himself he was getting too old for this line of work. When the job was finished, he was going to have to rethink his life.

* * *

Welcome To Glenwood.

Hannah stared at the sign and wondered if she was going to throw up. Her stomach, which had calmed down considerably in the afternoon, started acting up again. This time, it wasn't from the aftereffects of alcohol. It was nerves...and fear.

Nick pulled to the side of the road and turned off the engine. "What do you want to do? Find a hotel or find your mother?"

Her throat closed. She couldn't speak. Worse, she couldn't think. She opened her mouth. "I..." She drew in a breath and tried again. "The drive should have taken longer."

He brushed a finger against the side of her cheek. "I know. Sorry."

She shook her head. "It's not your fault." She'd had a turn at the wheel and discovered that his luxury car did make it amazingly easy to speed. "Give me a minute here. I'm not sure what to do." Her voice trembled. What had she been thinking when she decided to come up here? This was all a mistake.

Thoughts tumbled over and over in her mind. What to do? She glanced at Nick. He sat patiently waiting for her to decide. He'd been nice to her all day, even though she'd been difficult. She held back a sigh. She didn't mean to be callous and uncaring. Or so private it came across as paranoid. Even though it had been a lot of years, she had trouble letting go of the past. Trusting people was hard. Trusting someone like him was nearly impossible. But she must have, at least a little, or she wouldn't have brought him with her.

She rubbed her temples. She was putting off the inevitable. "Let's see if we can find my mother's street. If not, we'll check into a hotel and start again in the morning."

"No problem." He started the car and pulled back out on the main road.

Louise had sent directions to where she lived. Hannah pulled out her letter and clicked on the map light. "She rents a room," she said. "I'm guessing it's some kind of nursing home or retirement center. I don't know if that's going to be in a residential area or not."

"Depends on the zoning," Nick said.

She told him where to turn. They drove past a large park. In the twilight, she could just make out a pond with white ducks. Several families had come down to the sloping banks to enjoy the balmy May evening.

Families. Hannah felt a twinge in her chest. She'd been alone most of her life. That's what she was used to. Not depending on anyone. Now she had a mother. Would that change everything?

She spied a street sign. "Make a right here."

The residential area looked like something out of a television movie. Two-story houses with wide porches. Minivans in the driveways, bikes left on lawns. Shouts of laughter drifted into the car. Hannah felt her throat tighten. When Nick gave her hand a squeeze, she didn't push him away. Without wanting to admit it, even to herself, she took comfort in his presence.

They made another turn. The street got wider, the houses farther apart. Two-stories became three.

"Someone has money," she said.

"Maybe it's your mom." He grinned.

She smiled back. "Wouldn't you like that? You could get her involved in one of your land deals."

"Hey, people have made lots of money with me."

"Sure."

"I would never hurt your mother."

Oddly, she believed him.

"This is the street." Hannah stared at the houses, sure

something must be wrong. Louise couldn't live here, could she? It didn't make sense for one person. Maybe a large residence had been converted into apartments or something. "The address is 2301."

The car slowed to a crawl. "That one," Nick said, pointing to an especially large house.

In the gathering dusk, Hannah could just make out the shape of the peaked roof and wide porch. "It looks Victorian."

"Probably is. I think railroad barons first settled this part of the state. The houses might be restored."

There were so many cars in the driveway, there wasn't room for theirs. He pulled up to the curb.

Hannah stared at the structure. Her heart pounded rapidly, her palms were sweaty, and she felt as if she was going to be sick.

"What did you tell her about your arrival?" Nick asked quietly.

"I didn't know how long it was going to take to drive up. I thought we might do it in a couple of days. I just said sometime this weekend."

"So she's not expecting you tonight?"

"No. Why?"

He motioned to the cars. "I thought maybe she was throwing a welcome party for you."

"I doubt that."

"You want to go to the hotel and come back tomorrow?"

Yes! Yes! That would be great. She could sleep on it, figure out what to say. Slowly, she shook her head. That was the coward's way out. "I want to go in."

"Then let's get it over with."

He got out of the car and came around to her door. When she stepped out, he took her arm to steady her. Normally she would have slapped him away, or had a biting remark, but tonight her defenses were down. She was confident Nick would use this against her later, that he would tease her unmercifully. She didn't care. Right now he was a warm body she could cling to. He was the only person she knew in this strange little town. If he offered comfort and protection, she was going to leap at the chance to take it.

She drew the strap of her small purse over her shoulder. Nick closed the car door, then hit the button that activated the alarm. Before she could step toward the house, he moved in front of her and placed his hands on her shoulders.

"She's going to adore you," he said.

"You think so?"

"I'm sure of it. Just try to remember to smile."

She curled up her lips, but it felt like more of a grimace. Still, Nick grinned in return and she felt some of her tension ease. He grabbed her hand and started for the house.

As they climbed the steps of the porch, they could hear laughter. "Maybe it's a party," Hannah said. "We could be interrupting."

"I'm sure having you show up will just add to the joy of the occasion."

In spite of everything, she laughed. "You're very quick with those lines."

"They're effective, too." He winked.

"I'll just bet they are."

The wide front door looked imposing. Nick raised his free hand to knock, then glanced at her for approval. She sucked in a breath and nodded.

The sharp sound was followed by a burst of laughter, then a woman called, "I'll get it."

The porch light was bright, as was the light from the foyer. When the woman opened the door, Hannah could see her clearly.

She was on the tall side, maybe five-six, in her mid-forties. Hannah had a brief impression of blue eyes and a generous mouth before her attention focused on the woman's clothes. She wore lime green slacks and a turquoise shirt. A gold belt circled her waist twice. Heavy makeup highlighted her features and big dangling earrings hung below the layered edges of her short blond hair.

Hannah could feel herself shaking. The only stable part of her world was Nick's warm hand as he held on to her.

"Hi," she said, forcing the words past uncooperative lips. "I'm not sure if we have the right house or not, but I'm looking for—"

The woman caught her breath and clapped her hands together, effectively cutting Hannah off. "Oh, my. I would have recognized you anywhere. Hannah, honey, you're the spitting image of Earl and the boys."

Nick leaned close. "Who are Earl and the boys?"

Hannah shrugged helplessly. Obviously this woman knew her. A close friend of her mother's perhaps? Maybe a paid companion? "I'm afraid I don't understand," she said.

The woman smiled. "Of course not. Here I am talking about Earl and his sons, and I'm leaving out the most important part." Tears sprang to her eyes and she sniffed. "Hannah, honey, I'm your mother. Welcome home."

Wait a minute. This couldn't be her mother. Hannah straightened and stared. What happened to the old frail woman who was sick or possibly dying? The person in front of her looked fit and strong.

Hannah found herself being pulled into an embrace. The woman, Louise—Hannah couldn't really think of calling her Mom or Mother—stood in the doorway, about a half step above Hannah. That put them at the same height.

Strong arms drew Hannah close. She didn't like being hugged by people she knew, let alone strangers. Yet this embrace felt oddly right. Almost familiar.

Louise cupped Hannah's face in both hands. "You're so pretty. I tried to imagine what you'd look like, but I never could. You have Earl's eyes."

"My..."

Louise nodded. "Your father. Your hair color is mine." She tugged at a short blond strand. "I'm not a natural blonde, but you know what they say. I prefer it this way." She smiled. "I can't get over this. When I wrote you, I—" She looked past Hannah and gasped.

"Your husband. Darling, I didn't see you there. Welcome." She held her arms open again. Nick stepped easily into her embrace and she hugged him tightly. "Aren't you the handsomest man I've seen in a while. So tall."

Louise smiled. "Hannah, honey, you picked wisely with this one. I didn't always pick wisely, but I made sure they were pretty to look at."

Nick grinned. "I'm going to like you, Louise."

"Well, I hope so. I want you to know straight off, I'm not going to be a meddling mother-in-law." Her smile faded. "I'm just happy to have the chance to see you at last. Both of you." She took one of Hannah's hands and one of Nick's.

Hannah felt as if she'd been caught up in the middle of a tornado. She was being whirled around so fast, she couldn't catch her breath or her balance.

"What's going on, Louise?" a male voice called from inside the house.

Louise laughed. "I swear, it's a good thing all my body parts are attached or I would leave them behind. Imagine me forgetting my manners. Come in." She released their hands and stepped back, motioning them through the door. She patted Hannah's arm. "The boys are going to be so thrilled. They've been waiting to meet you."

Hannah swallowed. "Boys?"

"The Haynes brothers. Earl's sons with his wife. I know it's confusing, but you have four half brothers."

Nick draped his arm around Hannah's shoulders. "Great. With me, that's enough to play basketball."

"Actually, there's Austin, too, but he's not a real relative. More like an adopted member of the family." Louise frowned. "Oh, did I just put my foot in my mouth? You don't mind me saying adopted, do you?"

Numbly, Hannah shook her head.

They stepped into the living room. People were everywhere. Not just adults, but children. Lots of children. She couldn't begin to estimate the size of the crowd. Over twenty people. And they were all staring at her.

"Everyone, this is Hannah. My daughter." Louise's voice cracked and a tear slipped down her cheek. "Isn't she wonderful?"

Four men separated themselves from the group. They were tall, well over six foot, with dark hair and eyes. Hannah didn't need to look at her own reflection to see the resemblance.

Her heart stopped in her chest. She felt it *thunk* once and then freeze. She was going to die, which was a very good thing.

Cops. Her bothers were cops. Only two were in uniform, but the remaining two had the same look about them. Cops who, if they knew about Nick and his shady practices, not to mention the deal she'd made with him, wouldn't think twice about throwing them both in jail.

Chapter Four

Hannah stared unbelievingly at the four men in front of her. They stared back. Silence grew. She kept waiting to fall to the floor. After all, she still couldn't feel her heart beating. Then, in the quiet, she heard the faint thudding that told her not only was she still alive, but she was also probably going to live long enough to have to suffer through this weekend.

Nick gave her shoulder a quick squeeze, then stepped forward. "Hi. I'm Nick Archer, Hannah's husband."

The brother with a bit of gray at his temples smiled slightly. "Craig Haynes. Nice to meet you." The two men shook hands.

Hannah watched closely, but there didn't seem to be any kind of male-dominance test going on. At least not yet. The handshake was brief; she didn't notice any bulging tendons, a telltale sign that there was a pissing contest in progress.

Craig turned his attention to her. "We weren't sure what

to expect. Sorry, Louise, but she's a hundred percent Haynes.''

Louise slipped her arm through Hannah's. "Oh, there's a little Carberry in her, too. Your side doesn't get all the credit.''

Hannah shook her head. She'd always wondered about her "real" last name, about any family that might be around to claim her. Here they were, in the flesh. It should have been exciting. Instead, all she wanted to do was run for cover.

Craig motioned to the man on his left. "This is Travis, then Jordan and Kyle.'' He grinned. "We're actually standing in order of age. I'm the oldest, Kyle's the youngest.''

"Not anymore," Kyle said. "Now you get to be the baby, Hannah.''

"How nice," she murmured.

"We'll run through the rest of the family," Craig said. "I'm sure it's going to be confusing as hell, but at least you'll get a sense of who belongs to whom.''

At his words, wives came up to stand by their husbands and children collected in small groups. There were too many people, too many faces, too many names.

She tried to concentrate, but it was no use. She caught brief impressions. Craig's wife was a petite redhead who was very pregnant. They had three boys. Jordan's wife was also pregnant, but not so far along. There was another man introduced as "Austin Lucas, family, but not by blood." He was dark and dangerous-looking, an earring glinting from one ear. His wife, Rebecca, was beautiful, with a face that belonged on a cameo.

When the introductions were completed, everyone began talking at once. Louise pulled her close. "Don't worry about trying to sort everyone out. It's going to take a little while.''

Nick dropped a quick kiss on Hannah's head. She felt the heat all the way to her toes and hoped her pleasure and shock didn't show in her eyes. "Hannah and I will compare notes tonight. I'm sure between the two of us, we'll be able to keep everyone straight."

Hannah wasn't so sure. She stared at the huge living room. A large fireplace dominated the far wall. Navy drapes covered floor-to-ceiling windows. The same color was picked up in the four sofas forming a loose square. Striped wing chairs of navy and cream filled in the corners. The furniture and floor were light pine. Scattered rugs, paintings and the evidence of coffee and dessert gave the room a homey, lived-in look.

She couldn't imagine anyone living in a house this large, but it was obvious the Haynes family needed a lot of room. Hannah counted seventeen adults, eleven children, with two more on the way.

She glanced at Louise, who was talking to Nick, pointing out various individuals and giving a brief background. The children had started to chase each other around the room. The adults talked among themselves, all the while casting curious glances at her. She felt like the featured entertainer at a sideshow. The attention was uncomfortable. When Nick stepped close and placed his hand on the back of her neck under her braid, she didn't protest.

"Do you live here?" she asked Louise, remembering her vision of a frail old woman living in a nursing home.

Louise laughed. "I have my own place in town. An apartment. But I'm hardly ever there. These boys keep me busy."

Louise led them over to one of the sofas. They sat down, with Louise on one side of Hannah and Nick on the other.

"You work for the Haynes family?" Nick asked.

Louise nodded. "I have for several years. It started when

Travis here—'' she pointed to one of the brothers in uniform ''—needed a housekeeper. He and his first wife had divorced and he was rattling around in a house as big as this one. The boy couldn't cook anything. I was afraid he'd starve to death. So he hired me.''

The brother in question came over and sat on the coffee table in front of the sofa. His wavy dark hair was trimmed regulation short, not quite touching the back of his collar. The khaki uniform indicated that he was Glenwood's sheriff. Hannah fought back a shudder. Why couldn't her brothers have been plumbers or electricians?

''I'm Travis, remember?'' he said.

Hannah gave him a shaky smile. ''Yes, hi.''

''We're a loud bunch, but our hearts are in the right place. We've really been looking forward to meeting you.''

''You have the advantage,'' Nick said easily, with his arm around Hannah. ''We were expecting Hannah's mother to be by herself. This is an unexpected bonus.''

If Hannah hadn't been so nervous, she would have rolled her eyes. Nick had been born charming. Most of the time she didn't approve of those who skated through life using fancy words instead of work to get by. In this case, however, she was extremely grateful to have him along. Who would have thought she would be related to an entire herd of people?

''It's kind of interesting about Louise,'' Travis said and winked at the older woman. ''She's been a member of this family for years.''

''She was just mentioning that,'' Hannah said politely.

''Now you're related to both of us.''

Hannah wondered if anyone had thought this through. If she was Louise's daughter and the Haynes brothers' half sister, that meant they shared a father. Then Louise must have had a relationship with their father nearly twenty-eight years ago. Had he been married? If not, why hadn't Louise married him herself? Why had she, Hannah, been given up for adoption?

Travis said something to Nick, but Hannah wasn't listening anymore. She was looking around the room at the happy family. Adults clustered together, talking and laughing. Children played. The volume increased steadily as everyone tried to be heard. It was chaos in its most pleasant form.

Her family. She was related to many of these people by blood and to the rest of them by marriage. Louise had stayed and found a life for herself. Why had she given her child away?

She felt emotions piling up in her throat. As tired and shell-shocked as she was right now, she couldn't risk weakening. She might say something inappropriate. Or worse—she might burst into tears.

Nick moved his arm and began to stroke the skin at the back of her neck. The contact was comforting and erotic—an intriguing combination. She leaned toward him and let her left hand rest on his thigh. His muscles were rock hard, his body warm. In an uncontrollable situation, he was the only stable point of reference. Right now, she didn't care if he was a criminal with a record or even a tattoo. For some crazy reason, she trusted him to keep her safe. She, who never dared trust anyone. She didn't want to think how much she was going to regret this later.

"Hey, Hannah." The other brother in uniform walked over. "I'm Kyle." He looked a lot like Travis, maybe a tiny bit better-looking. Obviously, this was a gene pool that treated its men very well.

She glanced at the badge on his chest. "You work for the Glenwood sheriff's department, too?"

"Sure thing." Kyle pulled up one of the striped wing

chairs and sat down. "I used to work in San Francisco, but Travis offered me a job here in Glenwood. I was glad to come home."

Travis shrugged. "I couldn't have my baby brother off making trouble in the big city."

"Hannah's the youngest now," Kyle said, sounding pleased with the fact. "We have a little sister."

"I don't feel very little," Hannah said.

Kyle leaned forward in the chair. "Yeah, but we're still bigger. If this guy starts hassling you, you just let us know and we'll take care of him."

Everyone laughed.

"Don't you start any trouble with my son-in-law," Louise said. "Nick looks very nice."

Travis winked. "I don't know, Louise. He's kinda pale. Like he hasn't been out in the sun."

Hannah glanced at Nick's lightly tanned skin, then at his blond hair. He was certainly different from all the men here, she realized. But she liked the contrast.

"Maybe we should drag him outside," Kyle said.

"Don't even think about it." Hannah held up one hand in warning. "I like him just the way he is."

Nick's hand continued to stroke the back of her neck. Shivers started at her shoulders and worked their way down to her toes. She felt him looking at her, but she didn't dare meet his gaze. She didn't want to know what he was thinking. There would be hell to pay as it was. However, she couldn't risk being separated from him so soon. Not until they got their stories straight. Oh, Lord, why hadn't she thought Louise might be part of a big family? And why had she resisted so much when Nick had asked for personal information? It was her stupid independence and stubbornness. She hated having to depend on anyone for anything.

The other two brothers drifted toward them. Soon most

of the adults were gathered around their sofa. More chairs were moved close by until everyone was seated and listening intently.

She was starting to figure out who was who. At least with her half brothers. Travis and Kyle seemed the most easygoing. Craig had the hint of gray at his temples and Jordan was quiet.

"Do you work?" Travis asked.

Nick started to say something. Hannah elbowed him discreetly, afraid of what he would say. "Yes," she answered. "I'm a communications officer in Southport Beach. That's in Orange County, near Huntington Beach."

"She's a cop, too." Kyle grinned. "We all are." He motioned to his brothers. "Except for Jordan. He's the black sheep of the family. He's a firefighter."

"That's great," she said weakly. As she'd suspected. Law enforcement officers. Except for Jordan. If the truth came out... She shook her head. She didn't even want to think about that.

"Dad was a cop," Craig said. He sat on the floor while his very pregnant wife leaned back in a wing chair. "Third generation."

"Where is my—your father?" she asked. The brothers exchanged glances. Hannah turned to Louise. "I'm sorry. I didn't mean to ask something inappropriate."

"It's all right." Louise patted her hand. "Earl Haynes moved to Florida some years back. He doesn't visit here. I haven't had contact with him for about sixteen years. The boys might have heard something."

Travis shook his head. "Not really. We aren't very close."

Hannah sensed undercurrents of tension in the room, but she didn't know what they were about. Obviously, Earl

Haynes wasn't anyone's favorite person. Were they upset because of her?

Jordan sat with his wife on his lap. He played with her fingers. "What do you do, Nick?"

The panic was instantaneous. Hannah opened her mouth, but didn't know what to say. Nick didn't have any such hesitation.

"I'm in real estate. I just finished up a project developing some residential houses on a cliff by Newport."

"How long have you two known each other?" Louise asked.

Nick slid his fingers down Hannah's back, then picked up the hand resting on his thigh. He brought it to his mouth and kissed the back. Had she been standing, the moist heat from his mouth would have driven her to her knees. Damn the man for taking advantage of the situation.

"The time has gone by so quickly," he said. "It feels like it was only yesterday when we had our first conversation."

She wanted to slap him. She wanted to scream. She wanted to disappear and never be heard from again. He held her hand loosely, circling her palm with his thumb. If she protested, everyone would know something was wrong. No doubt Nick had worked that out, too.

"It was about five years ago," he said at last.

"How did you meet?" one of the wives asked. Hannah wasn't sure, but she thought her name might be Elizabeth. She had medium brown hair and pretty eyes.

Nick smiled at Hannah. "Do you want to tell the story, darling?"

At this moment in time, she could barely remember where she was, let alone come up with some tall tale about their meeting. "You do it so much better," she murmured. "Go ahead."

The slight smile warned her he was about to pay her back for not wanting to share personal information on the drive north. She sent up a quick prayer that it wasn't too awful.

"We met on a cruise. Actually, we were in port at the time, St. Thomas," he began.

Someone sighed. Hannah breathed a sigh of relief.

"It was very romantic," he continued. "The sea, the sand, Hannah throwing up in the bushes."

She straightened and glared at him. His smile was so sweet. He was loving every minute of this torture.

"I know you don't like me to tell the story, honey, but this is family. They can handle it." He glanced at her brothers. "Hannah's not much of a drinker. A couple of those umbrella drinks and she's under the table. Or in this case, over the bushes."

Hannah could feel everyone's attention on them. A heated flush started to crawl up her cheeks.

"I took her back to the ship and took care of her." He leaned over and kissed her cheek. "For me, it was love at first sight. Hannah didn't see it that way. She resisted me, but in the end I wore her down." He lowered his voice conspiratorially. "Hannah doesn't trust easily, but she was worth the effort."

A couple of the women sighed. "That is so romantic," said Jill, who was obviously nine months pregnant. "I know it's just the hormones, but I think I'm going to cry." She sniffed loudly.

Kyle's wife—Hannah wasn't sure of her name—handed her a tissue from her pocket. "We should all have romantic stories to tell."

"Our story is romantic, Sandy," Kyle said. "At least I think it is."

Sandy laughed. "You go on thinking that," she teased. "No one is going to tell you differently."

Hannah listened to the banter. She was still stunned by Nick's story. Everything had been a complete fabrication until the end. She really didn't trust anyone easily. How had he figured that out?

The conversation died down and Hannah could see they were in for another round of questions. Rather than face that, she tried to distract them. "There are a lot of children here," she said. "You like large families."

Craig rubbed his wife's swollen belly. "We seem to be a fertile group."

Hannah had to agree with that. It's a good thing she'd never played fast and loose with birth control.

"You doing all right, honey?" Louise asked.

"I'm fine. Just a little overwhelmed."

"If it gets to be too much, remember you can always duck outside. They'll understand."

Hannah looked at the woman who had given birth to her. She was filled with questions. Why had she sent her child away? What were the circumstances around her pregnancy? Did Earl Haynes know he had a daughter?

There were even more questions, but she knew this was neither the time nor the place. It was too public. She was going to be around for a couple of weeks. She and Louise would have plenty of chances to talk alone.

Louise clapped her hands together. "What have I been thinking? I'll bet the two of you drove straight through, didn't you? Did you even stop for dinner?"

"Not exactly," Hannah said.

"You must be hungry."

"No, we're not—"

"I'm starved," Nick interrupted cheerfully.

Louise stood up. "Come with me," she said firmly.

"There are plenty of leftovers. We had a potluck, so you'll have a wide choice. Fortunately, all the boys married women who are great cooks."

Hannah found herself standing up and following Louise. Nick was right behind her, as was the rest of the family. She held in a whimper. It had been bad enough that everyone wanted to sit around and talk to them. Now they were going to have an audience while they ate dinner.

The kitchen was as large and well proportioned as the living room. A huge greenhouse window stretched out above the sink. The cabinets were bleached oak, the countertops alternating white and cobalt blue tiles. One end of the center island held a cooktop, while at the other was an eating area with tall bar stools.

"Sit here," Louise said, ushering them toward the island. "I'll have everything put together in a minute."

A couple of older kids had followed the adults in, hoping for extra dessert, but they were quickly shooed upstairs.

Louise checked the contents of the extrawide refrigerator on the wall at right angles to the sink. "We've got roast beef, some ham, salads, vegetables, bread, baked beans. Anything you don't like?"

"I'm easy," Nick said, sliding onto a stool.

Hannah settled next to him. "Anything is fine. We appreciate this. You don't have to go to any trouble."

Louise paused and smiled at her. "You're my baby girl. Nothing is too much trouble."

She moved quickly around the kitchen, familiar with the layout. Holly, who Hannah had figured out was married to Jordan, helped. Apparently, this was their house. In less than five minutes, steaming plates were removed from the microwave, cold salad was heaped into bowls, and Elizabeth—or was it Sandy?—offered wine.

Hannah shuddered at the thought of liquor. She hadn't

completely recovered from the previous night. Louise poured ice water for her and a beer for Nick. Just as Hannah wondered if everyone was going to stand there watching her and Nick eat, Louise said, "Baseball."

Travis looked at her. "What?"

"Basketball? Isn't there a sporting event on television tonight?"

Kyle grinned. "I think she's trying to tell us something." He leaned over the island and grabbed Nick's plate. "Come on. The women are throwing us out. Let's go to the den. There's a big-screen television in there. You can eat in peace."

Nick hesitated. Hannah stared at him. If he left, she would be alone. Their eyes met. She read concern and compassion in his gaze. If she didn't know better, she would swear he really cared about what happened to her. Which was a completely crazy idea. Nick only cared about himself. Right?

She thought about all he'd already done for her and it was only the first day. He was worth a whole lot more than four hundred dollars. Or three hundred and ninety, a little voice whispered in her head as she remembered the heat and pleasure of their ten-dollar kiss.

"I'll be fine," she said.

He touched her cheek with the back of his fingers. For one oddly unsettling moment, she wanted the contact to be real and not simply because he was playing a part. Then he followed the men and she was left alone with six strange women.

Her appetite deserted her and she set down her fork. Now what?

Louise took the seat next to her. The two pregnant half sisters-in-law, if that was the relationship, took the other two. The remaining three leaned against the counter.

"You look lost and confused," said one. She had long brown hair and pretty eyes. "I'll make it easy," the woman continued. "I'm Elizabeth. Brown hair, brown eyes. Average-looking."

The other women hooted at that remark. "Oh, sure. Average," Jill said. She was easy to remember because she looked like she was going to give birth at any moment. She shifted on the stool. "I'm Jill. Red hair, short."

"And pregnant," Hannah said.

Jill patted her tummy. "Any day now."

Hannah turned to the other pregnant woman. "Holly, right?"

"That's me. Jordan's my husband and this is our house." She smiled shyly. "We were just married in January."

Elizabeth moved next to Holly and hugged her. "Newlyweds and this one already five months pregnant. Do these boys know how to get the job done, or what?"

Hannah laughed.

"I'm Sandy." She was about Elizabeth's height and age, with shoulder-length hair, freckles and huge green eyes. "I'm married to the baby. That's Kyle."

"Which leaves only me. I'm Rebecca." Rebecca was tall and slender, with thick curly hair that spilled over her shoulders nearly to her waist. Her perfect face belonged on an eighteenth-century portrait. "I'm married to Austin, who is a Haynes brother in spirit if not in blood."

Hannah stared from one to the other. "I'm not sure I'll ever sort you all out, but I'll try."

Louise gave her a quick hug. "I'll make everyone wear name tags."

Elizabeth stared at Hannah. "You have the Haynes features, all right."

"She's very pretty," Louise said proudly. "I knew she would be."

"I don't think I'd use the word *pretty*," Hannah protested.

"Oh, I would." Sandy grinned. "And your husband is very handsome."

"For a guy with blond hair," Elizabeth teased.

"I happen to like Nick's blond hair," Hannah said.

Elizabeth leaned close. "He's a natural blond, right?"

All the women shrieked with laughter. Hannah joined in, feeling vaguely uncomfortable. Not with the teasing. She liked these women. What made her stomach clench was the fact that everything about her was a lie. Would they be as open and friendly if they knew the truth?

She always worried about people being whom they pretended to be. Despite being married to cops, none of these women seemed to have doubts about her story or to wonder if she might not be telling the truth. They trusted her.

For a half second, she thought about coming clean. Then Louise raised her glass and said, "I'd like to propose a toast. To my beautiful daughter and her charming husband."

Hannah had no choice but to raise her glass of ice water and drink.

Louise urged her to eat, then leaned back on her stool. "I'm a very content old woman."

"You're not old," Elizabeth told her. "Barely what? Forty-one?"

Louise chuckled. "You always were my favorite. No, I'm going to be forty-seven very soon. All right. I'll retract the old, but not the rest of it." Her expression turned serious. "Thank you for coming to visit me, Hannah. You've made me very happy."

When Hannah's eyes burned, she told herself it was only because she was tired. She'd barely gotten any sleep the previous night. It wasn't emotion. She didn't know this woman or these people. They certainly didn't matter to her.

Conversation flowed around her. The women had obviously spent a lot of time together. Hannah enjoyed listening to them. She would have liked to grow up in this kind of family. To be part of something.

She finished her dinner. Her stomach full, she felt the exhaustion of the day finally catch up with her. She yawned. "Oh, excuse me," she said and covered her mouth.

Louise frowned. "You made that drive all in one day. No wonder you're tired. Come on. Let's collect that husband of yours. We can visit more in the morning."

The women trooped into the den. It was nearly as spacious as the living room. The leather furniture all faced the big-screen TV on the far wall.

She and Louise led the way. As they entered the room, the men were laughing. Hannah noticed their attention was focused on Nick and not on the basketball game. What had he been telling them? After the cruise story, she wasn't sure she wanted to know.

Nick glanced up and saw her. "Hi, honey."

"Hi. I thought maybe it was time for us to head off to the hotel." Where she would have her own private room with a shower. Where she could finally be alone.

"Good idea."

But before Nick could stand, Travis pushed to his feet. "It's early. You can't leave so soon."

"They're tired," Louise said. "They're going to be here two weeks. We'll all have time to get to know each other."

"I agree."

Hannah thought the brother speaking was Jordan. As he stepped into the light, she was sure.

"But you're not going to a hotel," he said. "We have plenty of room right here."

"We have room, too," Travis said. "Right, Elizabeth?"

His wife joined in the invitation. "Yes, of course, you're welcome to stay. The guest bathroom has a wonderful claw-footed tub. It's very romantic."

Hannah fought down panic. She wasn't interested in romance. She wanted, needed, some time alone. She and Nick could not share a room. It wasn't possible.

"You're all very sweet, but we can't impose," she murmured, not daring to look at Nick. She could just imagine what he was thinking about their sharing a room.

Craig glanced at her. "You're safe from us. Jill and I live too far from here to bug you about staying. Although you'd be more than welcome."

"The hotel is—"

"Wait!" Sandy walked to the middle of the room. "I have the perfect solution. I understand Hannah wanting to stay at a hotel. After all, the family is a little scary at first."

There were murmurs of agreement.

"As a compromise, I'd like to offer our gatehouse. It's currently empty and furnished." She smiled at Hannah and Nick. "It's a fully equipped one-bedroom apartment. You'd be close by and staying with family, but you'd have some privacy. You guys might have been married for five years, but you're still acting like honeymooners."

Nick moved close to Hannah and dropped a kiss on her nose. "She's right, honey. I know the thrill is still there for me."

Hannah wanted to punch him. She settled on a tight smile. "Me, too, darling."

Louise nodded. "It's really perfect. Sandy redid the entire apartment just a couple of months ago. You'll love it."

Hannah doubted that. "A hotel is really fine with us. We don't want to be any trouble."

Louise touched her arm. "You're not trouble. You're family. We like taking care of each other. That's the best part of being together. Now, there'll be no more talk of staying at a hotel."

Hannah looked at each of their faces. They seemed genuinely glad to meet her and Nick. They'd welcomed them with open arms, no questions asked.

"You're very gracious," Nick said. "We'd love to stay at the apartment."

It took a couple of minutes for Sandy and Kyle to round up their children. Everyone walked them to the car. Hannah and Nick were to follow the minivan to their temporary home.

Louise hugged Hannah. "Thank you for coming back to me. I know you have a lot of questions about what happened all those years ago and what's happened since. I'll tell you everything I can." She blinked, then brushed away a tear that slipped down her cheek. "I'm so happy."

Emotions tightened Hannah's throat. She managed to whisper, "Me, too," then hugged the older woman back. Louise wasn't "Mom" yet, but a connection had been established. In time, it would become stronger.

Hannah found herself passed from person to person, hugged, kissed, squeezed and generally made to feel like a favorite rag doll. Nick got some attention of his own, with a few slaps on the back from the men.

She sank into the passenger seat, then waved as Travis shut the door. For a moment, there was only silence.

"Pretty amazing, huh?" Nick said and winked. "I especially like the hugging and kissing at the end."

"You would."

"And the *one-bedroom* apartment sounds really attractive."

"I don't want to talk about it."

"Honey, you don't have to talk about it. After all, we're going to live in it."

Chapter Five

Nick waited for the minivan to pull out into the street. Hannah was quiet beside him. He was still shell-shocked from all that had happened in the past couple of hours. She must feel as if she'd been swept into another dimension.

"You did well," he said.

Hannah glanced at him. Despite the dark interior of the car and the fact that he couldn't read her expression, he knew what she was thinking. Should she go with the compliment or should she berate him for presuming to pass judgment on her performance? He suspected it was a battle of principles and exhaustion. Exhaustion won.

"Thanks," she murmured. "I still can't believe it. Brothers. I have four brothers."

"Cops, too. That makes the whole thing interesting."

The minivan backed out of the driveway and headed down the road. Nick followed. It was nearly 10:00 p.m. and the residential streets were quiet.

"*Interesting* isn't the word I'd use," she said. "Do you know what will happen if they find out the truth?"

"No."

She sighed and sagged against the seat. "Me, neither, but I'm sure it won't be good. I should have thought this through better. I should have—oh, I don't know. Something. Maybe they won't find out."

"They won't. Not until you tell them. By then, they'll adore you so much, they won't mind that you fudged on a detail or two."

"We come from very different worlds. To you this might be fudging details, but where I'm from, and I suspect where they're from, too, lying about being married is more than a detail. I should have come clean from the beginning."

He was glad she hadn't. If Hannah hadn't needed a temporary husband, she wouldn't have hired him. Instead of sharing this time with her, he would have been trapped in some casino in Las Vegas.

Undercover work was a hell of a lot more difficult than most people realized. Every reference, every thought about a former life had to be suppressed. He was required to live, eat and breathe the job. Nick Archer wouldn't think twice about "fudging details." He had to remember that. He had to focus on who he was supposed to be and not what he wanted to be. But for a brief moment, less than a heartbeat, he wished he could just be himself.

"It's funny how the five of you look so much alike," he said.

"I agree. Wow. I sure wasn't expecting that. It's so odd to think I have brothers. They've been walking around for all these years and I never knew. And the way we resemble one another...well, it takes some getting used to."

"Several of your nieces and nephews have the 'Haynes' look, too."

Hannah chuckled. "There were so many children. Don't these people believe in birth control?"

The van in front slowed for a stop sign. Nick stepped on the brake. "The kids are great. Don't you want any?"

"I haven't really thought about it. I sort of assumed I wouldn't have any." She paused for a second. "I don't think I'm very maternal. You can't tell me *you* want children."

"Of course. Dozens."

She laughed. "No way."

"All right. Maybe just two or three. But I do want children."

"You?"

Her surprised, slightly patronizing tone got under his skin. "What's so strange about that?" he asked.

"Nothing. Only I wouldn't have pictured you as the type."

"I would be a great dad." He would do exactly the opposite of what his father had done to him. It was a simple formula for success. "I love children."

"Yeah, right."

She was still laughing when they pulled into a long driveway. As the main house came into view, her laughter turned into a strangled cough. This house was just as big as Jordan's. Three stories, peaked roofs, a porch wide enough to host a dance.

"Cops make a lot more money up here than they do in Southport Beach," she murmured.

"Hell, if I'd known the money was this good, *I* would have joined the force. What's the name of this town?"

"Glenwood. This is amazing."

Nick slowed the car and stared out the windshield. There was no way either brother could afford their homes on city salaries. There had to be another income source. For a half second he wondered if the family was into something dirty. Then he dismissed the thought. It had to be something else.

"Maybe an inheritance," he said, thinking aloud.

"Or someone married money."

"There's a plan."

She shot him an impatient look.

He raised his hands in surrender. "It's not like you're going to keep me around for long, dollface."

"Just try to keep your libido on hold until the weekend is over."

The minivan stopped in front of a small gatehouse. Nick looked at it and wondered if Hannah would be willing to work off some more of her debt in trade. He thought about suggesting it, then figured she would object. He wouldn't mind the verbal or even physical wrestling match sure to follow, but he would prefer either to be in private.

Kyle and Sandy got out of the van. Sandy approached the passenger side of Nick's Mercedes, and Hannah rolled down the window.

"I'm going to get the kids in bed," Sandy said. "Kyle will show you where everything is." She reached in and squeezed Hannah's arm. "I'm so glad you're here. Welcome to the family."

"Thanks."

Kyle motioned to a spot next to the gatehouse. As Nick pulled in, Sandy got in the driver's side of the minivan and headed for the main house.

Kyle waited at the rear of the car. When Nick opened the trunk, Kyle reached in for the luggage. With Hannah carrying the smallest bag, they made it to the front door in one trip.

"I've got the key right here," Kyle said, pulling a set of keys out of his khaki trousers. He slipped one off and used it to open the front door. "We were going to use this as a rental,'' he explained as everyone stepped inside. ''Sandy just finished redecorating the inside, but we haven't had a chance to run an ad in the paper. Great timing, huh?''

''We really hate to put you out,'' Hannah said.

Kyle set down the suitcases and reached for a switch by the front door. Light flooded the room. A long hunter green sofa sat across from a television. The end tables were oak, as was the floor. There were two large windows and even a fireplace.

Kyle took them on a quick tour. The kitchen was small but adequate, with refinished cabinets and an eating area. They continued into the bedroom, which had a king-size bed. Two people could be very comfortable there, Nick imagined, then figured he would never get the chance to test the firmness of the mattress.

They returned to the living room. ''Would you like to sit for a minute?'' Hannah asked Kyle.

''Sure.''

Kyle settled on one end of the sofa. Hannah took the cream-and-green-flecked easy chair. Nick sat on the other end of the sofa and figured Hannah would want to keep Kyle around for as long as possible. Not only to get information about her family, but to avoid being alone with her pretend husband.

Kyle stared at Hannah for several seconds, then laughed. ''Sorry. I've known about you for a few months now, but it's strange to actually have you here.''

''It feels weird to be here,'' she said and clasped her hands together. ''I have so many questions, but I don't know where to start.''

Kyle shrugged. ''Start wherever. We don't have any secrets.''

Hannah's body stiffened at that remark. Nick knew she was thinking about her own secrets—about him and their so-called marriage. If she'd chosen to sit on the sofa instead of the easy chair, he could have moved close and offered support. But she was too far away for him to touch her. No doubt she'd planned that deliberately, not wanting to give in to weakness.

He liked her strength and her stubbornness nearly as much as he liked the softness she kept hidden from the rest of the world. If he ever told her that, she would either assume he was trying to make fun of her, or haul off and slug him. Nothing about Hannah was easy, but he suspected she was worth the effort. Too bad his stay in her life was only temporary.

"What about my—our—father?" she asked, her voice low and uncertain. "You never see him?"

"No." Kyle leaned back on the sofa and crossed one ankle over his opposite knee. "None of us has gone to visit him since he moved to Florida and he hasn't been back. Sometimes he sends one of us a card, but that's about it."

"You don't mind?"

Kyle's features tightened. His mouth pulled into a straight line. "No. We don't mind. Earl Haynes isn't exactly a model father. I wish I could tell you he was a kind man, or a loving husband, but none of it's true. He never cared about anyone but himself. He was a real—"

He stopped abruptly and glanced at her. "I'll mention this to my brothers and the five of us can talk about him together. We can get out the photo albums if you want to see what he looks like. I'm sure there are some good memories."

Hannah didn't wear much makeup and what she'd applied that morning had long since worn off. Nick could see the shadows under her eyes. Pale skin made the irises appear even darker brown. A single strand of hair had dared to escape her neat braid. It was the first time he'd ever seen that happen. The strand fluttered around her neck.

Nick looked from half brother to half sister. He could see the similarities in eye and hair color, in the shape of their mouths, the straight noses, the set of their shoulders. Hannah was a beautiful, feminine version of her brothers.

"I'm sure Louise will be happy to talk about Earl, too," Kyle said.

"They weren't married, were they?"

"No. If they had been, she wouldn't have had to give you up."

Hannah nodded.

Kyle dropped his foot to the floor and leaned toward her. "Don't judge Louise. She was very young and very much in love with my father. He had a way of charming women. We don't blame her, and you shouldn't, either."

"I don't," Hannah said, but Nick wasn't sure she was telling the truth. The brothers were enjoying having a new sister in the family. Hannah had to deal with the fact that her own mother had given her away. Understanding the past and trying to forgive were going to be long and difficult tasks.

Kyle rose to his feet. "I don't want to keep you two up any longer."

Hannah stood. "Oh, it's fine. You don't have to go. Really."

Nick heard the note of panic in her voice.

Kyle grinned. "We'll have plenty of time to catch up." He came over and gave her a hug. "Welcome to the family." Then he kissed her cheek.

Nick saw him to the door. "Thanks for everything," he said. "The house is terrific."

"Let us know if you need anything," Kyle said. "We're right up the driveway."

Nick waved, then closed the door and returned to the living room. Hannah had sunk back in her chair.

"It's been a hell of a day," he said.

She nodded. "I feel as if I've been through a war."

"I've got just the thing to make you feel better."

She eyed him suspiciously. "Like I believe that."

"Would your own husband lie to you?"

"In a heartbeat."

He walked over to the pile of luggage still by the door and opened his small bag. When he pulled out a fifth of Scotch, he said, "Sarcastic people don't get a drink."

The corners of her mouth tilted up. "I take it all back. Every word. You're a prince without equal."

"Better. Much better. Say something about being good-looking. Guys always like that."

But instead of giving him a quick retort, she flushed slightly and glanced away. Interesting, Nick thought, strangely pleased by her reticence. He liked making her nervous. Keeping her off guard evened the playing field.

In the kitchen, the cabinet above the dishwasher yielded octagonal-shaped glasses. He snagged two and carried them back into the living room. After opening the bottle and pouring them each an inch of amber liquid, he handed her a glass, then raised his.

"To family found," he said.

She nodded and took a sip. A small shudder rippled through her. She closed her eyes for a second, then exhaled. "Here I was expecting a lonely old woman and I found the Waltons."

"Four John-boys for the price of one."

"I wonder if I've made a mistake."

"Coming up here?" he asked, leaning back against the sofa.

"All of it. Coming up here, getting involved with them and their lives."

"Don't you want to be a part of this family?" He tried not to think about the fact that he didn't belong anywhere himself. His old man had passed away about ten years ago. Most of the time, Nick didn't give him more than a passing thought, but occasionally he wondered about all he'd missed when he was growing up. When he considered raising a family, there was always a large group involved. It was, he acknowledged, a stupid fantasy for a man who never stayed long enough to get involved. Relationships required a commitment, and that was where his plan broke down. He'd been burned enough to know he wasn't going to give anyone the chance to get close again.

"I'm not sure what I want," she said.

"Are you angry at Louise?"

She raised her eyebrows. "Just when I get used to thinking of you as a selfish, myopic jerk, you go and say something perceptive."

"Hey, I'm an amazing guy."

She pulled her feet up, shifted and tucked her legs under her. "I think I might have a little anger toward the woman who gave me up for adoption. Yet I came willingly when she invited me. I suppose I'm wrestling with ambivalence."

"Did you tell her about losing your adoptive parents?"

"No. She doesn't know."

So Louise didn't know about Hannah's being raised in foster homes. The woman was going to be heartsick and blame herself when she found out the truth.

Hannah leaned back in the chair. "Every orphan dreams about her birth parents coming back to rescue her. I had the same fantasy about my parents. But they never came to get me. In some ways, it was worse knowing they were alive and didn't care."

"Your father probably didn't know about you."

"I assumed that from what everyone said." She took another sip. "You think he's as bad as they say?"

"Yes."

Her gaze met his. "How do you know?"

"I've seen the results of parents who didn't care. I've learned to recognize the scars." He didn't bother mentioning he had a few of his own.

"Louise isn't anything like I thought she'd be," Hannah said. "What happened to the frail old woman?"

"You're twenty-seven, right?"

She nodded.

"Most women in their forties don't have to give up children for adoption," he said. "She was a kid when you were born."

Abruptly, Hannah rose to her feet. She set the glass on the end table and started to pace the length of the room. When she reached the fireplace, she turned and walked to the hallway, only to repeat the circuit again.

"I want to ask why she did it," she said. "I just don't know how."

"Say the words. I'm sure the story is pretty simple. Teenager gets involved with a married man, then gets pregnant. Glenwood is a small town. If she'd stayed, she would have caused a scandal."

"I suppose you're right." She raised her hands and covered her eyes. "Why did I think coming here would be easy?"

"You never thought that. You knew it would be tough, but worth it. That's what you have to remember."

She stopped in front of him and lowered her hands to her sides. "When did you join my side?"

He was tempted to tell her he'd always been on her side, but didn't think she'd believe him. "When you offered me four hundred dollars in cash." He raised his eyebrows. "Make that three ninety."

At the reminder of their kiss that morning, she spun on her heel and resumed pacing. On her next pass, he stood up and grabbed her hands. She was tall, but he was taller. He towered over her by a good five or six inches. With her, he needed the advantage.

"It's going to be okay," he promised. He held her fingers firmly and stroked her knuckles with his thumbs. She didn't pull away. She didn't react at all. If it wasn't for the fluttering pulse he could see at the base of her throat, he might have thought his touching her didn't affect her in the least.

"I want to believe that," she said softly. "I'm just not sure. This is so much more than I expected."

"It must be scary."

Her dark eyes widened. "Terrifying. If I'd known what I was getting myself into, I would have come clean about the divorce right away."

"You still can." God, he hated it when he got noble.

She shook her head. "No. It would be too difficult to explain. I can't imagine what I would say."

"I could tell them."

"Oh, right." She rolled her eyes. "Don't make me laugh."

Her assessment irritated him, but he ignored the flicker of hurt feelings.

"We'll stick with the original plan," she said. "You stay here tomorrow, then the day after—Sunday—you pretend to get a business call that requires your return to Southport Beach. I'll stay up here for a couple of weeks. Once I've established a relationship with Louise and my brothers, I'll explain everything.''

Her plan was never going to work. "Sounds great," he muttered.

She glared at him. "What? What are you thinking? You don't think I can pull it off?''

He gave one last squeeze on her fingers. She was going to pull away fast enough to give him rope burn. Just as soon as he said what he was thinking. Too bad. Being close to Hannah had a warming effect on his whole body. Some parts were downright steamy.

"Establishing relationships isn't your strong suit," he said.

As expected, she jerked free of his touch, then backed up a couple of steps. "What are you talking about?" she asked between clenched teeth. "I'm a very friendly person.''

"Uh-huh. That's why you date so much.''

"Until a few months ago, I was a married woman.''

"A separated woman, Hannah. There are plenty of men interested, so don't give me any bull about that. You chase them off because you don't want to get close.''

"I do not. I don't believe in dating anyone at the station. I don't want to be talked about.''

"You don't want to risk getting close.''

She planted her hands on her hips, nearly vibrating with fury. The wayward strand of hair fluttered by her neck. He wished he could smooth it back over her ear, but if he got that close to her right now, he would put several body parts at risk.

"I don't see you with a wife and three kids.''

Touché. "Not that you know about.''

She turned her back on him. "I'll have you know I have lots of friends.''

"Name five."

"It's none of your business."

"Name one."

"Alice."

"Where is Alice?"

"She lives in Chicago. We went to college together. So I've not only established a relationship, I've maintained it." She stalked to the fireplace and stared at the neatly stacked logs.

"When was the last time you spoke to her?"

She cleared her throat. "It's not the quantity of time in a relationship that counts. It's the quality."

"So it's been what, a year?"

"Christmas," she snapped, facing him. "We spoke at Christmas."

"That's not a close friend, honey. That's a pen pal."

"Don't honey me, and don't pass judgment on my relationships. You don't know what you're talking about."

But he did. He knew all about Hannah Pace and how she held the world at bay. He'd known from the first time he'd seen the wariness in her eyes. The wall she'd built around her was hard to break....

"Dealing with a large family is going to be difficult," he warned.

"I'm more than up to the task." Her hands returned to her hips and she raised her chin. "Where exactly do you get off telling me my faults as you see them?"

"I know what you're good at and it's not lying."

Amazingly, she smiled. "You're right. But you're an expert, right? So I'll run any false stories by you first."

"Good idea. Let's start by getting our stories straight."

"If this is a ploy to get personal information out of me, you can just forget it."

It was clear she'd been badly hurt. Was it a particular

individual or some unfortunate turn of events? He hoped she would risk caring enough to let her family in. They could be her salvation.

He thought about taking on that job himself but knew it was way out of his league. Better for both of them if he did what he'd agreed to and moved on.

She glanced at her watch. "It's late. We should go to bed."

"No problem," he said. "Which side do you want?"

She grabbed his arm before he could head to the bedroom. "Just a minute, Romeo. We're not sharing the bed."

"No?" He tried to look innocent. "I wouldn't mind. You can even take advantage of me."

"Gee, thanks. I think I'll pass."

"I'm willing to let you work off another ten bucks for a kiss."

Her gaze dropped to his mouth. He felt it as intensely as if she'd stroked him with her fingers. Desire flickered in her eyes. She blinked it quickly away, but he'd seen it. He was pleased to know he wasn't the only one who was thinking how great they would be together.

Sweet Hannah. He had a sneaking suspicion that she would be half shy innocent, half wild temptress in bed. He couldn't wait to find out if he was right. But not tonight.

She took a step toward him and leaned close. For a second, he thought she was going to kiss him, then she grinned. "I'd rather pay the money."

He reached over and tucked the loose strand of hair behind her ear. "Liar."

She walked into the bedroom, then returned carrying a pillow and a blanket. She tossed both at him. "The sofa looks really comfortable, Nick. Enjoy."

Chapter Six

"I can't believe I'm sitting here having coffee with my mother," Hannah said.

Louise smiled and leaned forward to pat her hand. "I'm just as surprised. A few months ago, I was sure I'd never see you. Now here you are."

Sunlight poured into the small, bright kitchen. It was a beautiful late-spring morning with warm temperatures and clear skies.

"Do you think Nick is going to be all right?" Hannah asked. When Louise had called and suggested they spend the morning together, Hannah had agreed. They had a lot to talk about. Jordan had dropped off Louise at the gatehouse, then had asked Nick to come along to help with the restoration on Jordan's Victorian house.

Hannah would have preferred Nick to stay nearby where she could monitor his conversations, but he'd left before she could protest. Now she watched the clock and wondered what exactly he was talking about. No doubt her brothers wanted to grill him about his life and their marriage. Would Nick come up with more absurd stories as he had yesterday? Maybe she should have given in and provided him with a little personal information when he'd asked.

Too late for second thoughts now, she reminded herself.

Louise smiled. "Nick will be just fine. The boys will take care of him. Besides, men love building things together. Next to sports, it's the ultimate male bonding experience."

"I suppose. Although it's hard to think of my half brothers as boys. They're all grown-up."

"I guess they are. To me, they'll always be the Haynes boys."

Hannah took a sip of her coffee. "Jordan's house. That's where we were last night?"

Louise nodded. "I'm staying with them because Holly has her own store and doesn't want to give up working until she can't be on her feet anymore. I'm helping around the house so she doesn't have to work all day, then come home and worry about that. Over the past five or six years, I've worked for all the Haynes boys."

"I wonder if I'll ever get them straight. Okay, I know Holly and Jordan, and this is Sandy and Kyle's place."

"Right."

Hannah drew in a breath and frowned. "One of the women was very pregnant. Whom is she married to?"

"That's Jill, and her husband is Craig. He's the oldest. They live outside of Sacramento."

"All these couples having babies." She shook her head in wonder.

Louise laughed. "Once those boys learn how to do a thing, they just keep doing it. In this case, they've figured out how to fall in love and have children." The older woman gazed at her fondly. "You've already managed the first part, haven't you? Nick is quite a charmer."

"Charming is what he does best," Hannah agreed, feeling vaguely uncomfortable. She didn't want to get into a discussion about the love she and her pretend husband supposedly had for each other. The whole concept unnerved her. Love was one of those things that was really fun to read about, but in real life it often fell short of the mark. She'd seen the things people did in the name of love. In her mind, it was a whole lot smarter to stay out of trouble and not get involved.

Louise studied her for a minute. In the bright morning light, Hannah could see the lines around her eyes and mouth. She didn't look old, but she wasn't a young woman anymore, despite how great she looked in a fuchsia T-shirt and tight-fitting jeans.

"You must have lots of questions for me, Hannah. I want you to feel free to ask me anything. After all these years, I'm tired of keeping secrets." Louise's blue eyes darkened. "I daresay you're more than a little angry with me, too."

Hannah didn't want to admit to any strong emotions, even anger. She clasped her hands around the coffee mug. "I'm not sure what to ask."

"Then I'll start with what happened, and you stop me if you think of anything you want to know. Is that fair?"

Hannah nodded. This conversation made her nervous. She was still wrestling with the reality that this stranger actually was her mother. She knew that Louise had been quite young when she'd been forced to give up her child and was only in her forties now, but Hannah couldn't shake the image of a frail old woman as her parent.

Louise drew in a deep breath. "I was seventeen when I caught your daddy's eye. Earl Haynes—" she paused and smiled "—well, let's just say he was better-looking than all his sons put together. Oh, some might say I was exaggerating, but that's how I felt about him. He was a handsome man. Charming. He came to the high school to talk to the senior class about drinking and driving. A couple years before, a teenager had been killed in a car accident. Ever since, the adults had taken underage drinking really seriously."

She brushed her short blond hair away from her face. Hannah noticed her earrings were beautiful and unique. A tiny teapot dangled from one ear, while a cup and saucer sparkled from the other.

"He made his presentation to each of our history classes. I was right in front of the room. I remember thinking he was older, but so handsome. He had a smile that made me melt like butter on a hot griddle." Her face flushed. "I'll admit that I was just seventeen and innocent, but I knew his reputation and I knew he was married. In class, I couldn't stop looking at him and I had the feeling he'd noticed me, too. That afternoon, when I walked home, he was waiting for me at the house. Sitting bold as you please, right there on the front porch."

She shrugged. "Mama worked in a bar at the edge of town. She left right before I got home from school and didn't get back till after midnight. I'd always been a good girl. Never got into trouble. Until then. There was that whole big empty house with no one in it but me and Earl. I just couldn't resist him."

She took a last drink of coffee, then rose to her feet. "The affair went on for some time," she continued. "Until after I graduated from high school. For a long while, I didn't think anyone knew, then I started to hear the whispers." She moved to the kitchen sink. "I was so embarrassed. I wanted to stop, but I loved him. Or thought I did.

And he said he loved me. So I continued to see him. Then I found out I was pregnant."

She ran the water and washed out the cup. Instead of facing the room, she continued to stare out the window. "My mother found me crying in my room one night. She wanted to know if Earl had dumped me. It was the first time I realized my mother knew what was going on. She told me later that the bar had had some trouble with its liquor license. Earl could have shut it down at any time. He told my mother he would have, too, if she interfered."

Louise turned back to Hannah. "She needed that job. She didn't have any other skills. I found out later that she was sick. She died of cancer a few years after that, but back then, the symptoms were starting. She couldn't chance being laid off. So no one stopped Earl. Not even me."

Hannah didn't know what to think. She hadn't thought about the circumstances of her conception. An older married man taking advantage of a young woman. The notion left a bad taste in her mouth.

"This is a small town," she said slowly. "There must have been a lot of gossip."

"Plenty. Once I knew I was having a baby, I left. I never told Earl why. I just said I was tired of it and that I was moving on." Her mouth twisted down. The bright fuchsia lipstick that had seemed flattering a few moments ago now stood out garishly against her pale skin. "He begged me not to go. Said he loved me. I didn't believe him. I knew his reputation. I knew that what I'd done was wrong, but I was finally going to make it right. I went to one of those homes for unwed mothers. They took care of everything. I learned to type and do office work. Their agency found a nice couple to adopt you." Tears welled up in her eyes. She raised her chin and blinked rapidly. "They were a nice couple, weren't they?"

Hannah nodded. "Very nice. Lovely people." Her throat started to tighten.

"I'm glad. Really. It was for the best. I know it was. The only thing is..." A tear slipped down her cheek. She brushed it away and sniffed. "The only thing is, they wouldn't let me hold you. They said you were a healthy little girl and they took you a-away." Her voice cracked. "I thought that was wrong. They should have let me hold you."

The simple story had been acted out by thousands of women thousands of times all over the world. Innocent girls seduced and left pregnant gave up their babies every day. This shouldn't be any different. Yet Hannah found herself fighting tears. Her anger faded, drained away by sadness.

"Tell me about them," Louise said. "The people who adopted you. What are they like? Are you a close family? Did you tell them about my letters?"

"I..." She wasn't sure what to say, then decided the truth would be easiest. "They were killed in a car accident when I was four."

Louise gasped and covered her mouth.

Hannah shrugged. "There wasn't any other family. I was raised in foster homes."

"No," Louise murmured. Tears spilled onto her cheeks. "Oh, no. Hannah. No. I can't... Oh, that's so wrong. It's so unfair."

Louise crossed toward her. Hannah didn't remember standing, but suddenly she was in her mother's arms. They were both crying, Louise with great choking sobs and Hannah silently.

None of it had been fair, she thought grimly. Not what happened to Louise and not what happened to her.

"I'm so sorry," Louise apologized tearfully. "This is all my fault."

Hannah drew in a deep breath and straightened. She brushed her tears away and tried to smile. "It's no one's fault. It just happened. I turned out fine."

"But I wanted more than fine for you. I wanted the best." She moved to the counter, tore off a paper towel and handed it to Hannah, then took one for herself. "I wish I'd known. I would have come for you. All those wasted years."

"We're together now."

Louise wiped her face and offered a shaky smile. "So we are. You're right. That's what's important. We can't do anything to change what happened."

They both returned to the kitchen table. Hannah fought against unfamiliar emotions. She hadn't believed she could be affected by details from the past. Nor had she expected any of it to matter to her. Obviously she'd been wrong.

"I'm glad you wrote to me," she said impulsively.

Louise leaned back in her chair. "It was your brothers' idea. As soon as they found out about you, they wanted me to find you. I'd thought about it for a long time, but I'd been afraid. They gave me the encouragement I needed."

"I'm surprised they were so willing to have a stranger invade their lives. And under such difficult circumstances. It can't be easy for them to think about the past."

"Probably not." Louise smiled sadly. "They're sweet enough not to blame me completely. They know what their father is like. I wasn't the first woman he…well, there were plenty of others. Still, they're happy to meet you, although your being female complicated everything."

"Why? What difference would that make?"

"I think I'll let them explain about that."

Hannah decided not to pursue the matter. She had other, more pressing questions. She sorted through them in her mind and found the one that concerned her the most. "Are you very ill?"

Louise raised her eyebrows. "Ill? No. Why?"

"In your letter you said we should get together while there was still time. At first I assumed it was because you were old and frail. But that's obviously not it, so I decided you must be sick."

Soft laughter filled the kitchen. Louise smiled broadly. "I'm disgustingly healthy. All I meant by that was that we'd wasted so much time already. Twenty-seven years apart. I didn't want to go another day without knowing my daughter."

She stretched out her arms, sliding her hands across the table. Hannah hesitated for a moment, then placed her palms on top of the other woman's fingers. They clasped hands.

"I'm so glad you came," Louise said.

"Me, too."

Hannah was pleased to find that she meant it. Things were working out better than she'd hoped. She liked her mother. Now that she understood a little about the circumstances of her birth, she could see that Louise hadn't had many options about her child. The anger was still there, but it was fading. She had a whole family to meet and be a part of. Until they found out the truth.

Her good spirits faded quickly, squashed by the weight of her lies. Nick. What was she going to do about him? What was there to say? She cleared her throat to try.

"About Nick and me," she began.

"Oh, he's wonderful," Louise said. "Very good-looking. Of course, the women in our family do have an eye for handsome men. Sometimes much to our regret. But in your case, you chose wisely. He cares about you. That's obvious in the way he looks at you."

Hannah shifted uncomfortably. Great. Her mother applauded her taste in men. What would happen when Louise found out Nick was nothing but a common thief and that her only daughter was a liar? As for Nick caring about her, well, Hannah didn't know what Louise saw in his gaze. Lust, maybe. If he watched her at all, it was to make sure he knew where she was so she wouldn't run off without paying him.

"Now what about Nick?" Louise asked.

Hannah forced herself to smile. She couldn't tell the truth just yet. It would spoil everything. "I'm glad you like him," she said lamely.

"Me, too. I'm so pleased he's staying with you while you're here. We'll be able to spend lots of time together."

Another burst of conscience tightened her chest. Another lie. Nick would be getting his "phone call" tomorrow and heading back to Southport Beach. At least then Hannah would be able to draw in a breath without worrying about what he was going to say or do. But instead of feeling relief, something oddly like regret filled her as a tiny voice whispered she might actually miss Nick when he was gone.

"Where did you go to college?" Travis asked.

Nick lowered the measuring tape and made a note on the paper he'd placed on the windowsill. He turned to face the man who would have been his half brother-in-law if he and Hannah were really married.

"University of California at Santa Barbara," he said because it was true. He had a four-year degree, in economics of all things. It hadn't done him a damn bit of good when he'd first joined the Santa Barbara Police Department, although all those business courses had come in handy in the past year.

While working the scams necessary to bring down the

bad guys, he'd actually bought and sold land, planned subdivisions and made a presentation to Southport Beach city planners about a shopping center he wanted to develop.

He remeasured the top of the window, wanting to get it right. When he'd double-checked the pencil marks on the pale yellow walls, he reached for a hammer.

Behind him, Travis and Kyle smoothed the wallpaper border that they'd applied halfway up the wall. Its circus animals danced across the paper. Pudgy lions played trumpets, the giraffes had trombones, and hippos in tutus waltzed with zebras in top hats. Craig was installing cream-colored miniblinds while Jordan supervised everyone's work.

The baby's room was good-size. Maybe fourteen by sixteen. Under normal circumstances, it would have felt spacious, especially empty of furniture. But with five guys in it, all moving around and trying to work, the space seemed confined. It had taken Nick a couple of minutes to figure out he was here to be grilled. The casual questions had started a couple of hours ago and so far hadn't let up.

He didn't mind. If Hannah had been his sister, he would have done the same thing.

After making a small hole in the plaster with a nail, he pulled it out and tapped screw anchors into place. Next he lined up the brass bracket with the marks on the wall and secured it in place. There were three lengths of fabric in the closet. Jordan had explained that Holly wanted miniblinds to keep out the light, then fabric matching the border print would be draped around the windows. Nick had a vague idea of what it was all going to turn out like, although he'd never understood how women could take some cloth, tie a couple of knots and make the whole thing look like it was out of a magazine photo shoot. But he did know how to install brackets.

"How long has Hannah been a cop?" Jordan asked.

"Since she graduated from college."

Kyle stepped back to admire the wallpaper border and grinned. "That proves she's a Haynes. Except for that traitor there—" he motioned to Jordan "—we're all cops."

"I know," Nick said.

Craig finished screwing in the supports and bent down to grab the last miniblind. "That doesn't make you nervous, Nick, does it?"

"Being surrounded by Glenwood's finest?" He shook his head. "Not me. My conscience is clear. I sleep like a baby at night."

Except for last night when he had lain awake knowing Hannah was only a few feet away. He'd tried to relax, but questions about what she'd worn to bed and how she would look sleeping had kept him tossing and turning on the too-short sofa.

"It shouldn't bother him," Kyle said. "After all, he's married to a cop."

"That's right. Hannah keeps me in line."

Kyle measured the distance from the bedroom door to the closet, then called the number to Travis. "Hannah is the first girl born to the family in four generations."

Nick tapped a screw anchor into place. "That's unusual."

"Maybe, but it's true. Our father is one of six brothers. His grandfather is one of five, and his great-grandfather is one of eight boys."

"But you four have daughters."

"Not me," Craig said quickly. "At least not yet. Jill is going to have a girl."

"Holly and I don't have children yet," Jordan added. "But hers will be a girl, too."

The four brothers exchanged a look, but Nick didn't

know what it meant. There was some kind of secret in the air. He wasn't sure if he should pursue it or not. Then he decided if they wanted him to know, they would tell him.

"You and Hannah think about having children?" Travis asked.

Nick set the brass bracket against the wall. "We've talked about it. I'd like children but the timing just hasn't been right."

Most of the time, lying was easy, but sometimes, like now, it was damn hard. Travis accepted the explanation without question, yet Nick found himself wanting to say more. He liked these men. More important, he respected them. He wanted the feeling to be mutual. Maybe it was, but anything they thought about him now would change if they knew the truth.

He grimaced. Which truth? That he was pretending to be Hannah's husband, or that he was pretending to be a criminal? They were cops. They would understand about undercover work. The need to confide in them almost overwhelmed him. He fought against it. Too risky. He'd spent the past year setting up the deal—he wasn't going to blow it just so Hannah's brothers could slap him on the back.

Until the job was finished and everyone was in jail, he was going to stay Nick Archer, shady character.

He glanced around at the men in the room. With their dark hair and eyes, they reminded him of Hannah. Knowing that he was here with her brothers must be making her crazy.

"How's the real-estate market?" Travis asked.

"Coming back," Nick answered. "We've had a few slow years, but the recovery has started. I didn't lose much money because I work the beach areas. Waterfront property is always at a premium."

"Swindle anybody lately?" Kyle asked, grinning.

Nick returned his smile. "Not this week."

He finished installing the last bracket and climbed down the step stool. The wallpaper border was nearly complete. Craig released the miniblind so it zipped down, covering the window. He turned the handle, opening the slats, and sunlight filled the room.

"Looks great," Jordan said, surveying their work. "I guess the women will be over later to take care of the drapes."

Travis and Kyle smoothed the remaining wallpaper into place. Craig leaned over and punched Jordan in the arm. "You getting scared yet?"

Jordan didn't smile. "Terrified. When we're in bed at night, I can feel the baby kicking against my side. What do I know about being a father?"

Kyle nodded. "I know the feeling, but if I can do it, you'll be fine. You sort of learn as you go. Besides, we'll all be here."

Nick listened to their conversation. These men had a special bond. They cared for each other and they would care for Hannah. If she let them.

She'd spent most of her life assuming the worst about people. She'd concluded that if they tried to get close, they must want something from her. So much of her energy was consumed in attempting to hide her feelings. Her whole outlook would have been different if she'd been raised in this warm, close-knit family. Knowing Hannah as he did, he was sure she was going to resist believing something this great had happened to her. She would get all prickly and try to scare them off. Unless something—or someone—stopped her.

As he had a thousand times before, he wondered why he cared so much about Hannah Pace. She sure as hell didn't go out of her way to be pleasant to him. The combination of strength and insecurity was appealing. As was the sway of her hips and the flash of intelligence in her eyes. Maybe it was because she hadn't been easy. Most women gave in too quickly to his charm. Never Hannah. She would rather live with roaches than date him.

At first, he'd started teasing her because she seemed such an ice queen. It gave him pleasure to rattle her cage. Then he'd found he liked her snappy retorts and he'd begun looking forward to seeing her. Somewhere along the line, teasing respect had turned to affection. Maybe because he knew it was safe. With Hannah, it would never be real.

If he was honest with himself, he would have to admit his desire to help her fit in with her family wasn't completely altruistic. If he smoothed the way for her, she would remember him fondly, even after he was gone.

"I've got cold beer in the fridge," Jordan said. "Louise left some sandwiches."

The men started down the stairs. Nick followed last. As their conversation drifted back to him, he began wondering what it would be like if this was for real. If he were married to Hannah and a part of this family.

He shook his head. Whom was he trying to kid? He had still been in elementary school when he'd learned the most important lesson of all—not to get attached. He'd lived by that rule and it had served him well.

Hannah frowned at her reflection. It wasn't that she didn't like what she saw in the mirror. It was the fact that her hands trembled.

"I can't believe this," she muttered. "All it takes is one family dinner and I'm a basket case."

She drew in a deep breath. It was only dinner with people she'd already met. No big deal. All right, so Louise had mentioned everyone would be dressing. Not formally, just not jeans. So this time they were expecting her and might have had time to think up difficult questions. She would survive. It wouldn't be so bad.

She opened her eye shadow compact and lifted out the tiny brush. Her fingers shook visibly and she bit back a curse. She was a trained professional. What happened to performing under pressure?

She leaned forward and closed her left eye. As she positioned the brush over her lid, the bathroom door opened and Nick stepped inside. He wore a blue T-shirt tucked into worn jeans. The color of the shirt matched the irises of his eyes and did amazing things to her already-rapid heart rate. He'd shaved that morning, but there was a faint darkening around his cheeks and jaws as the stubble highlighted his bone structure.

"You going to be much longer?" he asked.

She stared at his reflection, meeting his gaze. "Maybe you didn't notice, but the door was closed."

"I noticed. That's why I came in. How much longer are you going to hog the bathroom?"

"I just need to finish my makeup. A closed door is usually a request for privacy. You could have knocked."

"Yeah, I could have."

He leaned against the wall by the shower and folded his arms over his chest. The action brought his firm muscles into relief. The tiny brush slipped from her fingers and dropped to the counter. She leaned her forehead against the mirror.

"I'm never going to finish," she muttered.

"Then you'll just have to share," he said and pulled the hem of his T-shirt out of his jeans.

She couldn't bear to think about his undressing in her presence. She grabbed the brush. "Never mind, I'll hurry."

She ignored his knowing smile and focused on her eye-lid. Using every available ounce of concentration, she was able to smooth a stroke of shadow right in the crease. She smudged it with her ring finger, then straightened to study the effect.

"Beautiful," he said.

She ignored his comment. "What happened with my brothers?"

"The usual. I mentioned how you liked to visit me in prison and that you had a tattoo with my initials right here." He pointed to his backside. "Oh, and I told them about the threesome we had with my cell mate, Bubba, on your last conjugal visit."

In spite of herself, she felt her lips turn up in a smile. "I'm trying to have a serious conversation."

"I'm trying not to." He held up his hands. "Okay, you win. Serious. They asked about real estate, your college. We discussed the baseball season and whether or not the international commodities market is ever going to stabilize."

She closed her right eye and started to apply the makeup. "So nothing dangerous?"

"Not a word. However, tonight could be a different story. It's the banquet for the prodigal daughter. There'll be a fatted calf and tons of questions. So do you want to discuss our stories or should I wing it again?"

She thought about his description of their supposed first meeting. He'd painted such a vivid picture of her hangover on some tropical island that she'd nearly believed him herself. But she couldn't risk more outrageous tales. Not if she planned on coming clean later.

She closed the compact and reached for a pencil eyeliner. "I would need your word that this information would be kept strictly confidential," she warned, still suspicious of his motives.

He stalked toward the counter. She turned to stare at him.

"What are you so damned afraid of?" he asked, obviously irritated. "You can't simply answer the question. You always have to qualify everything. Gee, Hannah, are you afraid you might accidentally reveal something of yourself? The world would probably end if you let someone get to know you, right? In case you haven't noticed, I'm up here because of *you*. I'm doing this for *you*. I don't get a damn thing out of it, so maybe you could start acting a little more like a team player and a little less like the lady of the manor."

His harsh words shocked her, mostly because they hit so close to home. "You're not doing it for me," she snapped. "Don't pretend you are. You're just in it for the money."

"Four hundred bucks? Compared to what I normally make in a few days? Get real."

She stared at him. He had her there. He made and lost millions every month. Why *was* he doing this? It couldn't be for her. Somehow that thought was more terrifying than a grilling quiz by all her relatives.

"Listen, Nick. I don't care why you're here. I'm paying you to look good and keep your mouth shut. That's our deal. If you're not up to it, then leave."

The sharp retort came from fear and she would have given anything to call it back. Something flickered in his blue eyes. Something dark and cold. If she hadn't known better, she would have thought she'd hurt his feelings.

Yeah, right. Nick Archer didn't care about her. He couldn't.

He turned away. She placed her hand on his back to keep him from leaving. His thick muscles bunched against her fingers and her mouth got dry. She would have paid a whole lot more than ten dollars if he would kiss her right now.

"I'm sorry," she said softly. "You're right. I am afraid." He would think she was referring to her family, when in truth they were a lot less scary than her confusing feelings about him. "I didn't mean it. This whole thing has me rattled. Maybe if it was only my mom. But there's everyone else, too. I spoke without thinking." She let her hand fall to her side.

Just when she expected he would walk out of the room and out of her life, he faced her and shrugged. "No big deal. Favorite food?"

"Scallops."

He shuddered. "Little white round things. No thanks. I don't even want to think about eating them. Least favorite food?"

She returned to the mirror and penciled in eyeliner. "Brussels sprouts."

"I'll agree with you on that one. When and where did you lose your virginity?"

She laughed. "Don't push it, buster."

"Hey, they might ask."

"Yeah. When and where did you lose yours?"

"The back seat of a Mustang. Her name was Mary and she had these..." He cupped his hands in front of his chest, then grinned. "I was barely seventeen, so I was impressed. I think it took all of fifteen seconds."

She reached for her mascara. "Is there anything you won't talk about?"

"Sexually? Nope."

"And sex is the most important thing in your life?"

He winked. "What did you have in mind?"

"You're hopeless."

"You're not the first one to notice."

He pulled his T-shirt over his head. Hannah stared at his reflection in the mirror. Gold blond hair covered his chest.

Her fingers started to tremble again, but this time it wasn't from fear.

"Wh-what are you doing?"

His expression was carefully blank. "We don't have that much time." He motioned to his bare chest. "I was going to take a quick shower. We don't want to be late. Unless I'm bothering you."

She forced herself to concentrate on darkening her eyelashes. If he didn't mind getting naked in front of her, she refused to mind watching. "Be my guest."

As he reached for his button fly, she reminded herself he wasn't the first man she'd seen naked. There had been Shawn, and before him, Jimmy, the guy she'd gone out with in college. She knew what the male form looked like.

Which didn't stop her from nearly poking herself in the eye when he dropped his briefs on the floor.

She jerked her head back and tried to see if her lashes were clumped. Instead, she found herself watching him. Wide shoulders and a broad chest narrowing at the waist and hips. He had long legs, also covered with gold blond hair. While he wasn't aroused, he was still impressive, and she felt a flicker of heat in her belly.

He turned toward the shower and reached for the knob. She had a perfect view of his back and rear. Her fingers itched to squeeze the high, round flesh.

She forced her attention back to her makeup. The mascara she'd already applied would have to be enough. She didn't trust herself with anything near her eyes right now. She reached for the blush and colored her cheekbones. The last item she needed was lipstick.

While she finished her makeup, Nick adjusted the shower temperature. She was surprised at how long it took to find the right combination of hot and cold. Speaking of which, she was running completely on hot. Waves of heat rippled through her, making her knees melt and her thighs quiver. He was beautiful enough to take her breath away when he was dressed. Naked, he made her think about committing borderline illegal acts.

She eyed the lipstick, then realized she was in no condition to apply it. She would be safer if she got out of the bathroom and back under control. As she collected her belongings, he finally stepped into the spray.

She walked toward the door.

"You were looking," Nick called. "That's gonna cost you five bucks."

He stood under the water and grinned. Two seconds later, the door slammed shut. Oh, Hannah, what you do to me, he thought, well pleased by her staring.

Five minutes later, he turned off the water, stepped out and reached for a towel. There on the counter, right next to his shaving kit, was a flat, crisp, five-dollar bill.

Chapter Seven

Hannah approached the large, formally set dining-room table. Her heart pounded in her chest and her palms felt sweaty. She would like to think it was a reaction to having seen Nick naked, and the fact that even as she walked into the dining room, his hand rested on the small of her back. Some of it was, but most of it was nerves. It had only been twenty-four hours and she hadn't adjusted to being part of the Haynes family.

Elizabeth motioned to the empty chairs. "Sit where you'd like. I counted a couple of times and made Travis count with me. We should have enough place settings." She frowned faintly and shook her head. "This family is getting bigger by the day."

"It could be worse," Travis said, coming up behind her and wrapping his arms around her waist.

Hannah watched as Elizabeth leaned into her husband's embrace. Their love was as tangible as one of the dining-room chairs. She admired what they had found together and was willing to admit to a hint of envy. What would it be like to have someone love her the way Travis loved Elizabeth, or Craig loved Jill, or the way any of her brothers loved their wives? How had they solved that great mystery? Her lone attempt at a serious relationship—marriage—had ended after five pitiful days.

"I'll sit next to Hannah," Kyle said, giving her a wink.

"I'm the oldest," Craig said. "I'm sure she wants me to tell her about the family."

Elizabeth looked at Jordan. "What's your reasoning for sitting next to your new sister?"

"I'm the most interesting."

Despite her nerves, Hannah smiled. She appreciated the attempt to make her feel welcome. However, there were so many of them. She took a half step closer to Nick, willing him to protect her from these strangers.

His blue-eyed gaze settled on her face. He'd shaved for dinner and was wearing one of his expensive suits. They'd all dressed up for the occasion. Hannah had put on a cream silk blouse tucked into tailored black pants. Nick was tall enough for her to wear pumps with the outfit. Actually, all the men were tall—and handsome. Her brothers and their friend, Austin, with his strong features and dark hair and eyes. Nick, with his blond hair.

He slipped his hand to her arm and down to her wrist, then took her hand in his. She knew the gesture was two parts performance and one part comfort. Even so, they'd done it enough times that their laced fingers felt familiar. As if they really were a couple.

Louise came into the dining room. This was the third time Hannah had seen her mother. She was prepared for the almost-spiky bold blond hair and the not-so-subtle makeup. It was the colors of her outfit that gave her pause.

Tonight, Louise wore a red long-sleeved blouse. Embroidered from her left shoulder across her midsection to her right hip was a bright green parrot. Her flowing skirt reached almost to her ankles. It was the same silky material with the same red background, only this fabric was covered with miniature versions of the same gaudy parrot. Hannah didn't consider herself much of a fashion plate, but even she was startled by Louise's wardrobe choices. Still, they looked right on the curvy woman. They certainly suited her personality.

She glanced at everyone standing around. "Why aren't you sitting down?" she asked, then held up a wine bottle in each hand. "I'm ready to take requests."

"They can't decide who sits next to Hannah," Elizabeth explained.

"That's easy. Her husband deserves to be on one side and I'll take the other."

The brothers groaned good-naturedly and began pulling out chairs for their wives. In a few minutes, everyone was seated. Louise poured wine while Sandy gave Elizabeth a hand in the kitchen.

Hannah started to stand up. "Let me do something," she offered.

Elizabeth came through the doorway holding a huge bowl of salad. "Don't be silly. You're the honored guest. Trust me, you want to take advantage. Once we're used to you, we'll put you to work and you'll look back and remember this time fondly."

Jill, petite and very pregnant, smiled. "She's telling the truth. The first couple of times Craig brought me to meet everyone, I couldn't believe how kind they were. Then everything changed."

"Hey, we're swell guys," Kyle said, giving his sister-in-law a soft mock punch to the arm. She blew him a kiss and he squeezed her shoulder in a gesture of affection.

Hannah watched the scene and realized it was being repeated around the table. This family touched. Not just husbands and wives, but everyone. Brothers exchanged playful blows; the women hugged.

At first, these contacts made Hannah feel as if she was trapped in some bizarre petting zoo. Then she watched more closely, noticing the love lighting everyone's eyes. These people were a genuine family. They truly cared about each other. It was something she'd missed her whole life. How odd to have found it now...under false pretenses.

Sandy carried in another large bowl of salad, along with rolls. Soon food was being passed around and conversation flowed.

"Where are the children?" Hannah asked, accepting the salad and placing some on her plate.

Jill pointed toward the ceiling. "The older ones are with friends. The younger ones have a sitter to look after them."

Hannah remembered how many children there had been last night. "Just one sitter?"

Rebecca, Austin's wife, smiled. "Candace is an old pro at baby-sitting for our brood. She's great at organizing games and keeping everyone under control. She gets a dollar a child per hour. If you do the math, you can see it's well worth her while."

Kyle nodded. "I noticed she just bought herself a car. I'm sure we paid for it."

Sandy touched his shoulder. "Honey, she earned every penny. You know what our four are like at home. Add everyone else's kids to that. Would you want to baby-sit?"

Kyle held up his hands in a gesture of surrender. "No, thanks."

As Sandy and Elizabeth sat down, Louise raised her

glass. "To my beautiful daughter and my handsome son-in-law. Welcome home."

Hannah felt a faint blush creep up her cheeks as she and Nick became the focus of attention. She sipped from her glass.

"I'd like to propose a toast," her pretend husband announced. "To family found. I married Hannah because she's the most wonderful woman I've ever met. Now that I've met her family, I see where she gets it from. You have my heartfelt thanks."

He took her free hand and brought it to his mouth, then kissed the palm. She couldn't breathe, or talk, or do anything but stare at him and accept the heat that flashed down her arm. An audible sigh breezed through the room. She glanced around and saw Nick had entranced every woman at the table.

Louise touched her napkin to the corner of her eye. "Nick, you're a charmer, I'll give you that."

"I'm a sincere charmer. There's a difference."

Louise patted Hannah's arm. "Honey, do not let this one get away. There aren't many like him out there."

How true, Hannah thought, wondering why she so desperately wanted to believe Nick's words. He was good—nearly good enough to make her forget about their deal and the fact that she was paying him to perform. If only...

She shook off the thought before it formed. This kind of dangerous thinking would only get her in trouble.

Conversation flowed around the table. When the salad was finished, the men cleared the plates while their wives brought in bowls of potatoes, two kinds of vegetables and a large prime rib. Travis stood at the sideboard and carved according to requests.

"Rare," Nick called. "Hannah prefers medium."

She wanted to kick him under the table and tell him she

could order for herself. She wanted to snap out that she didn't like her meat medium, but she did. How had he known? He caught her gaze.

"Lucky guess," he murmured, reading her mind.

"How do you do that?"

"Know what you like or know what you're thinking?"

"Both."

He leaned so close, his breath tickled her ear. She could feel his heat and inhale the scent of the shampoo he'd used in the shower. Instantly, the image of his lean, naked body flashed in her mind. Her hands trembled as she thought about what it would have been like to touch him all over, to feel the skin rippling over well-defined muscle. Her stomach clenched and her thighs pressed together.

"You wouldn't believe me if I told you," he said.

She turned toward him. Their mouths were less than an inch apart. The rest of the room faded; even the sounds became faint, as if heard from a long distance. Her world was reduced to his face, the fire flickering in his eyes and the shape of his mouth.

She wanted him to kiss her. She wanted to feel his mouth on hers, to taste him, to wrap her arms around him, to hold and be held. She wanted—

"I'm so happy you two are here," Louise said, her voice cutting into the moment and breaking the spell. "My birthday is in two weeks and you'll be here for that."

Hannah blinked a couple of times and slowly brought the room into focus. She turned to her mother. "Your birthday?"

"I'm going to be forty-seven. Practically an old woman."

"Never that," Nick said. "You're the type of woman who'll be young when she's a hundred."

Louise laughed. "Flatterer. But this time, I choose to believe you're telling the truth."

"Where is the party going to be?" Kyle asked. "We can have it at our house."

"Jordan and Holly have already volunteered," Louise said. "Having my daughter and her husband with me is going to make it the best birthday ever."

Hannah took a sip of wine so she could avoid answering. She would still be here, but Nick would be leaving tomorrow. A flicker of disappointment filled her chest. She ignored it. He had to leave. It was difficult enough to pretend to be married for a couple of days. They would never make it work for two weeks. Besides, she barely knew the man. She wanted him gone, didn't she?

"Here you go." Sandy handed her a plate.

"Thanks."

As Hannah reached for it, Sandy stared at her hand. "You're not wearing a wedding ring."

Silence descended like night in the tropics, fast and without warning. The observation hung in the quiet and everyone turned to stare. Hannah's stomach dropped to her knees. Oh, Lord. Now what?

Nick took the plate and set it on the table. Then he reached for her left hand and brushed his thumb across her knuckles. "She doesn't wear jewelry at the police station," he said easily. "No rings, not even earrings." He pushed Hannah's hair over her shoulder and pointed. "See, no pierced ears."

Sandy frowned. "Why not?"

"It's dangerous," Travis said from his place by the sideboard. "If you're trying to subdue someone and you have a large ring or earrings, you're vulnerable. Earrings can be ripped out and rings can be jerked off."

Sandy shuddered. "That's awful. No wonder you don't want to risk it."

Nick smoothed her hair back in place. "Combine that habit with a poor memory and my Hannah constantly leaves the house without her wedding band." He brushed his mouth against her cheek. "I love her anyway."

Hannah felt as if she'd just escaped death by drowning. For one horrible minute, she assumed their cover had been blown. A wedding ring. Why hadn't she thought about that? But Nick had covered beautifully. The man sure knew how to think on his feet.

Sandy smiled. "Louise is right. You picked a good one."

"Hey!" Kyle jumped to his feet. "You picked a pretty good one, too."

She hugged her husband. "I picked the best one, honey. You know that."

"Better," Kyle said and drew his wife into the chair next to his. "Later you can make it up to me in private."

"I can't wait."

Hannah couldn't join in the laughter. She was still too stunned by their near exposure. When Elizabeth had set Nick's plate in front of him and moved off, Hannah glanced over.

"How did you know about the jewelry?" she asked, her voice quiet.

"I spend a lot of time in police stations."

His answer reminded her of what he really did for a living. Of the shady dealings and illegal transactions. She didn't want to think about that right now. She didn't want to have to not like him.

He leaned close. "Not remembering a wedding band was pretty dumb, huh?"

She couldn't resist his smile. "Yeah, that's what I was thinking, too."

Just for tonight, she was going to forget Nick's past and live in the moment. What harm could it do?

Elizabeth passed a bowl of green beans to Louise. "Why didn't you invite your friend the professor to join us?"

Louise pressed her napkin to her lips. "This is a family affair. I don't think Richard would be interested. Besides, he's out of town on business."

Jordan raised his eyebrows. "Richard, is it?"

Hannah glanced at her mother and was surprised when the older woman blushed.

"Oh, stop it." Louise patted Hannah's hand. "They're trying to make more of it than it is. Really. I went back to college last year."

"To get a degree?" Hannah asked.

Louise nodded. "In sociology. I know you probably think it's silly at my age and all, but it's something I've wanted my whole life and I decided to just do it. Like they say in those commercials."

"I think it's great that you're studying for your degree. Why does it matter how old you are?"

"That's what I say."

Elizabeth smiled at her. "Louise being Louise, of course she didn't just take classes. She met a guy."

"Richard Wilson is a nice man and sometimes we go out for coffee after the lecture. There were several students there."

"In the beginning," Jordan said. "But since that semester ended, it's only been the two of you." He smiled at Hannah. "Your mother is involved with a much younger man."

Louise glared at him. "Eleven years isn't all that much and we're not really dating."

Nick leaned around Hannah and patted Louise's shoulder. "I'm proud of you, Mom. Teach 'em everything you know. Turnabout's fair play."

Jill pushed back her seat and tried to stand up. Her large belly made her movements awkward. Craig sprang to his feet and assisted his wife. She stepped back and grabbed the chair. "It's like trying to balance with a watermelon attached to your midsection."

Holly pushed the food around on her plate. "Please don't say that."

Sandy leaned over and hugged her. "Holly, I've had four kids. It's not that bad. And once the baby's born, you'll forget all about it."

Holly didn't look convinced.

"When is your baby due?" Nick asked.

"Around the first of October."

Louise pointed at Jill. "I'm hoping this one holds out for my birthday."

Jill groaned. "Louise, I want to. You know that. But it's two weeks away. I don't think I can make it."

"Sure you can. Just think calm, relaxing thoughts."

A bit of movement caught Hannah's attention. She saw Austin, the brothers' best friend, whispering with his wife. Then Rebecca shook her head. Elizabeth saw it, too.

"What are you two hiding?"

Rebecca glanced up. Her face was flawless, her skin pale and her eyes large. "Nothing really."

"It's not nothing," Louise said. "Out with it."

Rebecca glanced at her husband. "Well, we don't want to take away from the excitement of having Hannah finally a part of the family, but—"

Austin put his arm around her. "Rebecca's pregnant."

Spontaneous applause filled the room.

"Congratulations." Travis pounded Austin on the back and kissed Rebecca's cheek.

"When?" Elizabeth asked.

"January 1," Rebecca replied. "A New Year's baby."

"I'm envious," Elizabeth said as she reached for the dirty plates. "At least you have a chance of having a boy."

Hannah looked at Nick questioningly. "Doesn't everyone have a chance of having a boy?" she asked.

He shrugged. "I thought so."

"Not in this family," Louise said. "At least, that's the rumor."

"It's not a rumor," Jordan said. "Don't you think Hannah proves it's true?"

Louise's smile faded. She looked uncomfortable. Jordan stretched his arm across the table and squeezed her hand. "Hey, it's okay. Really." He looked at Hannah. "No girls have been born into the Haynes family in four generations. In that time, the Haynes men became womanizers. They married but never loved their wives. Our father and his brothers were the worst of the lot. Everyone kept having babies, but only boys."

Elizabeth came back into the kitchen for a fresh load of dirty dishes. Hannah rose to help, but Elizabeth waved her back to her chair.

"Then I married Travis and we had a daughter," Elizabeth said, picking up the story. "Jordan decided it was because we were truly in love. Kyle and Sandy had a daughter."

"Mine is supposed to be a girl," Jill said, pointing to her belly.

Holly shrugged. "I don't know yet."

Jordan stroked her cheek. "*I* know."

Hannah was confused. "You really believe this?"

"Of course," Kyle said. "So you know what this means about you, Hannah?"

She stared at them. They were all staring back expectantly. Nick figured it out first. "You're the first girl child born to the family. Your parents were in love."

Hannah turned to Louise. The older woman stared at the table. "It was a long time ago. I'm not sure it matters."

Travis covered her hand with his. "Louise, we've all talked about this. We know Dad didn't love Mom. I'm sure they got married because she was pregnant. His wild ways would have caught up with him eventually. She happened to be the unlucky one. It's okay that he loved you."

Louise nodded but didn't speak. After a minute, she wiped away a tear. "You boys are good to me and I appreciate it." She sniffed. "Enough of this seriousness." She turned to Hannah. "When can I expect my first grandchild?"

Hannah couldn't have been more shocked if everyone had started taking off their clothes. She opened her mouth but couldn't think of a single thing to say.

Nick patted her hand. "We both want children, but right now Hannah and I are concentrating on our careers. In a few years, when we're where we want to be, we'll start a family."

"That sounds like a good plan," Louise said and began clearing her end of the table.

Hannah exhaled the breath she'd suddenly realized she'd been holding. Crisis averted again, thanks to Nick. She looked at him.

"What can I say? I'm good," he murmured. "I probably should have charged more."

She felt a smile tugging at the corner of her mouth. She wasn't sure if she should slap him or kiss him. If she was being honest, she would have to admit that the kissing sounded a whole lot more fun.

"Do you have any hobbies?" Louise asked.

"Sure. Hannah plays the piano and she sings."

"That's great," Travis said. "None of us can carry a tune."

Louise glanced at her. "Oh, honey, I wish I had a piano so I could hear you play."

Hannah choked on her response. Nick was paying her back in spades for being difficult. Like her half brothers, she couldn't carry a tune if it came in its own box. She'd never once sat down at a piano.

"It's been years," she mumbled. "I'm sure I've forgotten everything."

Nick beamed. "She has a lovely voice. Sing something."

Hannah glared at him and touched her throat. "I couldn't right after eating. Perhaps another time."

"I can't wait," he said with obvious pleasure.

Elizabeth went into the kitchen, then came back and announced that they'd just taken the last of the pies from the oven. It was going to be a few minutes while they cooled. She suggested everyone move to the living room.

Hannah used the time to escape. She excused herself and started toward the front door. Once outside, she leaned against the porch railing and stared up at the sky.

It was a beautiful, clear night. She could see familiar stars, bright points of light against black velvet. Trees thick with leaves stood like tall sentinels. She crossed her arms over her chest. Forty-eight hours ago, she didn't know any of these people existed, and now they were a part of her life. How had that happened?

An old, familiar emotion stirred deep inside. She recognized the longing. The Haynes family tempted her with their humor and their love. She wanted to step inside their circle and belong. But she'd already learned a hard truth. The people she cared for rejected her. It had happened her whole life. If she came to love them, this family would send her away, too. It was so much easier not to get involved. At least the pain of being lonely was familiar and bearable.

Footsteps on the porch made her turn. Nick joined her in the darkness. He came up behind her and tried to draw her back against him. She resisted.

"I'm not speaking to you," she said.

"Why? What did I do?"

She smiled at the outrage in his voice. The darkness and their positions—her in front of him—hid her expression. She kept her tone stern. "You told my family I could sing and play the piano."

"Can't you?"

"Of course not."

"Gee, Hannah, I just assumed you could. Hmm, I guess if you'd been willing to share a little personal information, this wouldn't have happened."

"I refuse to accept the blame for your stories."

He whispered against her ear. "Admit it. You like my stories almost as much as you like me."

A shiver rippled through her. She wouldn't dream of saying the words aloud, but he was right, damn him. She did like his stories and she did like him. Funny how she'd spent the past year resisting him, and when they were finally together, it wasn't so very difficult to be in his company. She enjoyed his humor and his view of the world.

Remember who and what he is, a voice in her head warned. But she didn't want to listen. Not tonight.

Still close to her ear, he murmured, "Thanks for the five bucks."

She remembered him naked. "The pleasure was all mine," she said without thinking, then would cheerfully have paid the amount a hundred times over to call the words back.

"I like your looking at me," he said. "Maybe tomorrow we can turn the tables."

"I don't think so." Her tone was frosty, but inside her the heat cranked up about twenty degrees. She didn't understand her attraction to him. He wasn't her type at all. Yet there was something about him. Something irresistible.

He wrapped his arms around her waist and drew her back against him. This time she didn't resist. He was easy to lean on. Solid and dependable. Not two words she would have imagined associating with Nick Archer.

"I know this is overwhelming," he said, "but it will get easier."

"You think so?"

"Promise. The 'getting to know you' stage is always the worst. They're already charmed by you."

"I think you're the one doing all the charming."

He suddenly turned her toward him. Before she could protest, he drew her close and tugged on her hands until they were around his neck. "We've got an audience," he said quietly and jerked his head toward some bushes. "A few of the children. We'd better make this good."

Make what good? she started to ask, then read the answer in his eyes. She glanced toward the bushes but didn't see or hear anything. "Are you sure?"

"I saw them."

She didn't know if she believed him or not. Maybe he was lying. Maybe this was an excuse to kiss her. She hoped it was. Then she closed her eyes and gave herself up to the moment.

He kissed the way he did everything else—with an ease, grace and charm that left her breathless. His mouth possessed hers gently. A sweet caress, a soft brush of sensitive skin against sensitive skin. Her fingers clutched at the thick muscles in his shoulders. His hands held on to her waist.

She wondered if he did so to keep her close or if he wanted to prevent her from running away. If she'd had any breath left, she would have told him there was nowhere else she would rather be. Fortunately for her, he didn't think to ask.

She was tall and used to feeling awkward in a man's embrace. Yet Nick made her feel petite and feminine. He kissed her as she had never been kissed before, as if he needed to woo her. His mouth moved back and forth, sending a fiery hunger along her arms and down her torso. Without meaning to, without planning it, she pressed into him, bringing their thighs and chests in contact.

His arms wrapped around her, hauling her still nearer. One hand gripped the back of her head; the other rested on her hip. She could feel the imprint of his fingers, the strength of him.

He touched the tip of his tongue to her bottom lip and she parted for him. He entered slowly, tasting her, teasing her, making her vibrate with passion. When his tongue brushed against hers, she felt the current jolt through her all the way to her toes. Her breasts began to ache, as did her thighs. Bones became liquid and she flowed against him.

They clung together as their need grew. She'd made love before, she understood about desire, but the need—the acute necessity to join with this man—surprised her. Even more startling was how much she wanted to trust him.

She wanted his hands everywhere. She wanted him naked, as he had been before. She wanted to touch him, feel him inside of her. She wanted him to take her to a place of surrender, to shatter her into oblivion and then reassemble her whole.

He broke their kiss and placed his mouth on her neck. Her breathing was rapid and shallow, as was his. They generated enough heat and energy to create a tropical storm.

The hand on her hip slipped lower to cup her derriere. The one on the back of her head kneaded her scalp and played with her long braid.

As she arched against him, she inhaled a prayer of thanks that he was leaving the next day. She would never be able to hold on to her control if he stayed.

"I think they're gone," he said, his words muffled against her skin.

"The imaginary children?"

He smiled at her. "They were real."

She let her hands slide down his arms, then she stepped back. "As real as my piano playing?" He started to speak, but she placed her index finger over his mouth. "It doesn't matter," she told him. "I don't mind."

She should mind, but she didn't. He was breaking down barriers and she couldn't make him stop. At least by tomorrow she would be safe. After all, what damage could he do from a few hundred miles away?

Chapter Eight

Hannah felt as if she'd been asked in to explain her behavior to the principal. As she entered Jordan's living room the next day, she found her four brothers and Louise waiting for her. Austin wasn't there, which increased the feeling of being sent to the office for some transgression. After all, he was nearly family and if he wasn't here...

She swallowed hard. They'd found out about Nick and were going to confront her. Perhaps it was better to get it out in the open now.

Craig saw her first, rose to his feet and motioned for her to enter the room. "Don't look so scared," he said and took her arm, leading her to the sofa. Louise sat at one end, Travis at the other. "This isn't the Spanish Inquisition," he continued. "We expect you have some questions about what happened in the past and about us. Talking about these things is difficult at first, but easier in the long run.

We've had a lifetime of secrets and we don't want to keep them anymore. Not from you. You're our sister.''

She stared up into his brown eyes. Eyes the same shape as her own. He was tall and good-looking, with a warm, kind smile. She wanted to throw herself at him and have him hold her until all the little hurts went away. What would it have been like to grow up with Craig as her big brother? She had a feeling it would have been wonderful.

"I…" She raised her hands, palms up. "This isn't about Nick?''

"Nick?'' Louise asked. "No. But if you'd be more comfortable with him here, we'll understand.''

"We figured just the five of us would be less intimidating,'' Travis said, also coming to his feet. Like the rest of his brothers, he was dressed in jeans and a T-shirt. The casual clothing emphasized his strength and muscular build. "Maybe we should go get Nick to even out the numbers.''

Hannah shook her head. Whatever they wanted, it obviously wasn't to confront her about her pretend marriage. "That's fine. I wasn't sure at first, but I think I can manage on my own.''

"Have a seat,'' Craig said.

She slipped past Louise and settled on the center sofa cushion. Travis was on her other side. Kyle and Jordan had pulled wing chairs close and Craig sat down on the coffee table in front of the sofa.

He rested his elbows on his knees. "I'm not sure where to begin.'' He glanced at Louise.

The older woman nodded. "I'll go first.'' She angled toward Hannah. "Earl—your father—doesn't know about you.''

Hannah was surprised to feel a rush of disappointment. "Why?''

"We don't talk anymore. It's been years. Since before

he retired and moved to Florida." Louise's blue eyes darkened with concern. "I wasn't sure what to say to him. You would have...complicated things. It's selfish of me, I know."

Hannah stared at her for a long time. She turned her attention to each of her brothers. No one would meet her gaze.

For a moment, she wondered what they were hiding, then the truth burst through and lit up her mind like a floodlight. "You think he's not going to care about me."

"That's not true," Louise said quickly.

Craig shook his head. "Louise, we discussed this before you ever wrote to Hannah."

"I know." Her voice was small. She cleared her throat, then continued. "I'm not sure what Earl will think about you. I don't want you hurt by him. He's not the most sensitive man."

Hannah hadn't realized she was hoping to meet her father until the chance was taken away from her.

"We all thought it was best to wait," Travis said. "Give yourself a couple of weeks to come to terms with all of this. When you're ready to get in touch with Earl, we'll be happy to give you his phone number and smooth the way."

"I'll call if that's what you want," Louise said.

"I'm overwhelmed," Hannah admitted. "I hadn't thought about getting in touch with him until now. I don't know what to think." She touched Louise's hand. "You loved him."

"That was a long time ago. He wasn't someone I could depend on."

"None of us could," Craig said bitterly. "My father used to brag that he spent every night in his own bed. The fact that he'd been with other women before he got to that bed didn't matter to him."

Kyle shifted in his chair. "Obviously we're not sorry he's gone."

"You've never tried to reconcile with him?" she asked. For her, it was inconceivable that a child would want to be apart from a parent. She'd spent so many years alone, praying for someone to come along who would care about her.

"He was violent," Jordan said simply.

Hannah repressed a shiver. She'd spent a few weeks at a foster home like that. What she remembered the most was being afraid all the time. Each breath had been thick with the fear that the next blow could come at any moment.

"How did you four turn out to be so normal? You're all married, with great wives and happy kids. Someone must have done something right."

Craig smiled. "It wasn't easy. We're not exactly experts at relationships. Our father and uncles didn't respect women or believe in love. We had to figure that out on our own. I tried to do the opposite of my father. Unfortunately, I ended up married to a woman just like him. My life was a disaster...until I met Jill."

Even his voice changed as he said her name. His love for her was a tangible force in the room. She wondered what it would be like to be loved that much, and then to have the courage to love that person back. The level of trust required amazed her. But people fell in love all the time. How could they risk everything based on a feeling?

Had Nick ever been in love? She didn't know very much about his past. Mostly because she hadn't bothered to ask. Maybe there was a special someone he'd lost along the way. Oddly enough, that thought made her uncomfortable.

"I never knew how to care about someone," Travis said. "I thought I knew what love was, but I was wrong."

"I left women before they left me," Kyle said. "I refused to let anyone walk out on me the way my mom did."

Louise sighed.

Kyle looked at her. "Sorry. I didn't mean—"

She cut him off with a wave of her hand. "It's not your fault, Kyle."

"It's not yours, either," Jordan said quickly.

"I know. Sometimes, though, it's hard." She looked at Hannah. "Sorry. I still feel guilty, I guess. I never wanted to cause the family any hurt. So when I found out the boys' mother left because Earl wanted to marry me..." She shook her head. "It was awful. I never encouraged him when I came back to town. I even refused to see him. It wasn't enough."

"It's over," Jordan reminded her.

"You're right. I have to keep telling myself that. At least I have my daughter here." She touched Hannah's hand.

"A girl," Kyle said. "The first one in four generations."

"You're not going to start with that silly legend again, are you?" Hannah asked. "You don't really believe it, about girls being born when Haynes men are in love?"

Jordan grinned. "We're not sure it's only Haynes *men*, so you'd better be careful."

She opened her mouth to tell him it wasn't likely to be a problem, then quickly caught herself. She'd nearly forgotten that no one knew her marriage was a sham or that she and Nick had never been intimate. Even if their kiss had been hot enough to make her bones melt and her...

She forced her mind away from that erotic train of thought just in time to notice Craig handing her four sheets of paper.

"What are these?" she asked, staring at the legal-looking documents.

"We're transferring stock to you."

"Stock in what?"

"Austin's company," Travis explained. "The four of us

own forty-nine percent. Years ago, when he was first starting up his research firm, he needed capital. We gave him
all we had in exchange for shares in the company."

Kyle grinned. "It's been a hell of an investment, Hannah. Austin is brilliant. We want you to share in that."

She continued to study the papers. "I don't understand.
Why would you do this?"

"You're family," Jordan said as if that answered everything.

"I couldn't," she said, confused by the gesture. What
was going on?

Louise gave her a look of concern. "Don't be so quick
to turn down the shares. Austin's company might be private, but it's worth millions. The shares pay a generous
dividend."

Hannah looked at her brothers, then at the woman who
had given birth to her. Too much was happening too fast.
"This is impossible," she said and thrust the papers at
Craig. "You know so little about me. I could be an awful
person, a fraud. You can't just give me this."

Craig touched her hand. "You're family," he said as if
that explained it all.

But she wasn't. Not really. She *was* a fraud and an awful
person. She was lying about her marriage—deceiving them
all. If they knew the truth...

She couldn't bear to think about it. "No," she said, rising to her feet. "I just can't. It's not right. I know you
don't understand, but it's true."

She felt burning behind her eyelids and knew tears
threatened. She refused to cry in front of them. Most of the
time, she refused to cry at all, but it didn't seem as if she
was going to get a choice in this matter.

"Hannah?" Louise said.

"What's wrong?" one of her brothers asked. She wasn't

sure which one. She didn't bother to look up and figure it out.

"Excuse me," she said and fled the room.

Nick found Hannah huddled in a corner of the wide porch. There was a beautiful restored antique swing, but she'd ignored that in favor of a plain straight-back chair tucked next to the kitchen window.

She had her arms wrapped around her body, her legs pressed tightly together. From the porch steps, he could feel her misery. As he walked closer, he saw the traces of tears on her cheeks.

She looked up as he approached. He saw the visible effort it took for her to pull herself together. Her shoulders straightened and she quickly wiped her face.

"Louise said I'd find you out here," he told her as he moved next to her and leaned against the porch. He glanced up at the blue sky. "It's a great afternoon. Warm, but not hot."

"Lovely weather," she murmured automatically. She twisted her fingers together and stared at her lap.

Her thick hair, pulled back in a sensible braid, gleamed in the bright light. Hannah was strong and capable, but right now she needed a good hug and maybe a couple of kisses to put the color back in her cheeks. He was just the man to do it, if only she would let him.

But he knew Hannah; she was prickly and stubborn. She would rather bleed to death than admit she'd been hurt and wanted comfort.

"Did she tell you what happened?" she asked, her voice barely audible.

"Yes."

Louise hadn't gone into details, but Nick heard enough to get the picture. Hannah wasn't reacting well to her instant family. She felt guilty about lying to them, confused by her mixed emotions. Their offer of stock shares had been more than she could handle.

"You probably think I'm crazy, right?" she asked. "I should just take the stock shares and pocket the proceeds. So what if I've been given them under false pretenses?"

"What's false? You're Louise's daughter and their half sister."

"But I'm not really your wife."

"A small detail."

She glared at him. "Maybe to you, but I don't act like that. I don't lie to people, cheat them, steal from orphans."

He raised his hand. "I've never stolen from an orphan in my life. Don't you think you're being a little overly dramatic?"

"Okay. Maybe just a little."

"Holly said they've got a couple of bikes. Why don't we go for a ride?"

Hannah sniffed. "I don't think that's a good idea."

"Your alternatives are to go back inside and face your brothers or go to the gatehouse and be alone with me."

He didn't bother pointing out that they would be alone on the bike ride. He figured in her book, that wasn't nearly the same as being along in a small gatehouse.

For a moment, he hoped she would opt for the apartment. An afternoon of passionate lovemaking was just what she needed to take her mind off her troubles. After the kiss they'd shared the previous evening, he was having some troubles of his own—mainly getting his mind off her. Without wanting to, he could feel her in his arms and taste her sweet kiss.

She'd responded with the passionate heat of a sensual woman. He wanted to explore all the possibilities their mutual attraction suggested. If that wasn't an option, he was willing to settle for a bike ride.

"A ride sounds great," she said, standing up and heading toward the porch stairs.

She moved with the easy grace of a natural athlete. Long legs, swinging arms, swaying hips. When they'd walked the bikes out to the driveway, she climbed onto hers and began pedaling.

"I haven't done this in years," she called over her shoulder. She wobbled a little, but by the time they reached the end of the long driveway, she was steady and pedaling easily.

Nick rode next to her when traffic allowed, dropping behind when cars approached. Sunday afternoon in Glenwood was quiet. He could hear families playing together outside and smell the tempting aroma of barbecues. Leafy green trees sprouted in front of houses and along the sidewalks. Some of the graceful branches stretched across the street and touched.

After about fifteen minutes, they reached a large, grassy park. There were picnic benches, a baseball diamond, more trees and a pond complete with a score of little ducks and toddlers offering bits of bread.

Hannah came to a stop and straddled her bike. She smiled at him when he caught up. Her face was flushed, her eyes bright. "Thank you," she said. "I needed to get away. This is great."

She wore a peach short-sleeved shirt tucked into worn jeans. Nothing fancy or obviously provocative, yet looking at her was enough to make him want her. He watched the rise and fall of her chest as she caught her breath. Her lips parted and he caught a glimpse of white teeth. A couple strands of hair had slipped free of her braid.

"You're beautiful," he said without thinking, then could have kicked himself.

Hannah reacted predictably. She rolled her eyes. "Yeah, right. I expected something more original out of you, Nick. Are you losing your touch?"

He was and she was the reason. Not that she would believe him if he told her the truth. "Simply stating the obvious," he said lightly, then glanced around the park. "What do you think of Glenwood?"

"Seems nice. Kind of small and quiet."

"Great when you're a kid or a parent, hell for teenagers. There's not a whole lot to do."

"You sound as if you speak from experience."

He motioned to an unoccupied bench by a jogging trail. They left their bikes at the edge of the grass and strolled toward the bench.

"I grew up in a town like this," he said. "It was a little north of Santa Barbara, close to the beach. Everybody knew everybody else, just like here."

She settled next to him on the bench. He looped his arm around her shoulders. When she started to squirm away, he whispered, "It's just for show, sweet thing. Don't panic."

It was as much a lie as his claim of an audience of children the previous night. Not exactly noble, but he was working against the clock. Besides, Hannah kissed pretty hot for someone who was not even supposed to like him.

"What was your family like when you were growing up?" she asked.

He played with a loose strand of her hair, drawing it back from her face and fingering the cool, silky curl, then tucking it behind her ear. "Small. My mom died when I was born and I didn't have any brothers or sisters."

She exhaled and leaned against him. "My brothers said some ugly things about their father...my father, I guess. No one has told him about me. They haven't come out and said it, but I get the impression they think he won't care about me.''

"Children, even when they've grown up, want their parents to be perfect. You have that mental image from all those years ago. You imagined a wonderful, loving family and it's difficult when reality doesn't match the dream.''

She nodded slowly. "Louise is great. Not at all the mother I'd pictured, but terrific all the same. I don't know what to do about getting in touch with Earl.''

"You don't have to make a decision today or even this week. You can think about it for a while, you know.''

"You're right. I suppose I'm feeling pressured to do it all now." She looked up at him and smiled. "Thanks, Nick.''

For that moment, it was real. There wasn't any caution in her eyes, no hesitancy, no judgment. He told himself she leaned against him because she wanted to. Because he offered her comfort, and maybe because he turned her on.

His whole life was a fraud, yet he lived it as if it were real. Why not this situation with Hannah? Why should it be any different?

"What was your father like?" she asked.

He let his fingers trail down her cheek. She didn't protest or pull back. Maybe it was just part of the game, but right now he didn't give a damn.

"When he was sober, he was the best dad in town. We'd play ball, go fishing, build a fire and cook dinner down on the beach." He smiled at the memories. "He was always there for me."

If, he reminded himself. His smile faded. If his father didn't start drinking. "When he was drunk, he was a mean son of a bitch who picked a fight with anyone." Even a seven-year-old kid. He had the broken bones to prove it.

Hannah straightened. Her dark eyes widened. "He beat you." It wasn't a question.

He shrugged. "Sometimes. He'd go on the wagon for a couple of months, then one day he'd reach for the bottle. I never knew when it was going to happen. Once, when I was ten, my dad came home really drunk. He staggered into the house. I got up to see if he was all right. I had a dog. Chester. A big ugly mutt. My dad tripped over Chester and got mad. So he tried to shoot him."

Nick spoke the words calmly, but inside he could still hear the sound of the bullet being chambered. "I had to give him to a friend. Later my dad said Chester could come back, but I knew better. The next time my old man would probably pull the trigger."

"No!" Hannah placed her hands on his chest. "That's so horrible. I'm sorry. Did you hate him after that?"

He couldn't look at her beautiful face and watch the compassion soften her features. Knowing she cared would be dangerous. He stared out at the green grass and trees. "I always understood it wasn't really his fault. Taking the first drink was, I guess, but what happened later—that wasn't my dad. He was sick. I guess I learned early not to trust anyone. After Chester, I avoided getting attached."

"Is that why you operate outside the law?" He glanced at her sharply. She pulled back and covered her mouth. "I'm sorry. I spoke without thinking. I didn't mean to pry."

He didn't know what to say without blowing his cover. Despite everything that had happened, he hadn't turned to a life of crime. The thought had never crossed his mind. His past was the reason he became a cop. To make it right. But he couldn't tell her that.

"I am sorry," she said.

"No big deal. Ask whatever you like. After all, we're married and you've seen me naked."

His statement got the expected results. She laughed and flushed slightly. The dark mood was broken.

"I believe I paid for that," she said. "Five whole dollars."

"I gave you a break because we're friends."

She raised her eyebrows. "What would you charge a stranger?"

"That would depend on her intentions."

"Somehow I think the worse her intentions, the less expensive the price."

He turned his head and brushed his lips against hers. The desire was immediate, as was his reaction. He ignored the pressure in his groin and the need to pull her closer and make love to her. "Exactly."

She laughed again and stared up at him. He read the invitation in her eyes. Did she know it was there and what she asked? He didn't think so.

"Hannah, you've got a real chance here," he said. "Don't blow it."

"What do you mean?"

"Your family. They're willing to accept you with open arms. They don't want anything and they won't hurt you."

She visibly withdrew, sliding back on the bench and putting distance between them. She folded her arms over her chest. "They offered me stock. Just like that. Apparently, Austin owns this successful company and they're all shareholders. They each signed over shares to me so I could have a part of it, too."

"What's so odd about that?"

She looked at him as if he were as crazy as the rest of them. "They don't know the first thing about me."

"Three of your brothers are cops. They're used to assessing people fairly quickly. Besides, I'm sure it wasn't difficult in your case. You're just like them."

"I am not. I'm different." She turned her face away. "This family stuff is highly overrated."

The words were a lie. He found the truth in her defensive posture. She desperately wanted to believe in her newfound family. She wanted to be a part of them, to belong. But she was afraid. Afraid that she didn't know how to start and maintain a connection. Afraid that if she cared about them, they would reject her, just like everyone else in her life had done.

He wanted to tell her it was going to be all right, but she wouldn't believe him. She needed him to show her the way. Then he smiled slightly as he imagined what she would say if she knew he felt she needed guidance from *him* of all people. She would verbally chop him up into little pieces and serve them for supper.

But she wasn't going to make it on her own. He would have to subtly set things right and there was only one way to do that.

Stay a while longer.

It wasn't a problem. He couldn't go back to Southport Beach until he'd heard the all-clear from Captain Rodriguez. Hannah might put up a fight, but he figured he could handle her. This was a short-term commitment and he did that well. It was the long-term emotional stuff that gave him trouble.

He and Hannah made a good team. She had the skills to fit in; she just didn't know how to use them. He had the skills and the knowledge, but he didn't bother. In a way, they were similar. They both avoided relationships. She was afraid to be rejected; he refused to ever be hurt that badly again. Neither was willing to trust.

Hell of a mess, he thought and rose to his feet. "I'll race you back," he said. "Winner gets to see the loser naked."

She jumped up and jogged toward her bike. "Give me a real incentive to win, Nick. Something I care about."

He grinned. "Tough decision, huh? Do you go slow and flaunt yourself in front of me, or go fast and get to see me again?"

She didn't answer, but as she pedaled past, he caught a smile on her lips. His spirits lifted. Now that he didn't have to leave tonight, he could afford to take his time with Hannah and seduce her slowly, the way she deserved.

For starters, he was going to let her win this race.

Hannah glanced at the grandfather clock in the corner of the dining room. It was 8:36. Two minutes later than the last time she'd checked. Most of the dinner dishes had been cleared and the children excused from the table. Only the adults remained to linger over coffee.

Sandy leaned back in her chair and folded her napkin. "I have to thank you, Hannah. In the past couple of days, our family has spent more time together than we have in months. I've really enjoyed these large dinners and being with everyone. We tend to get busy with our own lives and forget how lucky we are to have all this." She motioned to include everyone in her dining room, as well as the children playing upstairs.

"I agree." Elizabeth smiled. "It's been a treat."

Travis pushed his chair back. "Yeah, yeah, it's been great. But if you girls are going to get mushy, I think we men had better leave the room."

"Not so fast." Elizabeth grabbed his arm. "You *men* are in charge of cleaning up. Remember?"

"Anything for you, love." He dropped a quick kiss on

her mouth, then picked up the rest of the plates. "Come on, men. Let's get to it."

In the confusion of everyone standing up and either clearing the table or moving into the living room, Hannah took another peek at the clock, then moved toward Nick. "I have to talk to you," she said quietly.

"I should help with the dishes."

"Later. This is important."

She moved down the hallway to Kyle's study. They were in his and Sandy's house, not far from the gatehouse where she and Nick were staying. It would be safer to have this conversation there, but Hannah didn't want to make anyone suspicious.

When he entered the room, she closed the door behind him and leaned against it. "Why haven't you received your phone call?" she asked.

He folded his arms over his chest and stared down at her. She really hated that he could do that. She was as tall as many men, taller than some. She was used to being their equal. In low heels, as she wore tonight, she often felt like an awkward Amazonian who'd wandered by accident into the real world. But around Nick, she felt normal, damn him. Feminine even. And those feelings made her uncomfortable.

"I'm not leaving."

She was so intent on studying the perfect blue of his eyes and the shape of his tempting mouth that it took her a second to register his reply.

"You're what?" she shrieked, then consciously lowered her voice. "What do you mean you're not leaving?"

"Just what I said. There's not going to be a pretend phone call."

"There sure as hell is," she told him. "Even if I have to make it myself."

He shrugged, apparently unconcerned by the threat. "Go ahead. I'll disappear for a few minutes, then come back and tell everyone I've taken care of it. They won't ask questions. Your family likes me, Hannah. They want me to stay."

Unfortunately, he was telling the truth.

Now what? He had to go. He had to. She didn't think she could stand being around him for two whole weeks. Anything could happen. They could blow their cover. Or worse. The tingling she felt when he was around could become something even more dangerous. She could start to care. And she knew the price of that.

"Why are you doing this?" she asked. "Do you want to punish me for something?"

He shoved his hands in his jeans pockets. "You won't believe me, but I'm doing this *for* you, not to make you crazy. You need my help to connect with your family and I'm going to stay until you feel settled with them."

She was humiliated that he would think she was so socially inept, even if it was true. And a little voice in her head crowed with excitement at the thought of spending several more days in his company. She would have missed him terribly. But she refused to make it easy on him.

"I thought we had a deal," she said.

"Don't worry. I won't charge you extra for the time. And maybe I'll let you see me naked again."

Chapter Nine

Hannah was fuming. He could tell by the rapid rise and fall of her chest. Her thick braid hung over one shoulder and the tightly bound end teased the top of her breast. Nick would have liked to replace that rope of hair with his fingers, but doubted Hannah was much in the mood to be seduced by him or anyone.

She planted her hands on her hips. "How dare you go back on our agreement?"

He pretended to be shocked and hurt. "I'm doing you this big favor and you're angry with me? Lady, you got a problem here. I'm willing to stay and be your husband, and I'm not even asking for more money. Do you know how much I can make in a week? Do you know how many people—women—would be begging to have me around?"

"Then go be with one of them and satisfy their wildest desires."

Who satisfies your wildest desires? But he didn't ask the question.

"Face it, kid. You need me."

She stamped her foot. "I do not."

He grinned. "Yeah, because you're so mature and poised."

"I am mature." She stamped her foot again, then realized what she'd done and turned away. "Dammit, Nick, quit bringing out the worst in me."

The room grew silent. He walked toward her and placed his hands on her shoulders. "I mean it, Hannah. You need me. This family stuff scares you to death. You don't know what to do or say. There are too many of them and only one of you. I can help. You've seen that."

"By telling them I can sing and play the piano?"

"By being on your side. Trust me."

She turned toward him, and his hands fell to his sides. Her gaze searched his. "Why are you doing this? Why do you want to help?"

It would be easy to put her off with lies. He had a thousand at the ready. But this was Hannah, and for reasons he didn't want to think about, he needed to tell her the truth.

"Two reasons. Things are a little hot for me down south," he said. "I could head over to Vegas or Reno, but I'd rather stay here with you. No one's going to come looking for me in Glenwood."

She shivered slightly. If he hadn't been staring at her intently, he wouldn't have noticed. An involuntary reaction to the reminder that he was a criminal. A man on the wrong side of the law. He swore silently. He wanted to tell her the truth. But he wouldn't. Not just because he wasn't about to jeopardize his cover after all this time, but because if she knew the truth, then their situation would get about a hundred times more complicated.

"What's the second reason?" she asked.

"Because I care about you, and I sincerely want to help."

He braced himself for the inevitable scathing retort, but instead her eyes filled with pain.

"Don't joke about that," she said, then looked away. "I'm not at my best right now and it wouldn't take much to push me over the edge."

Before he could stop himself, he placed his arms around her and pulled her close. "I wasn't joking. I swear."

He'd told the truth. Saying he cared was flirting with danger, but it didn't cross the line. He could walk away from her in a second and never miss her. As long as that was true, he was safe.

"Don't," she said and pulled back. "Don't make it more than it is. We had a deal, nothing more." She moved to the door. "I hired you to play my husband for the weekend and that's all I want. I've got your money in my purse. I'll go get it and you can be on your way."

Before he could stop her, she pulled open the door and stepped into the hallway. He heard a gasp and quickly followed. Travis was standing in the middle of the hall. He glanced from Nick to Hannah.

"Is anything wrong?"

She wordlessly shook her head.

Travis nodded and headed for the kitchen. Nick watched him go. Danger signals flashed and his gut confirmed what he'd already guessed. Travis had heard some, maybe all, of the conversation.

Hannah tried not to hyperventilate as she sipped her coffee while sitting in the large, pleasantly furnished living room. Thoughts whirled through her head. Was Nick leaving? What if he wasn't? What if he really planned to stay?

If she'd realized how large and complicated her family was going to be, she would have come clean about not being married from the very beginning. But it was too late now. She felt trapped by a situation she could no longer control.

It wasn't just about Louise and the brothers, she admitted to herself as she smiled and attempted to make polite conversation with Holly. Although she regretted the lies, she would soon be making them right. The real danger came from another source completely. From Nick.

Because there was a part of her that didn't want him to leave. A part of her that had been thrilled when he'd said he was staying. She'd wanted to go to him and kiss him and confess that she often thought about their kisses and imagined doing so much more.

Lord help her, she liked him. Worse, she wanted him. Even as she tried to convince herself it was all right because he was funny and kind and he'd even said that he cared about her, she knew it was wrong.

Caring. What did caring matter in the face of who he was and what he did?

She glanced around the room, at her brothers and their wives, at Austin and Rebecca, finally at Louise. She desperately wanted to be a part of this family. With equal fervor, she was terrified it would all be snatched away from her. She knew that fear would cause her to hold herself back when she should be moving forward. This fear would make her seem cold and standoffish; it would make her question their motives.

Nick was right. She didn't know how to make the relationship with her family work. She needed him. She who had never needed anyone. But could she trust him?

More important, could she trust herself?

The questions continued to whirl. She remembered the

stock her brothers had tried to give her. What would these honorable men say if they knew she'd lied to them and Louise?

Her attention settled on Travis. He'd been standing right outside the study door when she'd opened it, but she didn't think he'd heard anything. If he had, surely he would have mentioned it. But he hadn't said a word.

A knock sounded at the front door. Louise glanced at her watch, sprang to her feet and announced, "I'll get it."

Jordan chuckled. "I can guess who that is."

"Hush," Louise hissed as she walked past him. "It's not a big deal. I swear, you boys are more trouble than you're worth."

Hannah looked at Nick sitting by the fireplace, but he just shrugged. Jordan caught their confused exchange. "Your mother has a beau," he explained.

"I do not," Louise called, then opened the front door. "Richard, ah, Professor Wilson, how kind of you to drop by."

Hannah strained to see into the foyer, but it was impossible from her place in the room.

A low voice said, "Louise. Sorry I'm late. My flight was delayed. I came directly from the airport. Is she here?"

"Yes, and her husband, too. You must come meet them."

Hannah stood up as Louise came in with a man. He was in his mid-to-late-thirties with sandy brown hair and hazel eyes. He had a pleasant face and an easy smile. He looked at her and came over to introduce himself.

"Hannah. I'm Richard Wilson. I'm so pleased to finally meet you. You're as pretty as your mother."

Hannah laughed. "And here I thought I looked like the Haynes brothers."

They shook hands.

"You must be Nick," Richard said.

She hadn't heard Nick approach, but there he stood, right beside her. He also shook hands, then someone pulled out a chair for the professor and brought him a cup of coffee.

"I'm sorry I'm late," he said. "I was speaking before a congressional committee most of the week, then I had a reception to attend last night. Then this morning..." He waved his hand. "Sorry. It's not important. The point is, I'm here now and I'm happy for both you and Louise."

He sat in the wing chair and Louise perched nervously on the arm. Hannah settled on the closest sofa, with Nick at her side. The rest of the family greeted Richard, then drifted out of the room to leave the four of them alone.

"I don't know that she looks all that much like me," Louise said, "but I'll agree with the pretty part."

"The eyes have the same shape, if not the color," Richard said. "And her smile is yours."

"We have the same hair color," Louise said in a mock whisper. "At least, we did until I learned that what they say about blondes is really true."

Richard smiled indulgently at her. Louise squeezed his hand. Although there was an obvious age difference between them, they looked right together—happy.

Hannah studied them for a second, then realized the room was silent. She searched her mind for something to say.

"You met in a college class?" Nick asked.

Hannah exhaled in relief. At least Nick wasn't a social retard. She could always count on him to come up with something.

"That's right," Richard said. "Louise was in my night class. I noticed her right away."

The older woman laughed and her bright red glass earrings bounced against her shoulders. Tonight, Louise was conservatively dressed, for her anyway. She wore a red Western-cut fringed shirt, tight black jeans and red boots. The narrow belt at her slender waist emphasized full hips and breasts. Hannah had inherited her general shape, although her attributes were much more modest.

Louise looked fondly at Richard. "He noticed me because I didn't agree with anything he said."

Richard nodded in agreement. "I teach sociology and in my evening classes I tend to use examples from real life. I also like to get discussions going."

"I told him he was a pompous pig who had never spent time poor, divorced or female, and he didn't know what he was talking about. Then he asked me to stay after class."

"To rake you over the coals?" Nick asked.

Louise shook her head. "No, to invite me for coffee with a few of his graduate students. I still didn't like him, but I wanted to meet some of the others. I figured I'd just avoid Richard."

He took her hand and kissed her knuckles. "And she did. For about three months. Until I confessed my feelings in the parking lot after class. I think it was raining."

Louise blushed. "He said that he found me interesting."

"I said more than that."

"Hush. This is my daughter. I don't want her to get the wrong idea." Louise paused. "I know what you're thinking."

"I doubt that," Hannah said, then clamped her lips together to keep from blurting out that she was jealous. Louise and Richard obviously had a special relationship. They adored each other. Hannah couldn't believe it, but her mother was actually glowing.

Louise shook her head. "You're shocked. Because Richard is so much younger."

"Is that important?" Hannah asked, baffled at the notion. "It happens all the time."

"The man is older," Louise said. "Not the woman."

Richard scowled. "I don't care, you don't care, your daughter doesn't care. Why is it a problem?"

"I'm just not sure."

"Stubborn woman." But he spoke the words affectionately.

Hannah glanced to her left and saw Kyle and Jordan hovering in the doorway, trying to watch what was going on in the living room. Kyle waved when she saw him, obviously unrepentant at being caught.

She returned her attention to her mother. Hannah felt drawn to this woman, drawn to the family. As far as she could tell, all they wanted was to care about her and have her care about them. She wanted to jump to her feet and call out that she was willing to take a chance. But she knew it wasn't true. The fear was stronger than the desire to belong. Then she felt Nick's hand on her own. He understood what she was thinking because she'd come to realize he understood everything about her.

Hannah lay on her solitary bed and listened to the silence. She stared into the darkness and wondered what she should do. Nick hadn't pretended to get a phone call. He really wasn't leaving. So what were her options?

She could protest his high-handedness and force him to go. Or she could give in graciously. Or she could tell the truth.

She didn't want to even think about the latter, so she rolled onto her stomach and punched her pillow. "Stupid man," she muttered. "Trying to complicate everything."

Had he been telling the truth? Was he really trying to help her because he cared? She really, really wanted to believe that. Of course, if it *was* true, she would be terrified. If he cared about her and she started to care about him a little, then they might actually have the beginnings of a relationship. She didn't think she could handle that.

With a heavy sigh, she got out of bed and walked into the dark living room. She could make out Nick on his side on the sofa. He pushed himself halfway up.

"What's wrong, Hannah?"

"Nothing. I just wanted to make sure. You're not going to leave, are you?"

"Nope. You're stuck with me for the next two weeks."

"I..." The words lodged in her throat. She tried again. "I think you *are* trying to help me."

"Don't sound so surprised. Why wouldn't I want to make it easy for you?"

"Because I haven't been very friendly."

He lay back down on the sofa and chuckled. "You are a little on the prickly side, aren't you?"

"I don't mean to be. It just happens."

"I know, honey. I even know why you do it. You're afraid. But now there's nothing to worry about. I'll be here and I'll make everything perfect. Go on back to bed."

She stood there for a couple of minutes, then did as he requested. As she stretched out on the mattress, she pictured him lying only a few feet away. Judging from the clean line of his silhouette, he hadn't been wearing anything above the waist. What did he wear below?

The question made her fingers tingle. What would it be like to make love with a man like him? She had a feeling he would make good on his word. That everything about the experience would be perfect.

Two weeks together. How was she going to resist him? And what would happen if she threw up her hands and gave in?

* * *

"This is what I like to see," Nick said as he leaned back in the kitchen chair. "My woman working hard to feed me."

Hannah gave him a mock glare. "My goodness. I married a chauvinist pig and I never knew it before." She pulled a bit of cookie dough from the bowl and tossed it at him.

He caught it in midflight and popped it in his mouth. "Delicious. Louise, you're a great cook. Have you ever thought about opening your own restaurant?"

She laughed. "Don't think that by being charming you'll get a larger share of the cookies."

"I'm serious." He licked the batter from his fingers. Hannah spooned dough onto cookie sheets, but the recipe had come from Louise.

The older woman wiped her hands on her apron. The broad white cloth covered her from shoulders to knees but didn't conceal her bright orange sleeves or cobalt blue pant legs.

"I've actually thought about opening my own place," she admitted slowly.

"Really?" Hannah set down her spoon. "You'd be great. Nick is right. Your cooking is wonderful. And with this family, you're certainly used to cooking for large groups of people."

Louise nodded, her spiky blond hair making the trip a half second after her head. "I've thought about a specialty place. You know, only breakfasts. Or maybe muffins. Or tea. I've always wanted to do a high tea. But I don't have a lot of money for start-up capital, and I don't have a head for business."

"You could learn," Nick said. "You're going back to college."

She wrinkled her nose. "I don't think I have the math background. I wasn't very good with numbers in high school and that was nearly thirty years ago. Oh, my. Thirty years. I can't believe it."

Hannah grabbed one of the full cookie sheets and started toward the oven. "Don't worry about it, Louise. You don't look your age, nor do you act it."

Hannah slipped past him and slid the tray into the oven. Before she could get around him again, he reached out and placed his hands on her hips, then moved his legs so she was trapped between them.

"What are you doing?" she asked.

"I would have thought that was obvious."

"It is from here," Louise said. "Give him a kiss, Hannah, so he'll let you go back to work. We've got a lot of cookies to bake before the kids get home from school."

Hannah stared at him. He held in a grin. He'd trapped her neatly, and not just with his legs. She couldn't very well protest what he was doing in front of her mother. Stealing kisses under false pretenses was pretty low, but she hadn't given him a whole lot of choice.

He tugged on the waistband of her jeans, pulling her closer. She bent forward and braced her hands on his shoulders. Their faces were inches apart. He couldn't move closer, so the kiss was up to her.

Interesting. Would she or wouldn't she?

"You want to," he murmured so only she could hear.

A light flared in her eyes. "In your dreams, buster."

"You've been there lots of times. Want to know what we were doing?"

"Shut up."

"Make me."

She pressed her mouth to his.

Heat flared between them hot enough to bake the cookies. He wanted to wrap his arms around her and haul her against him, but that wasn't an option. Not with Louise watching.

Their kiss was brief, chaste, yet it made him want more. It made him want all of her. Next to him, under him, naked, willing, wanting. His arousal was instant and painful, a throbbing need against the fly of his jeans.

As she was about to pull back, he gently caught her bottom lip in his teeth. A shudder rippled through her. She stared at him and he saw the fire of her desire.

In that moment, he wanted to make it all real and not just pretend. He wanted to be everything they said he was—her husband of several years, a successful real-estate mogul. He wanted them to be in love.

Hannah broke free and straightened. He glanced to his left. Louise was spooning out cookie dough as if nothing out of the ordinary had happened. In her eyes, it hadn't.

"Elizabeth says it's tacky, but I want to make my own birthday cake," Louise said.

"You shouldn't have to do the work," Hannah said breathlessly, moving away from him.

"That's what she tells me, but I don't want any of you girls worrying about it, and I don't want something store-bought."

Hannah walked over and touched her arm. "But it's no bother at all. I've already talked to Sandy and Elizabeth about it. We've got plans. Please let us do this."

Louise shrugged. "If it means so much to you."

"It does. Thank you."

Louise smiled. "While we're being honest, I want to know what you really think about Richard."

Hannah frowned and glanced at Nick as if asking what her mother was talking about. "We think he's fine, why?"

"Well, he is eleven years younger."

"I think it's great," Nick said. "If Hannah here ever gives me any trouble, I'm going to take up with a younger woman."

Hannah rolled her eyes. He could imagine what she was thinking but couldn't say. Of course, she would probably give him an earful later.

Louise dismissed him with a wave. "I'm being serious. It's different with men. People don't notice that kind of thing. But with a woman it's different."

"Louise, if you care about him, what does his age matter?"

"Maybe. I just hate not knowing for sure."

"What is it about the women in your family?" Nick asked. "You make it so hard on the guy. How long did you resist before finally going out with him?"

"A couple of months."

"Hannah ignored me for nearly a year."

Hannah snapped her head up and stared at Nick. What on earth was he going to say now? It wasn't enough that she was still ready to explode from the passion he'd ignited a few minutes before. Now he had to set her nerves on edge with one of his stories.

"A year?" Louise looked at her. "How could you do that?"

"I, ah—"

Nick cut her off. "After the cruise, I asked her out every week for a year. She never said yes. It nearly drove me crazy."

"How could you have turned him down?" Louise asked. "He's so good-looking and charming."

Nick preened.

Hannah was so impressed with his believable combination of truth and lies that she almost didn't notice the question.

"I didn't think he was serious." She realized it was the truth. Nick had been asking her out on dates, for drinks, to run away with him, issuing any number of invitations, but she hadn't believed he meant any of them.

She was still confused. The more she got to know Nick Archer, the more she liked him. There was no way for her to reconcile the generous, funny, caring man she'd brought on this trip with the criminal she knew from Southport Beach. Which Nick was real?

She kept trying to tell herself he was an awful person. Her head might still be convinced, but her heart wasn't buying the story. Liking was uncomfortable but still safe. What if her affections deepened? What if she gave in to the desire?

Louise gave her a quick hug. "At least you worked it out in the end. That's what's important. It doesn't matter if we grow older as long as we also grow smarter."

Nick grinned.

Hannah suspected he was thinking she hadn't gotten any smarter at all.

"Go check the cookies," Louise said.

Hannah crossed the kitchen floor and opened the oven door. "They need a couple more minutes."

Before she could return to the counter, Nick grabbed her again, this time pulling her onto his lap. She went willingly. It was just for show, she told herself as she snuggled close. In the safety of his arms, feeling welcome and secure for the first time in years, she let go of that lie and admitted the truth. She wanted to be exactly where she was. And she was very, very glad he was staying.

Chapter Ten

"Why do you look so terrified?" Hannah asked.

Nick shifted his weight and rolled his shoulders. "I'm fine."

She grinned. "Don't worry. It's not contagious."

"I'm just wondering if babies really need all this stuff."

He glanced around at the baby boutique. The large, well-stocked shop had a mezzanine level just for clothing. On the main floor, small rooms had been set up displaying several styles of cribs, rocking chairs, changing tables and an assortment of items at whose function he could only guess. Strollers and car seats lined one entire wall.

"You're asking the wrong person," she said and headed for a counter in the center of the room. "I have limited experience with babies. I like holding them, but I don't know anything about day-to-day child care. Louise said that Jill had picked out a few things here, and if we wanted to get a gift, this would be the best place."

He followed her, stepping around boxes, toys and bags of diapers. He hadn't felt this uncomfortable since he'd tried to buy something sexy for a woman he'd been seeing. All those feminine frills, lace and silk had sent him racing back into the safety of the mall.

"I just want to get out of here," he muttered.

She ignored him and approached the counter.

"May I help you?" the clerk asked. She was putting price tags on fluffy white bears.

Hannah nodded. "My sister-in-law is expecting a baby. I was told she'd picked out a few things from this store."

The clerk smiled and tucked her short red hair behind her ears. "We have everything on our computer. What's the last name?"

"Haynes."

The woman tapped a few keys on the computer, then glanced at Hannah, her eyes wide. "I guess I'm going to need a first name. There are four Hayneses listed here."

"It's Jill."

She tapped again, then the printer on her left began to spit out paper.

"There've been a lot of babies in your family," the clerk remarked.

"I know." Hannah took the offered sheet. "I come from a fertile family."

"The pattern she chose is in room twelve. Let me know if you need help finding anything."

"Thanks." Hannah turned to Nick. "Are you ready to shop?"

"Sure, but don't expect me to be much help. I don't know a thing about babies."

"I have to admit, with all the children and pregnant women running around in the family, I could get very nervous."

He dropped his arm over her shoulders and pulled her close. "I don't blame you. Sounds like people around here get pregnant simply by thinking about doing it."

"That seems unlikely." She pointed down a walkway. "I think room twelve is over here."

They paused in front of a three-sided alcove. The bleached-oak crib had a matching dresser and changing table. Each wall had been papered with a different print.

Hannah consulted the paper in her hand. "She picked teddy bears and unicorns."

Nick pointed. Fat brown teddy bears rode on cream unicorns across a pale sky. Fluffy clouds, bright suns and quarter moons brightened the background. "Not a football to be found," he said.

"Jill's having a girl."

"Yeah, right. That family legend. I'd forgotten."

Hannah smiled. "Well, that and she had an ultrasound. They're pretty certain it's a girl. Apparently, you can't tell for sure unless it's a boy and you see his, um, you know."

"Yeah, I know. I have one, too. Speaking of which..."

She raised her eyebrows. "That isn't what we were talking about."

"Uh-huh. Where's the ex in all of this?"

"What ex?"

"Your ex. Ex-husband. Why didn't you call him in for emergency duty? I'm sure he could have put off his business trip. After all, if you were separated all that time and didn't bother with a divorce, things can't be too bad between you."

She stared at him, then at the paper. "She's marked this lamp, but no one has bought it. We could get that."

"That's it?" he asked. "You're not going to answer the question?"

"It would appear that way."

"After all I've done for you?"

"Oh, yeah. You told my family I could play the piano and sing."

"A slight exaggeration."

"I think it's pretty," she said and picked up the lamp. The base was a porcelain unicorn. The shade picked up the pale lavender of the background.

Typical of Hannah. Why was she so damned stubborn? He didn't want details about her relationship with her ex. He just wanted… He shook his head. Whom was he kidding? Of course he wanted details. He wanted to know everything about all the men who had ever been in her life.

Maybe her ex broke her heart. Nick didn't want to think about that, but once the thought formed, he couldn't let it go. If some bastard had hurt Hannah, he was going to find him and rip his lungs out.

So much for not getting personally involved, he berated himself grimly. He was involved. The only good news was that he still planned to leave in nine days. He would go back to Southport Beach, finish his undercover assignment and get on with the rest of his life. He would never see Hannah again.

He should have felt reassured. Instead, he found himself wondering how much he would miss her.

She put down the lamp and picked up a stuffed teddy bear that matched the wallpaper. Overhead lights brought out faint hints of red in her dark hair. She wore a forest green T-shirt tucked into black jeans. Nothing special, nothing overly enticing, but he wanted her all the same.

He'd always enjoyed women, enjoyed their bodies and the pleasure they offered. But he'd never connected emotionally. There were lots of reasons. He'd never had a long-term relationship, never saw the need. Women were interchangeable. Long ago, he'd vowed never to hurt that badly again, which meant not falling in love. He wasn't sure he knew what love was. But he did understand respect and caring, and that's what he felt for Hannah. She wasn't an interchangeable person. Maybe that was the appeal. He saw her as uniquely herself.

"Is that for Jill?" a woman asked. She motioned to the wallpaper and furniture. "I recognize the print and style."

He turned and saw Rebecca Lucas standing at the entrance to the alcove.

Hannah pointed at the lamp. "We were thinking of getting that."

"I'm sure she'd love it." Rebecca came into the room and picked up the teddy bear. "There's always this fellow. You can never have enough stuffed animals."

Hannah glanced at him. "What do you think?"

He shrugged. "The lamp is more practical."

"Spoken like a man," Rebecca said. "Austin was exactly the same when I was pregnant. He didn't understand all the fuss over a baby. Then he held Jason in his arms and it made perfect sense." She smiled at Hannah. "I promise, Nick will be exactly the same when you have your first child together."

Nick couldn't shake the mental image Rebecca's words had invoked. Him holding a tiny baby, Hannah still in her hospital bed, exhausted but radiant from giving birth.

He shook off the picture. He and Hannah weren't a couple and there wasn't going to be a baby.

Rebecca placed her hand on Hannah's arm. "You look stunned. I didn't mean to upset you."

"I'm fine. The thought of having children is a little scary."

"Tell me about it." Rebecca touched her still-flat stomach. "I've already had a baby and I'm getting nervous thinking about going through that again." She motioned to the store. "That's why I'm here. Jason, our youngest, doesn't want to give up his room. I'd hoped to move him into a new bedroom and keep his old one for the baby, but that's not going to work. So now I have to decorate two rooms. I'm here to get some ideas."

"There's so much to think about," Hannah said. "All the furniture, clothes, stroller, car seat." She picked up the lamp. "I think we'll get this. At least I know what it is."

Rebecca laughed. "It's so interesting to watch you, Hannah. You remind me of your brothers, yet in a completely feminine way." She tilted her head. "Sort of like trying to read something from a reflection in the mirror."

Nick moved closer and leaned against the crib. "That's our Hannah. She's a product of her destiny and doesn't even know it. Her looks, her job."

The two women continued talking. Nick watched them. Rebecca was slender and delicate. Her flowing calf-length floral-print dress couldn't have been more different from Hannah's jeans. They were both attractive but in different ways. While Nick could appreciate Rebecca's beauty, Hannah was the one who appealed to him. He liked her toughness. Her strength made her vulnerability even more meaningful because he knew what it cost her to expose that side of herself.

Rebecca glanced at her watch. "I'd better look around while I can. In a little while I have to pick up Jason from his play group." She wrinkled her nose. "I trade with four other mothers a couple of mornings a week. We have two days with all the children, then eight days off. It's heaven."

She waved and walked toward another cluster of rooms. Hannah watched her go.

"Do you think it's true?" she asked. "Is this all destiny?"

"Maybe how you look, but the rest of it? I'm not sure."

"But I work in law enforcement. Don't you find that odd? And I look a lot more like my brothers than I look like Louise."

"Louise is blond," he said. "You'd probably look more like her if you had the same hair color."

She surprised him by laughing. "Are you saying I should dye my hair?"

He reached up and tugged on her braid. "Don't you dare. I like the color of your hair."

Her mouth parted slightly. She hugged the lamp close to her body. "Really?"

Self-protection required that he make a flippant remark. But he couldn't do it. He smoothed his palm down the thick length of her hair and wished he could see it loose. Just once. He touched the tip of her nose. "Yeah, really."

Hannah found herself forgetting to breathe. She could go entire hours without thinking about how handsome Nick was, then something would happen and she would notice all over again. It was very disconcerting to have the air ripped right out of her lungs.

She studied his face, trying to determine exactly what combination of features, bones, muscles and skin made him so perfect. Was it the vivid blue eyes? Perhaps his irises picked up the color from what he wore, but his shirt was white and his jeans had faded to nearly that color. Maybe it was the strong line of his jaw or his sensual mouth. She found herself studying his lips, remembering the feel of them against hers, the taste of him as he tempted her.

"As far as destinies go, it's not a bad one," he said.

She blinked several times before she could pull herself together to remember what they'd been talking about. "Law enforcement?" she asked.

"No, the family. Look at how happy your brothers are.

They have great wives and kids. That could be your destiny, too.''

"I never thought about it that way. With so many people, I was fighting the feeling of being trapped.''

"They don't want to hold you to keep you from going away,'' he said gently. "They want to hold you because they care about you.''

Just when she was on the verge of convincing herself her attraction to Nick was purely physical, he went and said something insightful and sensitive. Then she had to like him for himself. The man made her crazy. She didn't want to have feelings for him, except maybe disdain. Anything else was very risky for her.

She clutched the lamp to her chest. "I'm going to buy this. Maybe I'll have them gift wrap it. We should probably get a card, too.''

She led the way back to the counter. The clerk found the original box for the lamp and wrapped it up. Hannah glanced around the store. Rebecca had gone upstairs and was looking at baby clothes.

In her flowing dress and long, dark hair, she looked like a creature from another time. "She's so beautiful,'' Hannah said. "I could never dress like that.''

Nick came up behind her and placed his hands on her shoulders. "Why would you want to?''

"Don't you think she's lovely?''

"Of course, but so what? You're just as lovely. You shouldn't mind being different, Hannah. That's what makes you special.''

She wanted to laugh off his words, but she couldn't. Mostly because she wanted him to mean them. She wanted him to think she was special. She didn't dare turn around to see if he was teasing her. Instead, she repeated them silently to commit them to memory.

She knew she was being silly. Everything about their relationship was a house of cards and it was all going to come tumbling down around her ears. How was she supposed to hold it all together?

"I don't know what to do," she blurted out. "About my family, about getting in touch with my father, about going home, about telling them the truth."

He turned her until she was facing him, then touched a finger to her chin. "You don't have to do anything right now or even this week. You can just enjoy getting to know everyone. Later, it will be more clear and then you can decide."

"You promise?"

He nodded.

"And you don't think I should just confess everything? About us, I mean?"

"No. Not until you're ready."

She was secretly relieved by his answer. As long as they lived a lie, he would have reason to stay. As soon as the truth came out, Nick would leave. A few short days ago, she hadn't been able to imagine spending time with him at all. Now she couldn't picture a world without him.

Insults flowed freely around the large dining-room table. Hannah picked up her cards and grinned. "I know what it is, boys. You can't deal with the fact that a woman is whipping your collective fannies. Male pride. You're going to have to get over that."

Kyle pointed to the pile of chips in front of her. "I know she's not cheating, so how come she's winning every hand?"

Hannah arched her eyebrows. "Woman's intuition."

The five men at the table groaned. She was playing poker with her brothers and Austin. Nick had been invited to join the game, but he'd said he wanted to retire early and had walked back to the gatehouse. The women were in the living room making a baby quilt. Each of them crocheted a small square, which Louise then assembled into a larger piece. Even the older girls were helping. With so many hands, it should only take a few nights. Offered the opportunity to play cards, which Hannah already knew how to do, or learn how to crochet and expose her definite deficiency in the domestic arts, the choice had been clear.

She put one card facedown and slid it toward Jordan, who was taking his turn at dealer. He offered her another card in return. She added it to her hand and fought down a grin. Three ladies, a nine of spades and her new card...a nine of hearts. The bet was a quarter. She tossed one in from the impressive pile in front of her.

Austin had three of a kind; Travis, two pair; the rest, nothing. She swept the pot toward her and laughed.

"I need a break," Craig muttered, getting to his feet. He went over to Hannah and gave her a quick hug. "You're secretly a witch, aren't you?"

"You guessed. I never thought anyone would."

"I saw the broom in the back of your car."

She chuckled, then stood up and headed to the front porch. It had been a warm day and the house hadn't cooled off much. Outside, the stars were bright in the night sky.

She leaned against the railing and inhaled. The sweet air smelled of freshly cut grass and spring flowers. Whatever happened, she was pleased she'd come to Glenwood. She would remember this time forever.

"Did you come outside to give us a break?" Travis asked as he joined her.

"I wouldn't complain if I was dealt out of a hand or two. I can't believe how well I'm doing. I'm not usually that lucky at cards." She stared at him, his features shadowy in the faint light of the porch. "You're not all letting me win so I can feel better, are you?"

Travis held up his hands in a gesture of surrender. "We're not that nice. Ask anyone who knows us."

"Somehow I think people would say you *are* that nice."

"Maybe, but I promise we're not letting you win."

He settled next to her on the railing. Night creatures called to each other. Hannah felt herself relaxing. It had been a lazy day. All she needed was a warm bath and maybe a couple of kisses from Nick. She smiled. She could offer to work off some of the debt. She had a feeling he might not protest the exchange.

"Did you really meet Nick on a cruise?" Travis asked.

There was nothing in his tone to make her worry, but she stiffened and had to swallow before speaking. "Why do you ask?"

"Just curious. How long have you been married?"

Frantically, she tried to remember the lies. Nick had wanted to come up with a story together. She'd been too pigheaded to cooperate and now she was paying the price. Had they said how long they'd been married?

"We met on a cruise about four years ago."

"Nick said five."

Then she got it. Travis had overheard part—or all—of her conversation with Nick last weekend. She closed her eyes and prayed for direction. What was she supposed to say to him? What should she confess and what should she keep secret?

Maybe she should just tell him everything. But what would he think of her? What would he think of Nick? Would he want to take some action against him? She reminded herself that Nick wasn't really wanted for anything, at least not yet. But if she told the truth, what would happen? If she told the truth, Nick would leave.

"Where was he born?"

She exhaled. At least she had the right answer this time. "In a little town north of Santa Barbara. It was just him and his dad. His mother died when he was born."

Travis paced to the front of the house and back. He stopped in front of Hannah. "Try Philadelphia."

"What?"

"I ran him through the computer, Hannah. Nick Archer, born Nicholas Robert Archer, grew up in Philadelphia. Both his parents are dead, although his mother died only a couple of years ago."

Hannah felt the blood rushing from her head. The world tilted and she had the terrifying sensation of losing control. After a couple of deep breaths, she realized she wasn't going to faint, although the situation did call for desperate measures.

Had Nick lied to her about his family? She couldn't believe that. The way he'd talked about his father and the violence—that had to be real.

So why did the computer say differently?

"What else did the computer say?" she asked, barely able to speak the words. What hideous crimes had he concealed from her?

"He's clean." Travis sounded almost disappointed. "No outstanding warrants, no criminal record."

Thank goodness, she breathed silently.

"There are very few records at all," he said. "The ones there show that he's only been in Southport Beach about a year. And there's no mention of his being married."

She was tall, but her brother was taller. In the darkness, he was a large, dangerous man.

"Where do the two of you live?" Travis asked.

She gave her address, mostly because she didn't know Nick's.

"Funny, but that's not what's in the computer."

She wanted to die. She wanted to blurt out the truth. And in some strange way, she wanted to protect Nick. She knew instinctively that despite the bravado he put on about his criminal life, he wouldn't want her brothers to think badly of him.

"It's not what you think," she said quickly, then wondered what on earth she was going to say.

Travis folded his arms over his chest. "Then tell me what it is."

"He's..." She closed her eyes for a second, then received divine inspiration. "He's a private citizen working with local law enforcement on a sting operation. I can't go into details. It involves several beachfront developments in the area. Because of that, he has his own place. Most people don't know that we're married."

Travis didn't look as if he bought the story. She crossed her fingers behind her back and wondered if this lie was big enough to send her south when her time was up. She hoped not.

"He often has to come to the station and talk to Captain Rodriguez. The operation requires him to deal with a lot of criminal types. You can call down and check on that if you'd like. But please be careful. I don't want anything to happen to Nick."

Of everything she'd said, only the last sentence was true. She felt as if she were being ripped apart. Two voices screamed in her head. One demanded that she simply tell the truth. So what if Nick left and she never saw him again? Wasn't it more important that she not lie to her family? What had happened to honor?

The other voice merely whispered. It repeated all the kind things Nick had said and done on her behalf. It reminded her that he couldn't be all bad. It wasn't possible.

The voice spoke of how she felt in his arms and what it was like to laugh with him. If not for Nick...

"I'm sheriff here," Travis said. "I'm also your brother. I'm here for you if there's ever a problem. Of any kind. I want you to know that, Hannah."

Tears burned in her eyes. She felt lower than a snake's fanny pack.

He pulled her close and held her tightly against his chest. He didn't believe her. Who could believe that ridiculous story? Yet he wasn't calling her a liar, or throwing her out, or threatening to expose her. In fact, she was sure Travis hadn't discussed this matter with anyone.

"Thank you," she murmured.

"That's what family is for," he told her.

In his warm embrace, for the first time since she'd arrived nearly a week before, she felt as if she belonged.

Chapter Eleven

Nick put down the book he was reading and glanced at the clock on the mantel. It was after nine. Hannah had joined her brothers for a friendly game of poker, but he'd declined to participate.

He rose to his feet and crossed to the window. Was Hannah a good poker player? He could imagine she wouldn't have any trouble hiding her excitement or disappointment with her cards, but she might not have the courage to bluff well. The cautious lady probably played cautious cards.

The night was beautiful—clear, cool, quiet. Yet instead of enjoying the beauty, he fought an edgy restlessness. He'd spent too much time alone not to recognize the symptoms. The gnawing in his gut, the need to keep moving, no matter what. If he stayed still, if he allowed himself to listen to the silence, he would hear the faint whisper of pain.

He was tired of being lonely. He wanted to connect.

He swore softly, wondering when Hannah had first gotten under his skin. He knew it had started months before. Maybe the first day he'd noticed her and had invited her to run away with him. She'd been too startled to speak. Big doe eyes had widened as her mouth had parted in shock. Then she figured it was all a joke and had put him in his place with some scathing remark. He couldn't remember what she'd said. It didn't matter. He'd known then that he rattled her cage and he couldn't wait to do it again.

Teasing Hannah had been his favorite hobby. He'd looked forward to seeing her. But he'd never thought about making it real...until this past week. Until he'd spent time with her, had caught glimpses of the tenderness she kept concealed under layers of toughness. Until he'd held her in his arms and kissed her and begun to suspect this was a woman he might never forget.

He played a game, allowing himself to see what the future could have been like if he'd been someone else. A different kind of man.

He knew the past kept him trapped. Maybe he should think about letting it go. But he couldn't. Those images, that pain, were as much a part of him as his bones and skin. Imprinted on every cell were the beatings, the suffering, the uncertainty. The latter had been the worst. He'd never known when. Each morning, he'd awakened with the question—would his father drink today?

Sometimes they went weeks without an incident, even a couple of months. Then his father wouldn't come home from work and Nick would lie awake and wait. Hours or days later, he would return. Drunk, angry, mean. Broken and bleeding, Nick had vowed never to feel that much pain again, and he'd kept that vow. He'd never worried about being physically hurt. That wasn't the pain he feared. Instead it was the emotional betrayal—a loved one turning on him for no reason. He'd kept his promise to himself, too. He'd avoided getting involved.

With the hindsight of an adult, he knew it was time to make peace with that angry child from his past. It might even be time to take a chance on love.

Did he dare? Did he even know how? After all these years of withdrawing emotionally, did he know how to love anyone? He'd never tried.

He caught a flash of movement through the trees and turned toward the front door of the gatehouse. Hannah pushed it open and walked into the room.

Energy vibrated in the air around her. She crossed her arms protectively across her chest, her face pale. He moved to her side.

"What's wrong?"

"I..." She shook her head. "Nothing."

He wanted to pull her against him and hold her until whatever was troubling her went away. Yet something told him to wait and listen. He stood next to her, close enough to touch. He inhaled the scent of her body, sweet and familiar, and again felt the longing he'd experienced earlier.

She circled the room as if examining it, then moved to the sofa and sat down. He crouched next to her.

"Hannah?"

She squeezed her eyes shut, then opened them and stared at him. "Travis asked me about you."

"I'm not surprised. He overheard our conversation last Sunday."

"You knew? You knew and you didn't tell me?"

He settled next to her on the sofa. "I wasn't sure how much he'd heard or if he was going to say anything. I didn't want to upset you."

She covered her face with her hands. "It was awful. I

don't even want to think about it. He knows something's not right.''

''Tell me what happened.''

She shuddered. ''He asked how long we'd been married. I didn't know what to say. You're right. We should have come up with a story in advance. What was I thinking? I can't believe I was that stubborn.''

''I can. It's one of your more endearing qualities.''

She glared at him. ''This is no time for humor.''

''It's exactly the time for humor. Poor Hannah. I understand why you're upset. It's okay. What did Travis say when you told him the truth?''

She sprang to her feet and faced him. With her hands on her hips, her chin raised high, her eyes bright with anger, she looked like a pagan princess. He'd never wanted her more.

''I didn't tell him the truth.''

Nick couldn't have been more startled if she'd confessed to murder. ''You lied to Travis?''

''Yes. I did.'' Each word was clipped as if speaking was an effort. ''What did you expect me to do? Confess all?''

''Yeah. Why not?''

She turned away. ''I couldn't. He asked where you were born and I told him. I told him about your parents, about your mom dying when you were born and how you were raised by your dad.''

Nick winced. ''And he said it was all a lie.''

She nodded.

Dammit. Now what? Hannah had lied for him. He didn't understand why, but he knew what it had cost her. Honorable Hannah, who took herself and her job very seriously. What had he done to her?

He stood up and placed his hands on her shoulders. She flinched but didn't pull away. ''I know what's in my computer file," he murmured. "That I was born in Philadelphia. My parents died a while ago, my mother most recently. Of course there isn't any record of our 'marriage.'"

"You lied to me," she whispered.

She stood with her back to him. He wanted to turn her around so she faced him, but he knew she would resist that. Instead, he tried to tell her the truth with his touch on her shoulders and with his words.

"Never," he said, then realized that was the biggest lie of all. "I didn't lie about my family," he amended. "The computer files have been changed. I paid someone to do it."

"To hide a criminal record? Travis said you were clean."

"It was easier to start over," he said and hoped she wouldn't notice he hadn't answered the question.

She glanced at him over her shoulder. Dark, troubled eyes studied his face. "You told me the truth about your dad, what he did and all, and about your mom dying?"

"Yes. I swear, Hannah. That's all true."

"I suppose it's something."

He ached for her pain. If only he could tell her the truth. That was always the temptation on an undercover assignment. To tell one person. Then another, then another. He knew how it worked. His cover had to be absolute. Hannah would treat him differently if she knew. She might feel compelled to tell her brother. Nick couldn't risk it.

But he wanted to. If she knew who and what he really was, she would respect him, even let herself care about him. Perhaps it was just as well. He might have learned the wrong lessons from his childhood, but those lessons were firmly ingrained.

Hannah walked to the small fireplace and leaned against the mantel. "I told him the reason the computer records were so strange, not showing our marriage and listing an address different than mine, was that you were a civilian working with the Southport Beach Police Department on a sting operation. Something to do with beachfront property.''

She got it all out in one breath. He stared at her, barely able to comprehend what she'd said. ''You told him that?''

She nodded.

Her lies were so close to the truth, he started to laugh. One glance from her told him he'd made a mistake, but he couldn't stop. Except for the fact that he was a cop and not a civilian, she'd been one hundred percent accurate about him.

She glared. ''It's not funny.''

His laughter faded into slight chuckles. ''I know. I'm sorry. It's just—''

She spun toward him. ''It's just what? How dare you laugh at me? I lied for you, Nick Archer. I stood in front of my brother and deliberately withheld the truth. As a common criminal, I'm sure that's pretty meaningless to you. However, I don't share your loose moral code. I value my word and I always try to tell the truth.''

She was close to tears. He could tell by the tremor in her voice and the stiff set of her body.

''I know,'' he said quietly and moved toward her.

She took a step back. ''Don't touch me.''

He glanced around the room. ''There's no one else, Hannah. It's me or be alone.''

''I'd rather be alone.''

''I thought you said you didn't lie.''

She covered her mouth with her hand as if holding in a sob. He crossed to her and gathered her against him. She continued to hold herself stiffly as he put his arms around her and stroked her back.

"I can't believe you made me do this," she muttered.

He thought about pointing out that he hadn't made her do anything. She could have turned him in to Travis, but she hadn't. He wondered why. He would like to think it was because she was starting to feel something for him. He suspected it had something to do with the fact that he was her anchor in this strange situation. With him gone, she would have to face her family alone and that thought terrified her.

In time, she would adjust to them and not need him anymore, but he didn't want to think about that.

He also knew that part of the reason she'd withheld the truth was to protect him. She would think he didn't want her family knowing the truth, and in a way, she was right. He enjoyed his relationship with her brothers. If they thought he was a lowlife, everything would change.

Maybe it already had.

He continued to stroke her back and gradually she relaxed. Her hands rested on his waist. He took her wrists and drew them up over his shoulders. She buried her face in his neck.

"Damn you," she whispered. "I'll never forgive you for this."

Did she damn him for the lie, or for making her care?

"Sweet Hannah." He almost wished she had turned him in. Then he could get out of here. Before someone got hurt. "I don't deserve this."

She raised her head and looked at him. Tears swam in her eyes, but she blinked them back. "At least we agree on something."

He smiled faintly. "Not just because of who I am, but because..." He wasn't sure how to say it. "I want the best for you."

She frowned, not understanding his words. Then comprehension dawned. "And that's not you."

"Exactly."

"I know. Don't worry. My heart is quite safe." She took a step back. "Although I find the warning interesting. If you're trying to convince me you're one of the bad guys, you should have just used me and tossed me aside. Warning me off in advance doesn't exactly get you nominated as villain of the week."

His chest tightened and a peculiar aching began around his heart. "You're a hell of a woman."

"I know. Everyone says that. It's a real burden."

Her smile was a little shaky around the edges, but he wasn't going to comment on the fact. She would survive this because she was strong. He admired that.

She walked to the sofa and took a seat. "My head is spinning. I can't believe everything that's happened to me. I have a family, although God knows what Travis is thinking right now."

He settled next to her. "I'm sorry, Hannah."

"I believe you. You've been—" she glanced down at her hands "—you've been nice to me, Nick, and I appreciate that. For what it's worth, this past week with our pretending to be married has been a lot better than my real marriage."

"How long were you married?"

She sighed and mumbled something under her breath.

"What?" he asked.

She glared at him. "Five days, okay? Five days. Go ahead and laugh."

He didn't, although it was hard not to. "Five days. But you said you only got divorced a couple of months ago. What happened in between?"

She leaned back against the sofa. "I was pretending. I

somehow thought if I wasn't divorced, then I wasn't really alone."

He reached for her hand and stilled her twisting fingers. "I understand that."

"I'm glad someone does. It never made sense to me. It's not as if Shawn was a part of my life anymore."

"Where did you meet?"

"At the beach. I went with some friends to a little café and he was there." She smiled at the memory. "He was completely gorgeous. I don't know what he saw in me, but I wasn't going to ask any questions."

The hot, burning jab in his gut went unidentified until Nick caught his breath and realized he was suffering from acute jealousy. He released her fingers, but she didn't seem to notice.

"I had a huge crush on him," she continued. "When he asked me out, I wanted to die."

"Great." She hadn't wanted to die all the times *he'd* asked her out. She'd wanted to run far and fast in the opposite direction. Apparently, he'd gone about it all wrong.

"I was so excited to be part of a couple, I didn't notice we had nothing in common. After a few weeks, we decided to get married. Five days later, I realized I'd made a horrible mistake."

Nick didn't want to hear any more, but he couldn't keep from asking questions. "Why did Shawn agree to hold off getting a divorce?"

"He traveled a lot. Actually, for a couple of years, he wasn't in the country." She cleared her throat. "Shawn wasn't the kind of man who really worried about details like getting a divorce. If I hadn't gotten in touch with him, we would still be married."

Nick frowned. "Maybe he's secretly still in love with you and that's why he didn't want a divorce."

She laughed. "No, I don't think that's Shawn's style. He's much more into the flavor of the month. He's not marriage material."

"Hmm." So far he wasn't appeased. "So what does this Shawn do for a living?"

She didn't answer. He glanced over and saw her studying the floor. Color flared on her cheeks.

"Hannah?"

"Oh, what does it matter? He's not a part of my life."

"You're hiding something. Don't tell me he was in trouble with the law, too?"

"No. Shawn..." She drew in a deep breath. "Shawn is a professional surfer."

Laughter exploded out of him. He'd expected to hear that her ex-husband was an international banker, or an investigative reporter, or a successful businessman. "A surfer?"

"Yes. He was very good. You probably saw him on ESPN. He made a good living."

"A surfer?"

She glared at him. "Ha-ha. Very funny. I live to entertain. Can we change the subject?"

He shook his head and continued to laugh.

"Stop it!" she demanded.

"I can't," he gasped. "It's too good. A surfer."

She turned on him and pushed. He fell back across the cushions. She was on top of him, one knee between his hip and the sofa, the other between his thighs. She grabbed his hands and pinned them by his shoulders.

"I spill my guts to you and all you do is laugh?"

He shook his head helplessly. Chuckles continued to erupt. As long as he was laughing, he couldn't collect himself enough to push her off him. When he twisted his hands, she held on savagely, still glaring at him.

Then the laughter faded and it wasn't because she was

hurting him. Instead of pain, he felt a ripple of fire race through his body. He clamped his thighs around her knee, drawing her closer so that she pressed against the underside of his already-hard groin.

Her braid slipped off her shoulder to tickle and tease his chest. Their gazes locked. Her embarrassment and annoyance disappeared, replaced by an answering heat.

He wanted her. He'd always wanted her, from the first moment he'd seen her.

What would she say if he told her? Would she accept his words as truth? Would she question his motives? Would she make love with him? Or would she push him away?

"Nick," she breathed.

"Kiss me, Hannah."

The need inside him grew until it was a creature he barely controlled. She waited so long to respond, he thought she was going to move away. Instead, she lowered herself to him.

She didn't release his wrists, nor did she touch him anywhere else. There was just the brush of her mouth against his. Sweet heat. Warm pressure.

She kissed gently, tentatively, as if not completely sure of her reception. She shifted slightly and her breasts rested on his chest, her knee pressed against his inner thigh.

He parted his mouth and stroked his tongue against her lower lip. She gasped softly, then allowed him inside. She tasted of promise and surrender. He traced the tender skin on the inside of her lip, then moved past to touch her tongue with his.

The reaction was instantaneous. She released his wrists and cupped his face, holding him in place. She angled her head and opened to allow him in deeper. He obliged her, exploring her, tasting her, stroking her, arousing them both.

He brought his hands to her back and moved up and

down her spine. Sleek muscles rippled under his touch. Hannah was completely feminine, but never physically fragile. Her strength appealed to him. When they became lovers, they would be equals. He could give his all to her and not have to worry about holding back.

She raised her head and stared at him. Her lips were damp and swollen, her eyes dilated. "Damn you, Nick."

"What did I do?"

"You make me feel things. I don't want you."

He smiled. "Yeah, you do."

"You're right and I hate it."

His smile faded. "I'd never hurt you."

Dark eyes turned nearly black. "But you can't swear to that. You can't promise. You can only try. And I don't think trying is going to be good enough."

Somehow the conversation had moved from sex to caring and he wasn't sure how. "I want you. That I can promise." It wasn't enough, but it was the best he could do.

He placed his hands on her hips and shifted her so she straddled both his legs. Then he drew her down to stretch out on top of him. He rolled, bringing her with him, easing her between his body and the back of the sofa. She fitted him perfectly. Their chests pressed together, long legs tangling.

"There's something I've wanted to do for a long time," he said.

"I can just imagine what that is."

He kissed the corner of her mouth. "I'm willing to bet you're wrong."

He reached behind her and tugged on the end of her braid, freeing the ribbon holding the thick coil in place. She turned her head and tried to see what he was doing.

"Stay still," he ordered. "I'm unfastening your braid."

"Why?"

He looked into her big brown eyes. "I've known you for over a year and I've never once seen your hair down."

"That's it?"

"Don't be so dismissive. For me, this is going to be close to a religious experience."

"With my hair?"

He'd freed the ribbon and finger combed the thick strands. Next he drew them over her shoulder. "Beautiful. Just like I'd imagined."

"My hair?"

"Yes, your hair. Why are you so surprised?"

"I never thought it was anything special."

"Then you were wrong. Now shut up and kiss me."

Her eyebrows rose a little at his demand, but she complied. She leaned forward and touched her mouth to his. Desire spiraled between them, a thick, intoxicating brew that left him shaken and hard.

From her hair, his hand slipped down her arm to her hand. He brought it to his mouth, broke their kiss and nibbled on her fingertips.

She watched for a second, then slowly closed her eyes. "This is a bad idea."

"Uh-huh." Her skin was salty. He licked her palm. She shivered.

"No, I mean it, Nick. We have to stop."

"So stop."

"But I'm not the one doing anything."

He released her hand, then kissed her mouth again. She parted her lips instantly and swept her tongue inside. Electricity raced through him. Blood flowed hotter and faster. Need pressed against the button fly of his jeans.

He slipped his knee between hers and drew his leg up to the apex of her thighs. Her hips arched against him. She withdrew her tongue and he followed her back into her mouth. She clamped her lips around him and sucked.

His heart rate soared; her hips rocked faster. He placed his hand on her stomach and followed her rib cage up to her full breasts. She pressed into his palm. Even through her bra and T-shirt, he could feel her nipple tighten. He stroked his thumb over the taut peak.

They broke the kiss, both of them panting heavily. He was on fire. He shifted, rising into a kneeling position, letting her ease onto her back. Her hair fanned out over the sofa cushions. Dark eyes welcomed him.

He pulled her T-shirt free of her jeans and lifted it to her shoulders. Underneath she wore a lacy white bra. He could see the darker skin surrounding her nipples. His breath caught.

One of her hands came down on top of his. She urged him to release the shirt and move lower, to cup her breast. When he reached his goal, she gasped softly and arched into his caress.

A knock sounded at the door. "You guys still awake?" Kyle called.

Nick swore under his breath. "Yeah, we are. Just a second." He looked at Hannah. "You plan that?"

She was already pulling down her shirt. "Do I look like I planned it?"

He stood up and adjusted the front of his jeans. His erection throbbed painfully and bulged noticeably. "Maybe you should answer the door."

She glanced at him and flushed. Still tucking in her shirt, she hurried to the door and pulled it open. "Hi."

Nick moved so he was standing behind the easy chair. Sandy and Kyle were on the porch. They glanced inside the room, then at each other.

"Uh-oh," Sandy said. "Looks like we interrupted something."

Kyle dismissed her comment with a wave. "No big deal. They're married. They can do that anytime. Everyone just left, but it's such a great night out we thought we might go into town and get some ice cream. You want to join us?"

Nick knew one of two things would happen if they refused the invitation. He and Hannah would come to their senses and spend the next few hours feeling awkward around each other. Or they wouldn't come to their senses and they would make love. Each scenario had its own set of problems. It was probably the coward's way out, but avoiding the whole mess seemed like a brilliant idea.

"We'd love to," he said quickly. He had regained enough control to step out from behind the chair. "Is that all right with you?" he asked Hannah.

Her mouth was swollen, her eyes still unfocused. She had the look of a woman who had been thoroughly kissed. She reached up for her hair and brushed it back. "Sure. But I'm a mess. Give me a minute."

"You look great," he said and took her hand. He didn't want to give her the chance to pull her hair back into a tight braid. He might never get to see it loose again. "I've got the keys, so let's go."

She fingered her hair, then shrugged and followed him into the night.

Nick couldn't shake the feeling that he'd walked away from a dangerous situation. Hannah wasn't the kind of woman who made love lightly. If she gave her body, there was a good chance her heart wasn't far behind. The last thing he wanted was for her to fall in love with him. Wanting more than he was capable of giving would only cause them both pain.

* * *

Hannah licked the ice cream from her spoon. "Let me see if I get this straight. You fell in love with your wife when you were fourteen?"

Sandy laughed. "I think he only had a crush on me, but Kyle swears it was true love."

Kyle put his arm around Sandy. "It was. I knew the second she walked into my life. Of course, she was two years older and didn't even notice me. Not to mention the fact that she was dating my brother."

"Which brother?" Nick asked as he put his empty ice-cream cup on the tiny table. They sat in the balmy night air outside the Glenwood Ice Cream Shoppe. He and Hannah shared a bench pushed up against the plate-glass windows. Kyle and Sandy sat across from them.

"Jordan," Sandy said. "We went out for a couple of months. We weren't really an item, more like friends."

Kyle sighed dramatically. "You broke my heart."

She laughed. "We were children."

"What about after you moved back to Glenwood? You resisted me." He looked at Hannah. "She was very stubborn and refused to admit that she cared about me at all."

"Okay, yes. He's right about that. I couldn't believe someone as handsome and charming as Kyle would be interested in a single mother with three small children."

Kyle grinned. "She thinks I'm handsome and charming. This is why I keep her around."

The married couple exchanged a loving look, then Sandy turned to Hannah. "Your brothers are thrilled to have you here."

Except maybe Travis, Hannah thought. "I'm glad Louise finally got in touch with me. The family is a little overwhelming, but I'm getting used to everyone."

"Your brothers all look alike," Nick said. "It took me a couple of days to get everyone straight."

"It's true," Hannah agreed. "At least the wives are easier. We females look different."

"Jill and Holly said the same thing," Sandy said. "I guess I was lucky. I'd met the infamous Haynes brothers when I was in high school. When Elizabeth moved to town, she met them a couple at a time. The same for Rebecca. And Holly and Jill had already met one of the brothers before meeting any of the others. But you got everyone at once. At least Jill's easy to remember, what with being so pregnant and all."

"Any word on that?" Hannah asked.

"None. She's due any day. The poor kid. Louise wants her to hold out for her birthday, but Jill wants it over. She's so tiny, too. Within a week, she'll probably weigh the same as she did before she got pregnant. I hate that."

Kyle squeezed her hand. "Jill is a nice enough person, but so small I'm sure Craig loses her regularly in the house. I'd much rather have you exactly the way you are."

Nick raised his eyebrows. "That was great, Kyle. You think of that just now?"

"Sure. It's a gift. All the brothers have it." His mouth twisted as his good humor faded. "Not that it did us any good growing up." He stared into the distance. "We could have any girl we wanted, but that didn't make it any easier to go home. I remember thinking nothing could be worse than the screaming between my parents or my dad hitting me. Then, one day, my mother walked out. She didn't leave a note or anything. And I found out it *could* get a whole lot worse."

Hannah remembered hearing that story. "She left because your father wanted to marry Louise?"

"Yeah. After all those years of screwing around, the old

man was finally ready to settle down. Unfortunately, it wasn't with his wife."

"I'm sorry."

"It's not your fault. I don't blame Louise, either. My parents are both at fault. My father, of course, but I blame Mom some. She could have stayed in touch with her children. At least left a note." His voice was bitter.

Hannah pushed away her unfinished ice cream. "I look at you and your brothers and assume you had a perfect life, but I guess no one does. I was adopted when I was only a few days old. My parents were great. At least, that's how I remember them. They died when I was four." She briefly described growing up in foster homes.

Kyle leaned across the small table and took her hand. "If we'd known about you, we would have come and rescued you."

Her throat tightened with emotion. "I believe you. Thanks."

He released her and she leaned back. Her shoulder bumped Nick's. He put his arm around her and she snuggled close. Less than an hour before, they'd been about to make love. Now here she was spilling secrets about her past. She *never* talked about her childhood. What was happening to her? Everything was changing so quickly, she was having trouble keeping up.

She was wildly attracted to Nick, even though she knew it was a mistake. She had no regrets about what they'd done, only what they hadn't done. How was that possible? They'd only been together a few days. The intensity of her feelings frightened her. She didn't want to identify them, even though she knew what they were.

Nick played fast and loose with the law—and was virtually a stranger. Yet she trusted him. Perhaps foolishly.

How had someone so gentle and kind, so caring and honorable, ended up on the wrong side of the law?

She remembered the stories he'd told her about his past. About his father. Was that the reason?

"I think it's great that you're a cop like your brothers," Sandy said.

Hannah smiled. "I think it's a little odd. As if my destiny was chosen for me."

Sandy turned to Nick. "I know you're in real estate. Did you go to college?"

"Yes. I have a degree in economics."

They continued to talk. Hannah wondered if Nick really had a degree. Lies woven through truth. She wasn't sure what was real anymore. He wasn't her husband, or even her lover. They had nothing in common. She didn't want him to go but knew he had to leave. She had to make sure he was out of her life before she risked it all. Before she gave him her heart only to have him return it shattered forever.

Chapter Twelve

The phone rang and woke Nick from a sound sleep. As he reached for it on the end table, he instinctively glanced at his watch. Four-fifteen. He could only think of one person who would call at this time. Rodriguez. Either there had been a break in the case, or it had been blown wide open.

"Archer."

"Nick, it's Craig." The other man laughed. "I guess I woke you two up, right?"

Nick pushed the covers on the sofa aside and sat up. He rubbed his face. "Craig? What's wrong?"

"Nothing. I'm calling from the hospital. Jill had her baby. It's a girl, not that anyone is surprised by that."

The fog in his head cleared. "Congratulations. Everything okay?"

"Everything's great. The baby's perfect. Jill's doing fine. She didn't like the labor very much but swears the results were worth it." He paused. "I wasn't sure if I should phone you guys, but you're family now, so you got the call just like everyone else."

"I appreciate your letting us know. We'll be there as soon as we can. Tell me where the hospital is."

Craig gave him directions. Nick offered congratulations again, then placed the receiver back in the cradle. He glanced up and saw Hannah standing in the doorway.

If he hadn't been completely awake before, he sure as hell was now. She wore an oversize T-shirt that fell to the tops of her thighs and nothing else. Long hair tumbled over her shoulders. Her face was devoid of makeup, her eyes wide with questions. Desire slammed into him with all the subtlety of a tractor negotiating a china shop.

"What's going on?" she asked.

"That was Craig. Jill had her baby. A girl." He realized he was sitting on the sofa completely naked and aroused. Casually, he pulled the sheet over his lap.

Hannah pressed her hands together and grinned. "I want to go see them."

He glanced at his watch. "It's not quite four-thirty."

"I know, but I won't be able to get back to sleep, will you?"

He might have after the phone call, but not after staring at her legs. He shook his head.

"Then let's go. It will only take me a few minutes to get ready." Her sensuous mouth curved up in a smile. "I have a niece. Sort of. What would she be? A half niece?"

"Way too complicated a question for me to answer this early in the morning. You'll have to figure out the relationship on your own."

She laughed. "Nick, a baby. Isn't that great?"

"It's pretty cool." He thought for a second. "I doubt

five in the morning is the best time to go visiting. The hospital might not let us in.''

She tossed her head. "Don't worry about it. I'm a cop. I know how to act like I have a right to be somewhere. Besides, with all the children being born in this family, I'm sure we get a discount. I'm going to get dressed."

Forty minutes later, they walked into the hospital and followed the sign to the maternity ward. As they pushed open double swinging doors, a nurse stopped them.

"Visiting hours aren't until later in the morning."

"I know," Hannah said. "My brother and his wife just had a baby. We wanted to stop by briefly and congratulate them."

The nurse eyed her for a second, then shook her head. "I should have known. You're with the Haynes family." She laughed. "I suppose it will be your turn soon. Go on ahead. You can't miss them. The herd is in the maternity waiting room."

"Thanks." Hannah glanced up at him. "See?"

He had a box of doughnuts in one hand. He placed the other at the small of her back. "Which of your law enforcement skills did you use? I couldn't tell."

"I didn't have to use any."

"Too bad. I was looking forward to seeing you in action."

They rounded the corner and saw the open doorway of the maternity waiting room. Despite the early hour, conversation and laughter spilled out into the hallway.

"They amaze me," Hannah whispered. "So many people are here. You think they've done this for every birth?"

"Probably. It's just their way."

"Wow."

She stopped walking and stared into the room. Nick had a feeling she was a little overwhelmed. He couldn't blame her. Like her, he'd been a loner for a long time. Years ago, he'd stopped wishing for what he could never have. If someone had asked, he would have sworn families like this only existed on television.

But here they were, in the flesh. A living, breathing, loving family.

"I think I'm very lucky," Hannah said.

"You're right." He squeezed her waist. "Scared?"

"A little. At least I really like babies." She glanced at him. "Thanks for being here, Nick. I appreciate it."

"There's nowhere else I'd rather be."

"I bet I can think of a couple of places. How about Hawaii?"

"Nope."

"Tahiti?"

"I don't think so."

She frowned, trying to think of other exotic locations. He wanted to tell her the only place he would rather be was in her bed, loving her. That wasn't an option.

"How about—"

He dropped a kiss on her mouth to silence her.

"Is that all you two ever do?" a voice asked. Nick looked up and saw Kyle approach. The other man grinned. "It's five in the morning. Give it a rest."

Hannah laughed. "Nick can't help himself. He finds me irresistible."

"Why not?" Kyle asked. "You're a Haynes. The opposite sex always finds us irresistible."

"Gee, I could have used a little of this confidence during my gawky teenage years."

They entered the room. Nick fell into step beside them. "I'm sure you were stunning," he said.

"Oh, yeah. Stunningly awkward."

Kyle sniffed. "Do I smell fresh doughnuts?"

"Here." Nick handed over the box.

"Look," Kyle called. "Hannah, Nick and doughnuts."

Everyone turned toward them. There was a flurry of greetings. The family made quite a crowd. Three brothers and their wives, Austin and Rebecca, Louise and Richard—Nick wondered where the professor had been that he'd known about the early-morning birth—Hannah and himself.

He glanced at Travis, but there was nothing unusual in the other man's expression. Whatever Travis might think about Nick and his relationship with Hannah, he obviously wasn't going to discuss it here.

"We've got bagels, too," Elizabeth said and motioned to the white paper bags sitting on the coffee table in front of the sofa. "There's coffee, fruit, juice. We could open a restaurant."

Louise came over and gave Hannah a hug, then squeezed Nick's hand. "A beautiful little girl. Jill's doing well. She's sore, but happy."

"I'm so glad," Hannah said.

Elizabeth handed them coffee. Kyle circled the room with the box of doughnuts. Hannah was pulled aside to hear the details of the delivery.

"Does everyone have something to drink?" Jordan asked. There were murmurings of assent. He raised his plastic coffee cup. "To Craig and Jill. To the new baby. And to the Haynes legend."

Nick took a sip of coffee and studied the people in the room. From all that he'd heard, the brothers hadn't had a happy childhood. Their friend, Austin, had had it worse when he was growing up. They'd all managed to mess up relationships. Travis had been divorced before he'd met and married Elizabeth. Craig's first wife had left him, even though they had three children together. Three boys. If the legend was true, there had never been any love in that relationship.

So much pain and tragedy. An unfaithful father. A mother who simply disappeared. Yet through it all, they hadn't lost hope. Somehow, somewhere, they'd discovered the secret. They'd learned how to love and be loved in return.

Nick frowned. He'd never been in love. He'd wanted women, had enjoyed their company, but he'd never met anyone he couldn't leave behind. He'd never been willing to risk being hurt.

He often told himself that some kinds of fear were healthy. Better to respect an oncoming truck than to step in front of it. He knew his limitations. He knew the price of being wrong. So he hadn't taken a chance—not even once. And he hadn't regretted that until now. Until he'd seen what real happiness looked like. Until he'd watched this family and realized the emotional self-sufficiency he'd prided himself on meant spending the rest of his life alone.

What would it be like to stay in one place? To put down roots? To belong? What would it be like to commit to another person forever?

His gaze strayed to Hannah. She was laughing. She hadn't bothered to pull her hair back in a braid, and the soft waves framed her face. What would it be like to be married to Hannah for real?

"She's perfect," Hannah breathed as she pressed her fingers against the glass protecting the nursery from the outside world.

A nurse stood holding the tightly wrapped infant. The baby slept on, unaware of the adults watching over her. Hannah ached to hold her close and inhale the sweet baby scent of her.

"Six pounds, nine ounces," Elizabeth said. "Jill is so tiny herself. I know she was terrified of having a ten-pound baby."

Sandy shuddered. "I know the feeling. It's this pesky gene pool. The guys are so big."

"But we give good babies," Kyle said, slipping his arm around his wife's shoulders.

"That you do." Sandy smiled at him.

Louise moved closer. "I think she looks a little like her mother."

Elizabeth laughed. "That will be a pleasant change. Uh-oh, Nick, you're in trouble. Look."

Hannah glanced up and saw everyone staring at her. "What?"

"I recognize that expression," Elizabeth teased. "Be careful, Nick, or soon you'll be a daddy."

Hannah felt herself start to flush. She hadn't thought her feelings were that obvious. She couldn't bring herself to look at Nick. She didn't want him to think she was trying to trap him into anything. But Elizabeth was right—she did want a child of her own. A family. Did she have a chance of making that real?

"If what everyone says is true, I guess it wouldn't be a boy," Hannah said.

She risked glancing at him. He didn't look angry or even upset. She couldn't read the expression on his face, but some of her tension eased away.

"I'm so glad you're here to experience this with us," Louise said and pulled her close for a hug. "You, too, Nick." She drew him into the circle.

One by one, the brothers and their wives joined in.

"Group hug," Kyle joked. "Just like in the movies."

Hannah felt as if she *was* in a movie, or maybe a dream. Her heart swelled with emotions she didn't dare identify.

It was as if the protective shell she'd built around herself had started to crumble. She would have thought that would frighten her, but instead of fear, she felt renewed.

They separated and began talking. She saw Nick in conversation with Richard, Louise's beau. Her pretend husband was as tall and good-looking as any of her brothers. Feelings continued to burn hot inside of her. Was it love?

How could that be? she asked herself. Love Nick Archer? Had she handed over her heart? He was nothing she wanted in a man. She drew in a deep breath. He was *everything* she wanted in a man. Kind, gentle, smart, funny, sexy. He made her heart race and her knees buckle. He made her believe in possibilities.

Her gaze shifted and she saw Travis watching her. Her happiness faded slightly. She'd lied to her family. Not just once, when she'd first shown up, but every day. Even now, in this hospital waiting room, she lived a lie. She wanted to say it was because of Nick. She wanted to be able to blame him, but she couldn't. She was the one at fault. She had chosen to keep the truth from Travis and everyone else. She and Nick had no future together. But reality didn't stop her from wanting one.

Craig appeared in the doorway. He spotted Hannah and walked over. "You guys came."

"Of course. Why wouldn't we?" She smiled. "How's Jill doing?"

"Great. Why don't you come and say hi?" He motioned for Nick to join them, then led the way down the hall.

Jill was sitting up in her bed. She was pale, her short hair framing her pixie face. She waved as they came in the door. "Thanks for coming. Have you seen the baby?"

Hannah walked over to the bed and took her hand. "Yes. She's amazing. So perfect and pretty."

Nick moved to the other side of the bed, leaned over and

kissed Jill's cheek. "Thank God she looks like you and not her father."

"Hey." Craig grinned. "We're a good-looking bunch. I know you believe that. You married a Haynes."

Nick glanced at Hannah. "I didn't have a choice. She stole my heart when I wasn't looking."

"Oh, don't," Jill said and reached for the box of tissues on the table beside her bed. "I'm still fighting my hormones. It won't take much to get me to cry."

Hannah pulled up a chair. "How are you feeling?"

"Tender, but happy." Jill sniffed, then smiled. "Labor is the pits. Craig was with me. He kept promising it hurt him just as much to watch me as it did for me to go through the whole process."

"I doubt that," Hannah said.

"That's what I told him at the time." She sighed. "It's worth it, though. She's wonderful. And a girl. Just like Jordan said."

Craig moved to the foot of the bed. "I wonder how it will apply to you, Hannah. You're a Haynes, but female. What do you think?" he asked his wife.

Jill shrugged. "I'm not sure I even believe the legend, but so far it's working. You'll have to go ahead and get pregnant, Hannah. We're all going to be curious."

"What do you think about that, Nick?" Craig asked.

"I think we need to practice making babies a little more before we consider having one," he said lightly.

There was a knock at the door. Kyle and Sandy stepped in. "Are you up to more visitors?" Sandy asked.

"Sure," Jill said.

Hannah backed away from the bed, as did Nick. She watched him. He'd become a part of her family more easily than she had. As if he belonged. Travis and Elizabeth entered the room, then Rebecca and Austin. Nick left and she followed.

In the hallway, her throat tightened unexpectedly and her eyes filled with tears. Nick touched her face.

"Those hormones must be contagious," he murmured.

She nodded, unable to speak. When he pulled her close, she went willingly, never stopping to question why it felt so right to be in his arms.

"Have they already released Jill and the baby?" Hannah asked.

"This morning." Louise moved to the stove in Holly and Jordan's kitchen and stirred the simmering pot. "Usually I stay with the wives for a couple of weeks after they're released. Just to give them a break from taking care of the house." Louise grinned. "Not that being with a newborn is any kind of hardship for me." Her silver cowboy boot earrings glittered in the afternoon light.

"But Craig and Jill don't live in Glenwood," she continued. "So Rebecca is going to stay for a few days, then Elizabeth. I'll head up when you and Nick go back to Southport Beach."

Hannah nodded. When she'd first arrived, the two weeks had stretched before her, feeling seemingly endless. Now she had six days left. Six short days before she had to return to her real world.

"Karen seems like a good baby," she said.

"I know." Louise adjusted the burner, turning down the flame. "Jill's going to have her hands full, what with a newborn and the three boys Craig has from his previous marriage."

A timer went off. Hannah grabbed the pot holders, then walked to the oven and pulled out the bubbling casserole.

"She's going to have enough food for several weeks at least. How many dishes are you sending with them?"

"Five, counting this one." She tapped the pot. "I'm not sure how long they're going to last, though. You haven't seen those three boys eat."

"Does it bother you to be around all these children?"

Louise put down the stirring spoon and moved to the kitchen table. She sat down. "You'd think it would, but it really doesn't. I enjoy being with everyone's kids, especially the babies. Sometimes I think about what I gave up."

Hannah joined her at the table. She cupped her hands around her mug of coffee. "Did you see me after I was born?"

"Just for a minute. They wouldn't let me hold you. I wanted to, of course." Her blue eyes darkened with the memories. "I think they're afraid the young mothers will bond with their children. Maybe they're right. But I can't imagine I could have missed you any more than I did."

"You never had other children?"

"No." Louise shrugged. "I was married for a while. It was a mistake. I think I was looking for someone to fill that empty space inside of me. After a while, I figured out I had to find a way to fill it myself. So we got a divorce. It was friendly enough, I suppose. Then I had Alfred in my life."

"A boyfriend?"

"A basset hound."

Hannah was sipping her coffee when Louise answered and she nearly choked. "A dog?"

Louise smiled. "We were very close. Alfred passed away a couple of years ago. I still miss him."

"At least you found Richard to take his place."

"Oh, Richard is a little more company than a dog."

"But is he as well trained?"

They laughed together. Louise leaned back in her chair.

"I didn't like Richard at first. I thought he was pompous. Then I realized he was actually very shy. I'm just not sure about the age difference."

"If it were reversed, no one would think anything about it," Hannah said. "If you two are happy, why does it matter?"

"That's what I keep telling myself. But I have to decide if I believe it or not." She straightened her mouth. "I was very much in love with your father, Hannah. I knew it was wrong. I knew we could never be together. I've spent the past twenty-eight years regretting what I did to his family. Earl deserved what he had coming, but his wife didn't, nor did the boys."

"Do you think he loved you?"

"I don't know. He says he did. According to Jordan, the fact that you're female is proof."

"Do you believe that story?"

"I want to say I don't, but there have been a lot of girls born lately, and this after so many generations of boys."

Hannah stared out the window. The garden was bright with flowers. "I don't know what to do about him. Sometimes I think I should get in touch with him and tell him who I am. Other times, I can't face the thought of his rejecting me."

Louise touched her hand. "I can't promise he'll welcome you with open arms. I don't pretend to understand Earl. But when you're ready to talk to him, I'll do anything I can to help. I'll even call him first, if you'd like."

"Thank you."

Hannah was touched by the offer. It would be difficult for Louise to speak to her old lover after all these years. Confessing to a full-grown child wouldn't be easy, either.

She smiled. "I'm glad you wrote me."

"I'm glad you came to visit." Louise reached over and squeezed her fingers. "I'd like us to stay in touch."

"Of course. I was hoping you would come down and stay with me."

"I'd like that. I'm sure you and Nick have a wonderful place together."

Hannah stiffened. She'd forgotten it was all just pretend. Maybe it was time to tell the truth.

"Louise, I have something to tell—"

A sharp ring cut through the room. Louise stretched out her arm and snagged the phone from the wall.

"Haynes residence." She listened for a moment, then smiled. "I'm glad you made it safely. Yes, tell Craig I've already made two batches of his favorite kind of chicken. And tuna casserole for the boys. Uh-huh." She covered the mouthpiece. "It's Jill. They made it home safely."

"Tell her hi from me."

Louise nodded. "Is she sleeping? Good. Are you sleeping?" She laughed. "Rebecca will take care of you, but I'm afraid you're just going to have to wait the pain out. Try taking a warm bath. Oh, Hannah's here, she says hi." Louise listened, then held out the phone. "She wants to talk to you."

Hannah stood up and walked around the table. Louise moved to the stove to check on the stew.

"Hi," Hannah said. "How are you feeling?"

Jill laughed. "Actually, pretty good. The breast-feeding is strange. I feel like a twenty-four-hour convenience store."

"Sounds like fun. How's the baby?"

"Little Karen is doing great. I'm in her room right now and I want to thank you for the lamp. It goes perfectly and it's just…'' She sniffed. "Oh, here I go again. Crying my eyes out. I can't stand being this weepy."

"It's okay. I understand."

"What are you guys doing?"

"I'm cooking with my mom. We're making sure you have plenty to eat."

Jill sighed. "This is the best family, Hannah. No one has ever taken care of me like these people. I love them all. They're so w-wonderful. I can't believe I'm doing this again." Tears thickened her voice. "I'd better go. I'm a wreck. But thanks for the lamp. It's terrific. And come see me before you leave, okay?"

"I will. Take care." Hannah hung up the phone. She was feeling a little teary-eyed herself. "Jill's a sweetie," she said as she turned toward the stove. She stopped, shocked to see Louise wiping away a tear. "Nick's right," she said. "Hormones are contagious."

"It's not that," Louise said. "I'm being silly, I know, but when you said you were cooking with your mom, I realized that's me. You called me Mom." She waved her hand in the air. "You don't have to if you don't want to. I understand your adoptive mother will always be your real mother. But it was nice."

Hannah had to swallow before speaking. "I'd like to call you Mom. I didn't know if you'd want me to."

"Of course I do." She moved to Hannah and gave her a hug. "You're my daughter and I love you."

"I love you, too, Mom."

Hannah squeezed her eyes shut. A mix of emotions flooded her. Sweet, sweet affection tempered by the bitter taste of guilt. She still had to tell her mother the truth about Nick. Just not right now. It would spoil a very special moment.

Besides, the longer she put it off, the longer he would stay.

Nick looked up when the front door opened. Hannah stepped into the room. She gave him a bright smile, but he saw the evidence of tears.

"What's wrong?" he asked, springing to his feet. "What happened?"

"Nothing. Louise and I..." She wiped her face. "We said that we loved each other and I called her Mom. It was very emotional. I guess you had to be there."

Panic retreated. He squeezed her shoulder. "Way to go, kid. Soon you'll have normal relationships, just like everyone else."

"Don't hold your breath. I doubt I'll ever be very close to normal, but I'm trying." She walked into the kitchen and pulled a soda out of the refrigerator. "Poor Nick. You didn't expect this when you agreed to help out for a weekend."

"It's not so bad." He leaned against the entrance to the kitchen. "I never thought I'd see big, bad Hannah Pace in tears because she told her mother she loved her."

"No one will believe you, so don't even think about spreading rumors."

He grinned. "You're right. Everyone thinks you're so tough."

Since the night they'd almost made love and he'd admitted how much he liked seeing her hair loose, she'd worn it down. Now the silky brown strands cascaded to the middle of her back. He wanted to bury his fingers in her hair, kiss her until they both forgot to breathe and make love with her. Instead, he shoved his hands in his pockets.

Whatever happened or didn't happen between them,

when she thought of this time, she would remember him. He'd been a part of something good in her life.

She set the soda on the counter. "I'm not tough, though. How come you figured that one out?"

"I know your secrets."

She stared at him. "Why did you bother? There had to be other, more willing women around."

This conversation had moved a little too close to dangerous territory. He wasn't ready to answer that kind of question. "You were impossible not to tease," he said lightly.

She didn't smile. She took a step toward him. "A conscious act of seduction, Nick Archer. Why me?"

Because the moment he'd met her, he'd known instinctively she was hiding because she was afraid. The more he got to know her and saw the sweet person inside, the more he wanted her. He teased her and toyed with her because she wouldn't have accepted anything else. A serious pursuit would have sent her running in the opposite direction.

"I have this thing for big brown eyes."

"Good. I have this thing for big blue eyes." She took another step toward him. They were inches apart. "And blond hair. And strength. And guys with great butts."

He glanced over his shoulder. "You think I have a great butt?"

"Yeah."

He saw it in her eyes. The desire he could handle. Everything else scared him to death. His chest tightened as need warred with common sense. They couldn't do this. It would be a big mistake. What if she couldn't walk away when it was over? What if he couldn't?

But his body didn't cooperate. Need filled him, making it difficult to think. He tried to remind himself that everything about this relationship—including the so-called relationship itself—was a lie.

But his feelings were real, and that fact scared him to death.

"Don't look at me like that," he said, his voice low and gruff.

"I can't help it."

"It would be a mistake to get involved."

"We already are."

"I'm not."

She placed her hand on his chest. "Liar."

"Dammit, Hannah, I can't do this."

She didn't move. She continued to study his face, her sexy mouth curved up in a slight smile.

"You've got fifteen seconds to get out of here or I won't be responsible for my actions," he growled.

"I'm shaking," she said. "But it's not from fear."

He swore, grabbed her upper arms and hauled her against him. "Why the hell can't I resist you?" he asked.

"Because I don't want you to. Because—"

She never got the rest of it out. He silenced her with a kiss.

Chapter Thirteen

Hannah had been terrified. She'd never deliberately tried to seduce a man before. What if she'd been making a horrible mistake? What if he really didn't want her?

But at the first brush of his mouth against hers, she knew her fears were unfounded. He wanted her. He needed her. He trembled with desire.

His lips were warm, his kiss hot and hungry. Before, he had been gentle, almost tentative in his caress. This time, he devoured her, tracing her mouth with his tongue, then plunging inside. Their actions mimicked the act of love to follow. She clung to him, wanting to experience everything with him. Despite the lies, despite who and what he was, she trusted him. Perhaps more than she'd ever trusted anyone in her life.

He wrapped his arms around her shoulders and waist, pulling her closer. Her breasts flattened against his chest. He was strong and hard to her soft curves. Their legs brushed, the erotic sound of jeans against jeans filling the quiet.

She rested her hands on his shoulders, then moved them higher to his blond hair. The sleek, silky strands teased her fingertips. He angled his head and kissed her deeper. His tongue circled hers, sending liquid delight pouring through her body. Her thighs were on fire, as if she'd just run ten miles. Her arms were weak, her stomach tight with anticipation.

He broke the kiss. "I've got to get control," he muttered, his breathing harsh.

She stared at his handsome face, at the strong cheekbones, the vivid blue eyes, darker now as his pupils dilated with passion.

"Are you that close to being out of control?" she asked.

"You have no idea."

The concept pleased her. She still didn't understand why Nick was doing all this. Why he had come with her, why he was helping her, why he cared even a little. But she was glad. It was only for a short time and it was only pretend, but it was more than she'd ever had in her life.

Wanting to be sure he really was a man on the edge, she drew one hand over his shoulder and down his chest. His muscles rippled visibly, and when she reached the waistband of his jeans, he flinched, then swore.

Pure, perfect power filled her. She'd never been sure about her femininity. She was too tall, too physically strong, too determined and stubborn to be what she considered a typical female. Men either ignored her or tried to show her how macho they were. Nick seemed willing to accept her for who she was.

"You're going to make me cry again," she said.

"Why?"

"Because you really want me."

He brushed his thumb lightly over her mouth. "What the hell do you think all this has been about?"

"I don't know. I could never decide what you were thinking."

He drew her close and kissed her neck, then raised his head and drew her earlobe into his mouth. He sucked, then bit down gently on the tender skin. "Now do you know?" he asked.

"I'm starting to figure it out."

"Good."

He took both her hands in his and lifted them to his mouth. After kissing her knuckles, he backed out of the kitchen, still kissing her fingers. She barely noticed as they passed through the living room and into the bedroom.

He turned her hands palms up and brushed his thumbs over the sensitive skin. When the tingling shot up to her elbows, he bent his head and pressed his mouth to the base of her right thumb. He nibbled the fleshy spot, rose slightly and blew on the damp spot. She shivered in response.

He moved his mouth to her wrist and kissed the pulse point, went higher still to the sweet spot at the bend of her elbow.

Her breasts swelled, her knees shook. He held her other hand and touched his mouth to her arm. She could have easily stepped away. She could have stopped him, or demanded more, or any number of things. Yet he held her immobile with sensual magic.

No one had ever made love to her like this. While Shawn hadn't been the first man in her life, he'd only been the second. She hadn't been involved with anyone else since. She understood the workings of her body; she had found pleasure from time to time. The pattern was simple. Kissing, breast fondling, then "the act." No one had ever made her breathless simply by pressing his lips to her arm.

Nick raised his head and moved higher, nuzzling her neck, moving along her shoulder, then slipping down her other arm. He'd continued to circle her palm with his thumb, causing the small area of skin to heat and become sensitized. When he touched his tongue to the spot, she wanted to cry out. Her head arched back and every muscle in her body tightened with need. Her breathing came in short, rapid pants.

She wanted to grab him and demand that he get on with it. She couldn't take much more of this. She wanted to beg him never to stop.

He straightened and stared into her eyes. "Sweet Hannah."

Then he buried his fingers in her hair. She closed her eyes and absorbed the sensation. He tugged on the strands, drawing her head back. She went with the movement, arching her torso upward.

Sharp, exquisite fire cut through her right breast. She gasped and looked down. He held her erect nipple in his teeth. The layers of her shirt and bra, not to mention his gentleness, protected her from anything close to pain. Hot breath added to the sensation. She began to shake.

She grasped his shoulders, as much to hold on as to hold him in place. He moved his teeth back and forth, withdrew and repeated the procedure on the other breast.

His hands moved down her back, urging her to offer herself to him. She arched forward, needing more, wondering how it was possible to be so aroused and still have on all her clothing.

As if he'd read her mind, he slipped his hands lower to her waist, then moved them around to the front. He unfastened the button on her jeans and drew the zipper down. He tugged the jeans over her hips. She parted her legs slightly to help.

He abandoned her breasts and she nearly cried out in frustration. He knelt in front of her and pulled her jeans to her ankles, then pushed up her T-shirt and pressed his mouth to her belly.

The feel of his damp mouth on bare skin was her first indication that her panties had been removed with her jeans. She vaguely thought about protesting, but accepted that it was foolish at this point. Then he dipped his tongue into her belly button and she didn't really care what he did.

Between her legs, need pulsed in time with her heartbeat. She could feel the heat there, the desire making her body swell in anticipation. She couldn't focus on a single rational thought. All that mattered was what she felt, what he was doing to her and where they would soon go together.

He cupped her bare derriere and squeezed. She grabbed his shoulders to hold on, then moved one hand to stroke his head. He urged her legs apart. She tried to comply, but the jeans around her ankles restricted her. She was trapped and at his mercy. She prayed her surrender would be as wonderful as she imagined.

He kissed the skin below her belly button, nipped oh so gently on the protective folds around her femininity, then drew them open and pressed his tongue to her center.

She was unprepared for the sensual assault, for the fire that ripped through her. She nearly lost her balance as her knees buckled. He chuckled softly, his warm breath puffing against her private places.

She tightened her hold on his shoulders. He was the only stable part of a world that had started to spin.

Back and forth he flicked against her. Teasing, wet, sweet. She caught the rhythm of his caresses. Her muscles tensed, then relaxed in counterpoint to his attentions.

She couldn't move away or closer, she couldn't control

her reactions, she couldn't do anything but stand there and let him please her.

And please her he did. With a steady stroking that made her want to scream. Every part of her quivered. She needed more. She whimpered and held on to him tighter. Her hips tilted toward him, toward the magic, the promise of release.

Then, when she felt she couldn't stand it another second, when her legs really were about to give out and she didn't have the strength to breathe, he pressed his lips to her secret flesh and sucked on that tiny spot.

Pleasure exploded instantly. She had no idea what she did or what he did. The world could have ended. It didn't matter. Light poured through her, liquid and hot. Every muscle convulsed in a seemingly endless release of complete perfection.

When she regained conscious thought, she found herself sitting on the edge of the bed. Nick knelt at her feet, his hands on her thighs.

"I..." She paused, not sure there were words to express what she was feeling. She leaned toward him and cupped his face in her hands. "How did you do that?"

He raised one eyebrow and grinned. "Trade secret."

She kissed him. "Amazing."

He reached for her foot and untied her athletic shoe, then repeated the procedure and removed her socks. Her jeans and panties slipped over her ankles and she kicked them off. Before she could pull her shirt over her head, he took her hands in his.

"Did you bring any protection?" he asked.

He'd just touched her in the most intimate way possible, so why was she blushing after the fact? It was the question, of course. Protection. She shook her head.

He squeezed her fingers. "I'll be right back."

He left the room. She stared after him. He hadn't tried

to avoid the issue or convince her a condom wasn't necessary. He might be a con artist in his business life, but he conducted the rest of his affairs like a gentleman.

She pulled her T-shirt over her head and reached for the back closure on her bra.

"Wait!" he called as he stepped back into the room. "I want to do that."

"Why?"

He tossed a small box of condoms on the nightstand. "Taking off your clothes is the best part."

She grinned. "If you really think that, you've been doing it wrong."

"Nearly the best part."

As he kissed her, he reached around her and unfastened the bra. As it slipped down her arms, he moved onto the bed and settled himself behind her, her rear pressed up against his groin. She could feel his arousal though his jeans and his broad strength against her back.

He pushed her hair over one shoulder and dropped kisses on the other. Large, tanned hands rested on her midsection. She didn't get out much and her skin was pale. The vision of obviously male fingers touching her paleness, resting close to the dark hair at the apex of her thighs, aroused her.

He moved his hands higher and cupped her breasts. He held her gently, carefully, stroking the soft skin with his fingers. Around and around, sneaking nearer but never touching her taut nipples.

She decided to do some torturing of her own and rubbed her palms against his rock-hard thighs. He retaliated and finally brushed his thumbs against her nipples. She felt the contact all the way down to her toes. He did it again, then again, until the fire returned and all she could think about was how much she wanted him.

He moved his hand down her belly and touched his little finger to that secret place. She jumped.

"No," she cried and turned on the bed. "You're taking off your clothes, too."

He leaned back on his elbows and grinned. "I wouldn't have expected you to be pushy in bed. I'm pleasantly surprised."

"It's only fair."

"You're right." He straightened and pulled off his T-shirt. It went sailing across the room.

He was broad and muscled, tanned skin covered with gold hair. She pushed him onto his back and pressed a kiss in the center of his chest. He smelled masculine and tasted of temptation. She ran her palms up and down the hard ridges of his belly, savoring the strength and the way her touch made him jump.

She kissed a line from the center of his chest to his right shoulder, then bit down.

He groaned and tangled his hands in her hair. "You're even more beautiful than I thought. Kiss me."

She brought her mouth to his. Their tongues mated. She slipped her hand down his belly, over his jeans, then cupped his arousal. He was large, hard and pulsing. Between her legs, heat exploded. She wanted him there, claiming her.

He broke the kiss. "I wish you wanted this as much as I did."

"I do," she said, then smiled. "Trust me. I want you."

"But you haven't been dreaming about it."

She thought about the nights she'd lain awake listening for sounds from the living room, wondering what he slept in and if he ever thought of her. "It's crossed my mind a time or two."

He didn't look convinced.

She leaned closer, letting her bare breasts stroke his chest. "You sometimes wear a black suit. There's something about the cut. I can't explain it, but when you take off the jacket and throw it over your shoulder, my knees get weak."

"Yeah, right."

"I'm not kidding. You wear this white shirt and your shoulders are about a mile wide. I always watch you walk away from me when you wear that suit. The trousers really show off your butt. It should be illegal."

She felt wicked confessing these secrets, but the desire flaring in his eyes made it all worthwhile. He reached down and unfastened his jeans. She grabbed them and pulled them off. His erection sprang free. Without thinking, she reached for him, holding him gently and stroking the hard length of him.

"You've turned me on a time or two yourself," he said, his voice strained as he tried to maintain control while she touched him.

She laughed. "Like when?"

"Oh, just by breathing. You ever notice how I usually knock something to the floor when I sit at your desk?"

"Yes."

"I want to see you bend over and get it. You do your hair so the back of your neck is bare. I always think about kissing you there and I—"

She rubbed her fingers lightly over the sensitive tip of his arousal. He gasped sharply, then groaned.

Their eyes met. She knew in her heart she was making a huge mistake. Once she gave Nick her body, there was no going back. In time, she would be forced to pay for these few moments of exquisite pleasure. And yet, when she thought about what would happen in the future, she couldn't regret what she was about to do.

"Love me," she whispered and knew she meant more than just the physical fact of their joining.

He hastened to use the protection. When she was about to roll off him, he urged her to straddle his hips and lower herself onto him.

He filled her completely. His hands clasped her hips, urging her to ride him like some reckless, untamed creature. The heat in his gaze gave her courage and she moved up and down in a sensual rhythm designed to force them both into madness.

For once in her life, she was proud to be strong and tall. Her thigh muscles tightened with each thrust, allowing her to move faster without tiring. Her hair tumbled over her shoulders; her breasts bounced. She knew she looked like a wild woman and she didn't care.

When the need spiraled inside her, she surged toward it. When he reached a hand between her thighs and found her most sensitive place, she whispered for him to touch her. When she felt him collect himself, then hold back, waiting for her, she stared at his face, at the taut lines and muscles.

Without words, he begged her to find her release. She stopped, suspended by a connection so strong that nothing could sever it. His fingers danced over her center, moving gently on slick flesh. She saw the promise, closed her eyes and abandoned herself to her fate. His fingers moved in counterpoint to the thrusting. For the second time, she found paradise in his touch.

While she fought for breath and spasms of pleasure rippled through her, he stiffened and called out her name. Her body clenched tightly, bringing him the same release she had known.

When they'd caught their breath, she slid off him and settled next to him on the bed. Aftershocks swept through him, making a leg tremble, an arm jerk. Nick settled her head on his shoulder and stroked her hair. Her breasts nestled against his side; her knee rode his thigh.

"Amazing," he said, knowing he'd expected good and instead been blown away.

"I agree."

He wondered if she had any regrets. She didn't act like it. Maybe they would show up later. Maybe he should quit borrowing trouble and just enjoy the moment.

"To think I wasted a year resisting you," she said. "We could have been doing this all along."

The thought of it made him want to make love to her again. It also terrified him. "Hey, I said you were pretty. I never said you were bright." She pinched the lean skin around his waist and he twisted away. "Okay, okay, you're pretty and bright. Happy?"

She sighed. "Very."

He continued to stroke her hair, playing with the strands, twisting them around his fingers, then releasing them. "So how long have you had a thing for my butt?" he asked, remembering her earlier confession.

She turned toward him, resting her chin on his shoulder. "Since the first day I watched you walk away."

He winked. "I suspected that."

"Really?"

He kissed her forehead. "No, not really. You were very circumspect. I bet you thought I was a life-form slightly lower than a cockroach."

"Sometimes I did," she admitted. "At first I thought you were coming on to all the female officers. Then I figured out it was only me. I just never knew why."

They were treading very close to dangerous territory. As he often had with her before, he decided the truth would be the easiest answer.

"I liked you."

She studied him for a long time. "As simple as that?"

"Why make it complicated?"

"I don't think many people have liked me. I'm not sure I'm a likable person."

"Trust me, you have some wonderful qualities." He stroked the side of her breast.

She snuggled closer and relaxed her head. Silence filled the room. He stared at the ceiling and tried to convince himself he hadn't made a huge mistake. Even as he fought the panic at the back of his mind, he told himself he didn't actually feel emotionally connected to Hannah. They hadn't done more than make love. Okay, so maybe they'd become lovers, which was a little more, but it wasn't a permanent affiliation. When their time was up, he would walk away. As planned.

Lies and truth. Always lies and truth. If he walked he would be leaving a part of himself right here. He belonged in Hannah's arms. He felt it as surely as he felt the effects of gravity.

Belonging. Caring. Were they love?

Hell of a statement on his life. He was thirty-four years old and he didn't know what it meant to be in love. He couldn't define it and probably wouldn't recognize it if it came up and bit him.

He was sure of one thing. He didn't want to leave her. Make that two things. When their time together was up, he was out of here.

Better for both of them. He couldn't be what she wanted. He didn't know how. So he would walk away with nothing but the memory of how it *could* have been.

Hannah had finally grown used to dining with a large group of people. She realized she'd been truly accepted when one of the children pointed to the icing she'd left on her plate and asked if she was going to finish it.

Hannah laughed. "Help yourself," she said, passing the plate.

The routine was familiar. The children set the table, the women cooked and served, the men cleaned up. Once the bulk of the dishes were done, everyone came back to the table and ate dessert.

Tonight they were at Jordan's house. Holly led the way into the living room, where the adults settled in on the sofas. The children raced upstairs to play games.

Sandy flopped into a wing chair. "Can I leave my four with you, Holly? You could practice being a mother and give me the night off."

"Sure. I'd love it."

"Ha. That's because they'd be on their best behavior for you." Sandy shook her head. "I hate the last few weeks of school. The kids are getting excited about the summer holidays and having trouble concentrating on their classes. And I get to think about all that time at home with nothing for them to do but say 'We're bored. What can we do?'"

Holly looked at her. "Surely it's not that bad."

Elizabeth laughed. "It's worse."

As the conversation flowed around the room, Hannah was aware that Nick was still in the kitchen helping Louise with the dessert plates. Just thinking about him brought a smile to her lips. Had everyone been able to tell that they'd made love that afternoon? She'd felt sure her happiness was showing on her face. She hadn't been able to stop smiling all evening.

After she'd napped for about an hour, she awakened to find Nick nibbling his way up from her ankles. When he'd shown her that the first two times hadn't been a fluke, she'd gotten her own back by torturing him the same way. She'd never done that to a man before, had never taken him in her mouth and pleasured him. When she'd confessed her inadequacies, he'd told her he wouldn't mind being her first. She'd felt awkward in the beginning, then had relished the thrill of power as she'd driven him mad and led him to ecstasy.

So much had changed in only a few days. Nick had become a part of her life. How could she have survived without him?

The need to see him was too intense. She rose to her feet and headed for the kitchen. The door was partway open. She was about to enter when she heard Louise mention her name.

"Have you and Hannah given any thought to moving up here?" Louise laughed. "I know, I know. I'm being the cliché of a pushy mother-in-law. You both have careers. But it would be lovely to have you close by. There's plenty of family."

"Hannah could always go to work for her brothers," he said. "I'm not sure what I'd do."

Hannah felt as if she'd been stabbed. The lies continued. She could move if there was a job opening. But Nick wouldn't be coming with her. Their marriage was a sham. Worse, he was involved in criminal activities.

"Day care," Louise said. "The way this family has babies, you'd have clients for life."

"Maybe. There is something I've always wanted to do."

"What?"

He hesitated. Hannah moved closer to the partially open door. She could see Nick's back and part of his profile. Louise was at the sink and out of view.

"You'll laugh," he said.

"I won't. I swear."

Hannah cringed. What was he going to say?

"I've always wanted a bed-and-breakfast inn. You know, one of those old restored houses. Sort of like this one. Very upscale, very comfortable."

"I think it's a wonderful idea. There are plenty of houses like that around here. I'll tell you what. You run the bed-and-breakfast and I'll take care of the kitchen. We'll go into business together."

"Sounds like a great idea."

"Hannah can work for Travis. There. It's all settled."

Hannah bit her lower lip. It was a wonderful dream. If only it could come true.

"Louise, there's something I have to tell you about Hannah," Nick said.

Hannah held her breath, wondering what he would say.

"What is it? You sound serious."

"I am. She's a wonderful woman. I know you think you've already learned that about her, but there's more. She can be prickly on the outside. If she gets scared or threatened, she holds herself apart and is distant. Just when she needs a good hug, she takes off running."

"Instead of risking the pain of rejection," Louise said softly.

"Exactly. It comes from how she grew up. Hannah didn't have a lot of love in her life and she's not sure she believes in it. Of course, that's just for herself. She believes in it for others."

Hannah blinked several times before she realized she was holding back tears.

"She volunteers at the county hospital," he continued. "She goes in a couple of times a week and cuddles babies. The abandoned ones. Those born addicted to drugs, or AIDS babies. She loves them all when no one else will bother."

The tears fell and she was too stunned to brush them away. How did he know?

"You won't find anyone more kindhearted than your daughter. But she's put a wall between herself and the world. You're going to have to break that down. Whatever happens, no matter how long it takes, don't give up on her."

Hannah heard a dish *thunk*ing as it hit the bottom of the sink. "Dammit, Nick, you've made me cry and my mascara is running." Louise sniffed. "I know she's a wonderful woman."

"Yes, she is. Don't let her resist you."

"Why are you telling me this? It sounds like you're not expecting to be here when this happens."

Hannah had to clamp her lips together to keep from crying out. Nick was doing this for her because he *wasn't* going to be around.

"I'll be here. I just wanted you to know the truth about her."

Hannah took a step back, determined to get away before they caught her listening.

"She's lucky to have you," Louise said.

Hannah turned in the hall and ducked into the small guest bathroom tucked under the stairs. Her mother was right. She was lucky to have Nick in her life.

She stared at her reflection in the mirror above the sink. Tears rolled down her cheeks. How had he known? Who'd told him her secrets?

She didn't have any answers.

She continued to cry softly. For the truth he spoke, for the kindness in his words and for the realization that he'd been wrong about one thing. There was no wall. He'd already torn that down. She hadn't even noticed while it was happening.

There was nothing to hide behind. No escape from the knowledge that whoever he might be, whatever he might have done in the past, whatever he might yet do—she loved him.

Chapter Fourteen

Nick walked into the kitchen and poured a glass of water he didn't really want. As he stood there sipping it, he told himself he was acting like a fool. Or worse. He felt as nervous as a kid on his first date.

He and Hannah had become lovers that afternoon. He'd touched her and tasted her and taken them both to paradise. What happened now?

Had their time together been a one-shot deal? Had it meant anything to her? He placed the glass on the counter and closed his eyes. He wasn't being fair. Although he wanted their lovemaking to mean everything to her, he wasn't willing to make the same kind of statement himself. He didn't want to take the risk.

Even as he told himself it was a bad idea, even as he warned himself she could easily blow him out of the water, even as he prepared himself to fail, he turned and started for the bedroom.

He paused in the doorway. She sat on the edge of the bed staring at her hands.

"Hannah?"

She raised her head and looked at him. Her long, dark hair hung loosely around her face and shoulders. Her mouth twisted slightly and there were questions in her eyes.

His heart sank. She was having second thoughts. More than that, she didn't want him and didn't know how to tell him. He wasn't even aware he'd been anticipating being with her until disappointment flooded him. It was all he could do to keep from groaning aloud.

"I overheard you talking to Louise," she said softly. "You never told me."

He tried to remember what he'd said to her mother. "You mean about the bed-and-breakfast?"

"Yes, but that's not what I mean. How did you know about my work at the hospital?"

He leaned against the door frame and folded his arms over his chest. "A friend had a sick kid a few months ago. I went to visit and I saw you getting off another elevator on the same floor." He shrugged, feeling faintly self-conscious. "I couldn't imagine what you were doing there, so I asked a nurse. She told me."

She nodded. "That makes sense. I didn't understand how you'd know unless you'd followed me, but that's not really your style. You don't sneak around in the dark. You come out and say who and what you are."

Ouch. She might be paying him a compliment, but it stung like the lash of a whip. He *was* hiding in the dark—hiding who he really was. In the process, he was forcing her to question her beliefs. He had no right...and no choice.

She laced her fingers tightly together and continued to stare at him. "How did you know about the other thing? About the...wall?"

He wanted to go to her and hold her close. He wanted to promise he would always be there for her, protecting her from the world. Yet the person he most had to protect her from was himself.

"It's not difficult to see that you're holding yourself back from the world, Hannah. You want to belong, but you're afraid of being hurt. Everyone does it. I saw it in you because you're so strong in other ways. It's your only weak spot."

"I think you saw it because you were looking."

She had him there. He fought against flinching. "That, too."

"Do you really think I have a big heart?"

"Absolutely."

Maybe too big. He hoped she wasn't thinking of opening it to him. God help them both if she did.

She opened her mouth, then closed it. After drawing in a deep breath, she said, "Are you planning on spending the night with me?"

Pure honesty. She had ten times his courage. "I want to. It's your decision."

She stood up and pulled her shirt out of her jeans.

He was at her side in an instant. He lifted his hands and gently cupped her cheeks. "I don't deserve you. Whatever happens between us, please know that I care about you as much as I've ever cared about anyone. I don't want to hurt you."

Her gaze was steady. She nodded slightly. "But you will."

It was as inevitable as the tide. "I'm sorry," he whispered.

She pressed her mouth to his, perhaps to accept the apology, perhaps to silence him.

As they touched each other and began the life-changing

journey, she murmured his name and begged him to love her. He told himself she meant with his body, but in his heart he knew the truth. She meant true love, the kind that reached in and filled the soul.

She asked for the one thing he was too terrified to give.

Time was not her friend.

Hannah strode back and forth in the gatehouse living room and wished she could slow it or turn it back a few days. Her deal with Nick was nearly over and there was nothing she could do to change that.

She told herself she should be grateful. The sooner he was out of her life, the sooner she could get on with being over him. It was going to take a long time, so she needed to start the process as soon as possible.

She sank onto the sofa and covered her face with her hands. Whom was she kidding? She was never going to be over him. She loved him. Even though he broke the law. Even though their time together was a lie. The pain of not knowing what to do tore her apart, yet she couldn't turn her back on him.

She heard a car approach and raced to the window. It wasn't Nick. He'd gone out earlier with Louise. There was an old Victorian house for sale and she'd wanted him to see it. He'd agreed, keeping alive the fantasy that he and Hannah were married and that they might really have a chance at happiness together.

She frowned as her four half brothers got out of the car and approached the gatehouse. None of them looked happy. Her stomach tightened uncomfortably as she went to answer the front door.

"Hi," she said, staring at the four men.

They nodded and muttered greetings, then came in when she held open the door.

They filled the living room. Four tall, handsome, dark-haired men who looked unhappy and vaguely uncomfortable. The knot in her belly grew and she already knew what they wanted to talk to her about. Nick. Somehow, they'd learned the truth.

There wasn't seating for everyone in the living room. Jordan pulled in one of the kitchen chairs. Craig sat in the easy chair. Hannah settled in a corner of the sofa with Travis in the middle on her right and Kyle next to him. For the first time in her life, she felt physically insignificant.

It was like being in a strange kind of fun house and looking into one of those mirrors that distorts everything. They were dressed alike. Jeans, T-shirts, boots. Enough alike in looks to make everyone aware of their relationship. She knew she, too, was a Haynes, with the physical characteristics that went with the name. Someone seeing them together on the street would know she belonged to the family.

She tucked her feet under her and folded her hands on her lap.

"You know about Nick," she said quietly.

"We know about Nick," Kyle announced, then frowned. "What did you say?"

"Nothing. Go on."

"I went to check on your husband and he's no longer in the computer. Someone pulled his file." He sounded angry and he had a right to be.

Hannah didn't know what had happened and she wasn't sure she wanted to know.

Travis angled toward her. "I checked with a friend of a friend at Southport Beach Police Department. Nick isn't working with the police. He's a shady real-estate investor who's managed to avoid criminal charges through deals and high-priced lawyers."

"What's going on, Hannah?" Craig asked.

She looked at Jordan, waiting for him to pounce, too. Instead, he gave her a slight smile. "Whatever you have to say can't be worse than what we've imagined."

She nodded. "I know you're right. And everything you've said is true. All of it." She looked at Travis. "I probably should have told you the truth when you first mentioned all this to me."

Kyle frowned. "You *knew* about this?" he asked his brother. "You suspected something before I talked to you about it?"

"I overheard Nick and Hannah talking." Travis shrugged. "I figured it wasn't any of my business."

"But you still had Nick checked out," she said.

"I had to. He might be married to my sister."

Craig leaned forward. "Are you two married?"

Hannah wanted to run away. But there was nowhere to go. It was time to face the consequences of her actions. She sucked in a deep breath. "A few months ago, I got a letter from Louise. I'd thought about my birth mother, but I'd been afraid to try to find her. After all, if she'd given me up before, there was no reason to think she would want me now. You can imagine how thrilled I was to learn that she'd never forgotten me and wanted to be in touch. She said that she'd found me through a private investigator."

She went on to tell them about her separation from Shawn, how Louise assumed she was still married, and her own mistake in thinking Louise was a frail, dying woman. She told them about hiring Nick.

"I didn't set out to deceive anyone," she explained, "although, in telling the story, it certainly looks that way. I didn't want to disappoint my mother. I didn't think we'd have very much time together. I thought she'd be happier if she thought I was married. Later, when things were settled, I could tell her the truth. Then we arrived and everything got out of hand.''

There was a moment of silence.

"You're not married?'' Craig asked. He was obviously trying to control the tone and pitch of his voice. Cords tightened in his neck. "You never even dated him?''

She shook her head. "I knew him from the station. What with his criminal activities and associates, he spends a lot of time there. We'd spoken, but...''

She resisted the urge to bury her face in her hands. Telling the story like this made her see how stupid she'd been. She didn't know the first thing about Nick. He could have been a murderer. She'd blithely invited him into her private life. What on earth had she been thinking?

But she hadn't been thinking. She'd been reacting to a scary situation. At the time, being with Nick had been better than being alone. Now, nearly two weeks later, she thanked God for the quirk of fate that had brought them together.

Kyle jumped to his feet. "You and Nick are living here, together. And you're not married?''

His outrage made her smile.

"Fine. Think it's funny,'' he said, glowering. "When Sandy and I...'' He paced to one end of the living room and back. "Don't tell me you're *sleeping* together.'' He covered his ears. "Sex. I don't want to hear about it.''

Hannah felt color creep up her face. A few days ago, they hadn't been, but now they were. "It's not what you think.''

Travis stood up also. "My God, they *are*. That's it. I'm going to find Nick and beat the hell out of him. Nobody messes with my sister.''

"I'm with you,'' Craig said. "I can't believe this. It's an outrage.''

"Wait a minute," Hannah said. "What on earth are you talking about? I'm not some sixteen-year-old virgin. I'm a grown, *divorced* woman who has made choices. Choices, I might add, that are none of your business."

Travis glared at her. "Of course it's our business. You're our little sister."

She stood up. "Not so very little. I can take care of myself."

"Like you've done a good job so far? Coming up here, pretending to be married to that guy? Couldn't you have picked a cop at least?"

They stood toe-to-toe. Craig and Kyle hovered nearby, ready to jump in, but she wasn't sure if they were going to defend her or join in the attack.

She turned away first. "You don't understand."

"Then explain it," Craig said. "Or we'll get Nick to explain it. After we break his arms."

"That's mature," she muttered.

A sharp whistle filled the room. She glanced toward the sound and saw that Jordan was still in his chair.

"Now that I have your attention," he said, "let's try to be adults about this. Sit down."

Hannah resumed her seat because the alternative was running, and where was there to go?

When everyone was settled, Jordan looked at her. "I know we're coming on strong. It must be difficult for you. You were raised as an only child, but we've always had each other. What hurts one of us, hurts us all. You're our sister, Hannah. So the rule now includes you. We're here to fight your battles."

"I can fight my own battles."

"You can, but you don't have to anymore. That's the point." He glanced at his brothers, then returned his attention to her. "You know what we want. But beating up Nick isn't an option."

"Sure it is," Travis muttered.

Jordan silenced him with a glare, then turned back to her. "What do you want, Hannah?"

"I don't know. I..." Tears burned in her eyes. She blinked them away, but they spilled onto her cheeks. "I'm sorry. I can't help it. I love him."

She brushed her face and sniffed. "There. I've said it aloud. I know what he is. Probably better than you four. I've seen him at the station. I'm a cop. I can't believe any of this."

She turned to Travis. "Do you think I *like* what's happened? I picked him because there wasn't anyone else. I don't have a lot of friends. It's not that people don't like me. It's that I'm afraid to let them in. I worry about what they want and wonder how long they'll stick around. But Nick was there for me. When I needed him, he just came. He's been wonderful. Kind, gentle, sweet. He's an honorable man."

"He's a con artist," Craig said.

"I know. I know. If I could change it, I would. But I can't. Do you want me to stop loving him? I will. Just tell me how. There's no way it's going to work between us. Once he knows the truth is out, he'll leave and I'll probably never see him again. Or if I do—it won't matter. When we go back to Southport Beach, we'll be on opposite sides again. And I'll be alone again."

The tears flowed. She covered her face and tried to get back control.

Someone awkwardly patted her back. Weight shifted on the sofa and she was gathered into strong arms. She looked up and found Travis staring down at her.

"Don't cry," he said. "We'll make it work."

"How?"

He glanced around helplessly. "Guys?"

Kyle swallowed. "Well, if he's not in the computer anymore, he doesn't have a criminal record."

"He didn't have one before," Travis added.

"You're right," she said and wiped her face. "That's something."

"It's not that we don't like him," Craig said. "We do. Maybe we could show him the error of his ways."

"Yeah," Kyle said and grinned. "And if he doesn't agree, then we beat him up."

Despite everything, Hannah laughed. "Great plan." Her smile faded. "We can't make Nick change. He has to do it on his own. Why would he bother?"

"Because of you," Jordan said. "Because he doesn't want to lose you."

"I wish that were true. But it's not. He cares about me. He's been very sweet."

"There you are," Travis said.

She shook her head. "When I tell him you guys know the truth, he's going to leave and I'm going to let him." She patted Travis's arm and slid back. "I'm fine. Thanks for being concerned."

"He doesn't have to know just yet," Jordan said.

She frowned. "What are you talking about?"

"Louise's party is on Saturday, in three days. You two were going to leave Sunday morning. Why not stay with that original plan? We don't have to tell Nick what we know. You could do that on the drive home. It's a long ride with just the two of you trapped in the car together. If you told him how you feel about him, he might be persuaded to change his ways."

"Maybe." Although she had her doubts about the plan. She glanced at her brothers. They looked at her with matching expressions of hope and affection. She wouldn't share her concerns with them. Besides, if Nick didn't think his cover was blown, he would stay through the weekend. She would have three more days—and nights—with him.

"Then it's settled," Jordan said. He rose and crossed to the sofa, then took her hand. "If there's anything any of us can do, you let us know. We're happy to talk to Nick."

"Or beat him up," Craig added.

Kyle sighed. "Please tell me you're not sleeping together."

Hannah laughed, then carefully crossed her fingers and tucked her hand behind her back. "We're not."

Thursday evening, Nick slipped away from the group card game at Kyle's house and walked back to the gatehouse. Once there, he crossed to the phone in the living room and dialed a number.

"Rodriguez," the voice answered.

"It's Nick. Any news?"

"Hey, how's it going?"

Nick dropped onto the sofa and stretched out his legs. "I'm doing fine. Are the arrest warrants issued?"

"They were done this morning." Rodriguez laughed. "They had one for you, too, Nicky, but I took care of that. It seems unfair to ask you to go undercover for a year, then arrest you when it's all over."

"Gee, thanks."

"Everything is falling into place. Should be over by Saturday at the latest. But don't come back until you check with me. No one has been brought in."

"I know. I'm staying right here." He wanted to be here for Louise's party on Saturday. And he wanted to spend as much time as possible with Hannah.

"There was some computer activity on you," Rodriguez said. "Someone's been checking you out."

"I know." Hannah's brothers. "Don't worry about it."

"I didn't. I pulled the file. Just in case."

"Probably a good idea."

They talked business for a few more minutes, then hung up. Nick replaced the receiver and thought about Rodriguez's order that he continue to lay low. Nick had no plans to leave. He wouldn't mind a life sentence in Glenwood. What kind of crime would earn that as punishment?

He thought about the old Victorian house he and Louise had found a couple of days ago. It needed a lot of work. Remodeling, modernizing. The works. It would take the better part of a year if he did it himself. Of course, if he stayed, he would have help. All four Haynes brothers and Austin would be around offering advice and labor.

If it were real.

If it were real, he would ask Hannah to look for a job here. He would quit the Santa Barbara force and open the bed-and-breakfast with his mother-in-law. If it were real, he would start a college fund for the three kids he and Hannah would have. If it were real, he would love her forever.

He was going to love her forever anyway.

He reached for the light and clicked it off, then sat in the darkness. He loved her. He who had sworn never to love anyone. He who had promised never to risk getting hurt. He who, like Hannah, was terrified to trust, had fallen in love.

He didn't know when it had happened. He didn't understand the evolution of his emotions. He wasn't sure he was going to be very good at loving her, but there wasn't a choice. As long as he drew breath, she was part of his life.

In the back of his mind, a voice whispered he might turn

out to be just like his father. Nick silenced the voice. He would face his demons as they came. Until then, he would take his chances.

He stood up and walked to the door. When he looked outside, he could see the lights at Kyle's house and hear the sounds of conversation and laughter spilling from the open windows.

Envy filled him. He wanted what this family had. He wanted the love and security of belonging and he wanted it with Hannah. When all this was over, he was going to find a way to make it all come true. For both of them.

Chapter Fifteen

The sound of music and laughter filled Jordan's house. Bunches of balloons bounced in the corners and streamers crisscrossed the ceiling. The usual crowd of adults had been supplemented by a dozen or so children ranging from toddlers to teenagers.

Nick stood by the entrance to the kitchen and watched. Nearly two weeks ago, he'd decided to stay longer than the weekend originally planned so he could help Hannah fit in with her family. He thought he was doing her a favor. Little did he realize he would be the one to receive the gift of belonging. These people had welcomed them both with open arms.

Louise moved toward him. As the birthday girl, she was required to wear a gold cardboard crown on her head. She touched it as she approached. "I always wanted to enter one of those beauty pageants," she said and grinned. "I feel like I just won."

Nick bent down and kissed her cheek. "You did win. You're the most beautiful woman here. Except for Hannah, of course."

She slapped his arm. "Smooth talker. I'm in the mood to believe you. At least for tonight."

Richard walked over and shook hands with him. "None of that, Nick. No one is allowed to kiss Louise without my permission."

"Are you boys going to fight over me?"

Richard put his arm around her shoulders. "I would give my life for you."

Louise stared at him. Her smile faded and she touched his cheek. "That's the most wonderful thing anyone has ever said to me."

He pulled her close.

Nick left them alone and walked around the edge of the room. Family members stood talking in groups. He spotted Hannah talking with her brothers. As he got closer, he heard Travis mention stock shares.

"It's not right," Hannah said. "I don't want to take what belongs to you."

"We want to give it to you," Craig said. "We want to share our good fortune."

Hannah rolled her eyes. "Nick, explain it to them."

He put his hands on her shoulders. "Hannah is still afraid to completely belong. It's not her fault. Give her a little more time and she'll happily accept your generous gift."

"What?" She spun to face him and glared. "What are you saying?"

He might have exaggerated about Louise's being the second most beautiful woman in the room, but he'd been right about Hannah's being the first. She was lovely.

She'd spent part of the afternoon locked in the bathroom, grumbling about the pain of trying to look attractive. He'd caught a glimpse of her in hot curlers. The results were amazing. Shiny, thick curls tumbled down her back. Subtle makeup accentuated her eyes and mouth. She wore a little black dress that clung to her generous shape, emphasizing breasts and hips. They'd made love less than four hours before, but he wanted her as much as he ever had.

"I'm telling them the truth," he said and brought her hand to his mouth. He kissed her palm. "They love you. Trust them."

Those were the words he spoke. What he thought was *Love me and trust me as much as I love and trust you.* He wanted to tell her the truth. He'd nearly done it a hundred times in the past couple of days. Yet the moment had never seemed right.

After the party, he'd decided. When they were alone in bed, he would confess that he'd fallen in love with her. He would ask her to give him a little time, probably no more than a week. By then the arrests would be made and he could tell her who he really was. He would tell her he wanted to be with her always. Somehow they would find a way to make it work.

She covered his hand with hers and squeezed. "Oh, Nick. If you knew what you do to me."

"I have an idea."

"Yeah? I doubt you're even close."

They smiled at each other, then he remembered her brothers. When he glanced up, the Haynes brothers had left them alone, much as he had left Richard and Louise.

"It must be contagious," he said.

"What?" she asked.

"It's not important." He wrapped a curl around his finger. "Did I tell you how great you look?"

She glanced down. "Thanks. It's the dress, really. I'm usually in pants."

"It's not the dress. It's you."

Her dark eyes widened. "Thank you." Fire flared in their warm depths. Fire and need. He thought briefly about taking her back to the gatehouse and making love to her, then reminded himself the party would only last a few more hours. He could wait.

A couple of kids ran between them. Hannah laughed and stepped away. Before he could get close again, Elizabeth claimed her. He was about to follow when Holly touched him on the arm.

"You have a phone call," she said. "One of your business associates. He says it's important."

Nick's gut tightened. Was it Rodriguez? Had something happened? He prayed silently that the something was good news. Maybe the case had been wrapped up and he could confess everything to Hannah that night. He walked into the kitchen and picked up the receiver.

"Archer here."

"Ah, Nick. So this is where you've been hiding."

Every nerve went on alert. The sixth sense that had kept him alive this long now warned him that he was in serious danger. "Thompson. I told you I was going to take a few days off. Is there a problem?"

Thompson swore loudly. "No problem, you son of a bitch. How much did you tell them?"

"What are you talking about?"

"Don't play dumb with me. You think I'm stupid? You think I planned to play second banana to you all my life? I'm goin' somewhere. I'm gonna get rich and screw the rest of you."

Despite his pounding heart, Nick spoke calmly. "Everyone needs a goal."

"I've got a man on the inside," Thompson growled. "A

dirty cop. He told me about the arrest warrants. There wasn't one for you, Nick. Why? What did you tell them?"

Nick swore under his breath. At least Thompson didn't know he was an undercover cop. Except for the captain, no one at the station knew about that. He had a fighting chance.

"What's your point?"

"You sold us out. That means you took the money. Where is it, Nick? Where'd you put it?"

The money Thompson referred to was about seven million dollars, stolen in phony land deals. At this moment, it was tagged as evidence.

"You're gonna tell me," Thompson threatened. "I'm giving you a choice because I'm such a nice guy. You can meet me where I say, or I can come to the house and break up that great party you got goin'. It would be a shame if innocent people had to get hurt."

Nick thought fast. He didn't have a choice. Thompson wouldn't object to killing anyone who got in the way.

He grabbed a pencil from the counter next to the phone. A small message pad had been attached to the wall. "Tell me where," he said.

Thompson laughed. "I knew you'd see it my way." He gave an address. "Take the main highway south, out of town. There's a small industrial complex on the left. We'll be waiting there. If you take too long, we'll come and get you."

"I'll be there."

"I won't insult you by telling you to come alone."

"Thanks." His mind raced. He had a bad feeling about this. "How'd you find me?"

"My friend at the station saw some computer activity. He traced it back to the Glenwood sheriff's office. Have you been a bad boy, Nick?"

Nick leaned against the wall. Travis's investigation. Maybe there'd been more than one.

"You've got fifteen minutes," Thompson warned. "Then we come after you."

Nick hung up the phone. There wasn't much time.

He grabbed the top sheet off the pad, then headed for the living room. Hannah was still talking to Elizabeth. He excused himself, then pulled her toward the front door.

"What's going on?" she asked. "Something's happened? What?"

"I can't—" He swore. There wasn't any time.

He opened the door and shoved her onto the porch. Before she could protest, he kissed her hard, drawing her close and trying to store a lifetime's worth of memories in that single embrace. Then he broke the kiss.

"I love you," he said, holding on to her arms to keep her from moving. "Probably since the first day I saw you, although I just admitted it to myself a few days ago. I've never been in love before, so I didn't recognize the signs." She stared at him. When she was about to speak, he touched her mouth. "Let me," he said. "I want you to know that you're beautiful, funny, loyal and the best person I've ever known. I'll love you forever. Whatever happens, remember that."

"Nick?"

He released her and started down the stairs.

"You're leaving?" She stood looking at him. "Where are you going?"

He didn't answer. The Mercedes started easily. He would convince Thompson and the other men that the money was still in Southport Beach. Once they got there, well, he'd cross that bridge when he came to it. His priority was to get the danger as far from Hannah and her family as possible.

Hannah stared after him in disbelief. What was going on? First he said he loved her and now he was leaving? The sound of the car engine faded and she was left with nothing.

He loved her? He'd said he loved her. And then he'd left.

"Hannah?" She turned. Holly leaned out the front door. "There's a call for Nick. Jordan said the two of you came out here. Where is he?"

"He's gone." She couldn't believe the words even as she said them. Gone? It wasn't possible. Something was wrong. She felt it in her heart.

Holly frowned. "Do you want to talk to Captain Rodriguez? Isn't he your captain at the station? He's the one asking for Nick this time."

Hannah's instincts kicked in. "This time?"

Holly nodded. "Nick got another phone call just a couple of minutes ago. One of his business associates. He said it was important."

Hannah raced into the house. She paused.

"The kitchen," Holly yelled after her.

Several of the adults turned to stare. Hannah ignored them. She ran into the kitchen and picked up the receiver. "Captain? It's Hannah Pace."

"I must speak to Nick, Hannah. It's urgent."

"He's not here. He got a phone call and left. What's going on?"

Rodriguez swore. "They got to him first."

She broke out in a cold sweat. "Who got to him? Captain, you have to tell me."

"Nick is in danger. Listen to me, Hannah. Nick Archer is an undercover police officer working on a sting operation."

"What?" She couldn't have heard him correctly.

"I don't have time to explain," Rodriguez said quickly. "We were about to arrest everyone. One of my officers here was caught giving out information. Nick's associates know something is up and he's in trouble. You have to contact the local police there. Can you do that?"

She glanced up and saw her brothers standing in the kitchen. Three cops, including the sheriff of Glenwood. "Yes, that's the easy part. Now we have to find Nick."

"They're in the area. I know that much."

"We'll do our best," she said, then hung up.

She turned to Travis. "Nick's in danger. He's an undercover cop. Someone in the Southport Beach station told his associates he was staying here. They've come for him. We have to find him."

Even as she spoke the words, she didn't believe them. A cop? Too many emotions bubbled inside for her to identify any of them. First they had to get him back alive.

"Where would you meet someone if you wanted to kill him?" Travis asked, taking charge.

Hannah's blood ran cold. They were talking about Nick.

"Out of town," Craig said.

"Not too far," Kyle added. "Somewhere that didn't have a lot of people around but easy to find so Nick wouldn't get lost."

"It's Saturday night. What's deserted?" Travis asked.

Hannah turned her back on them and clutched her midsection. Please, God, don't let him die. She stared at the wall in front of her. The notepad was blank. She moved closer. There were faint indentations on it.

"I've got it," she said and jerked the pad from the wall. "He wrote down an address." She held the pad to the light. "I can't make it out."

Travis took it from her. "Two seven three one. The street name is a blur."

Jordan reached for the pencil on the counter. "Don't you cops watch television?" He grabbed the pad and rubbed it lightly with the pencil. The address popped out, thin, pale writing on a background of gray.

"The industrial complex," Travis said. "Let's go."

The five of them ran for the front door. Travis's sheriff's car was parked in the circular driveway. They piled in and Travis started the siren. The family spilled out of the house, but he ignored them. As they were leaving, Elizabeth yelled something about the radio.

Seconds later, Hannah heard Elizabeth's voice on the car radio. Travis quickly filled her in. Then he made a call to the station for backup.

In less than ten minutes, they were near the industrial complex. Travis switched off the siren and entered the first parking lot. "It's down here," he said, pointing to a side street. "The address is at the end. Let's go around and approach from the rear."

Hannah glanced down at her dress and high heels. Figures. The one day she dressed up, she would have to go in shooting.

Her mind had shut down and she preferred it that way. She was a communications officer and she didn't have street experience, but she'd been through the academy and knew enough to be afraid. She refused to think about Nick's being in danger. If she did, she would lose control and be of no use to anyone. Least of all him.

Travis killed the engine about a hundred yards from the last building. They coasted to a stop, then got out and headed around to the trunk. Travis opened it and passed them bulletproof vests. Travis and Craig had pulled out shotguns from the front. There were two more in the trunk, along with a couple of handguns. Hannah reached for a shotgun.

Travis looked at her.

She grimaced. "I know how to use it."

He nodded. "Ready?" he asked, then started for the building.

Hannah felt as if she had a bit part in a Clint Eastwood movie. They walked in a line, moving quickly but quietly. There were no windows in the rear of the building, so they couldn't be seen. As they approached the corner of the industrial structure, Travis went first, then motioned them around. She saw two cars parked in front. One of them was Nick's Mercedes.

Her heart thundered in her chest. Her mouth was dry and her legs trembled. Still, she forced herself to go on. She refused to stay behind and wait. Thank goodness she hadn't had to fight her brothers on that.

The glass door was closed but not locked. Once inside, they heard voices coming from the back. Travis led the way, motioning for them to stay well behind and go single file. Hannah was second to last; Craig brought up the rear.

The offices in front were empty and dark. Light spilled into a corridor leading to the warehouse. As they got closer, the voices became distinct.

"I'll tell you when we get back to Southport Beach," Nick said.

"You'll tell me now." The order was followed by a *crack.*

Hannah bit her lower lip to keep from screaming. The voices lowered, then there was another *crack* and a low moan.

Travis paused at the mouth of the corridor. The warehouse lights were on. Boxes of office supplies stretched up to the ceiling in disorganized rows. The area in front was clear. Hannah could see someone's back.

Travis inched closer and looked around the corner. He

ducked back, motioned for them to get ready to jump out, then lunged into the main warehouse.

"Freeze," he yelled. "You're under arrest."

Three armed men spun toward them. Hannah barely noticed as she searched for, then found Nick. He'd been tied to a chair. His face and torso were battered. Blood trickled from the corner of his mouth. His eyes were so swollen, he could barely get them open.

"What the hell," he said, the words thick. "Someone sent the cavalry."

The tallest of the men, maybe five-ten with broad football shoulders, grimaced. "Who the hell are you?"

"Glenwood Sheriff's Department, gentlemen. Put down your guns and kneel on the floor, hands behind your head."

The three men glanced at each other. Hannah tore her attention from Nick and raised the shotgun. "Please try to run," she said, so angry she was shaking. "One of you run. I want nothing better than to blow off your damn head."

One of the men took a step back. "Who the hell is she?"

"My wife," Nick said.

They stared at her. In the distance, they heard the sound of police sirens. Three pistols hit the concrete floor of the warehouse. The trio dropped to their knees and placed their hands behind their heads. Only when they were safely cuffed did Hannah lower her shotgun. She handed it to Jordan, then ran sobbing to Nick.

"You two going to be all right?" Louise asked. "I could stay."

Hannah liked the idea of someone acting as a buffer between her and Nick, but doubted he would agree. She walked her mother to the door of the gatehouse. "We'll be fine. The doctor at the hospital said he has some bruises, but nothing was broken. It's just going to take a few days for him to heal.'' They hugged, then Louise started toward Kyle's house.

Hannah closed the door behind her. The gatehouse was small. There was nowhere to go. Nowhere to hide. She simply had to turn around and face Nick.

She forced herself to smile and cleared her throat. ''That's the last of them,'' she said cheerfully. ''Now you can get some rest.'' She started for the bedroom. ''You'll probably be uncomfortable during the night. I'll let you have the bed and I'll sleep on the sofa.''

''Hannah, wait.''

His words were difficult to understand. She paused in the doorway, then returned to the living room and sat on the edge of the easy chair. Not wanting to look, yet knowing there was no way to avoid it, she raised her gaze to the sofa and the battered man lying there.

His eyes were puffy slits, his cheeks a mass of bruises. His bottom lip was split and there was a cut at the corner of his mouth. He dropped the ice bag onto the coffee table.

''We have to talk,'' he said and tried to straighten.

She was at his side in a second. ''Don't sit up.''

''I can't see you if I don't.''

She sank onto the edge of the sofa and pressed against his hip. ''Is this better?''

''Yeah.'' He touched her knee. She hadn't changed out of her dress yet. The black stockings offered little protection. It felt as if he were touching bare skin. Heat skittered through her. She ignored it.

''You're angry,'' he said.

''No. I'm confused.''

His gaze locked with hers. ''Because I'm a cop?''

The information hadn't sunk in yet. The whole evening felt like a strange dream. She was starting to come out of it and feel again. The first emotion she experienced was anger.

"I can't believe it," she said, throwing up her hands. "Dammit, Nick. A cop? Do you know how I agonized over you? I worried about what to tell my family. My brothers found out everything. I felt awful about that. I can't believe all the lies, all the pain. For nothing." She threw her hands in the air again. "My God, you must have had a great laugh at my expense. Did you like watching me squirm? Did it make you feel like a man? Nick, you nearly destroyed me. I was torn apart because I thought you were a crook. You made me go against everything I believe in. How could you do that?"

She fought against the urge to spring up and start pacing around the room. But she knew that he would try to sit up, and however much she hated him right now, she didn't want him to be in more pain because of her.

She sucked in a breath. "You made me betray my family."

He squeezed her fingers. "No, Hannah. You did that all by yourself. You did it when you decided to hire yourself a husband for a few days. I just came along for the ride."

She turned away. Her throat tightened. "I know," she whispered. "Everything started out so well. But it was all built on a lie. I suppose that's what makes it so difficult. I never meant to..."

She couldn't finish the sentence. She'd never meant to hurt anyone. She'd never meant to fall in love.

"I wasn't lying," he said.

She didn't have the courage to look at him. Instead, she stared at their joined fingers. "About what?"

"About loving you. I love you, Hannah. I'm probably not very good at it. This is my first time. But if you'll be patient with me, I promise to make it worth your while."

Love. She wanted to believe him. She wanted to think it was going to work out, but her life had never been that easy.

"I know what you're thinking," he said.

She glanced at him. "What?"

Despite the bruises and the swelling, his eyes twinkled. "You're afraid. You think I'm playing a game, or that I'm going to reject you like everyone else you've ever cared about. You've been lonely for so long, you've forgotten how to belong. You've closed yourself off from the world. I know because I did the same thing."

She looked doubtful. "That's hard to believe. You seem to find it easy to charm everyone you meet."

"On the surface, maybe. But no one gets inside. No one sees the real Nick Anderson."

"Anderson? Is that your last name?"

He nodded. "Nicholas Edward Anderson. Sounds like an accounting firm, huh?" He didn't wait for a reply. "Your family taught me a lot. I've seen how they care about each other and that's made me want to try again. Your brothers have shown me that with the right person at your side, anything is possible." The hold on her fingers tightened. "I love you, Hannah. I want to make this marriage real and I want to spend the rest of my life waking up next to you."

Her lips parted, but she couldn't think of a single thing to say. He didn't mean it. He couldn't. If Nick really loved her, *really* loved her, she was going to have to admit to loving him back. She was going to have to take a leap of faith and commit to him. She was going to have to risk feeling the fear. She was going to have to trust.

She stared at him, at his blond hair and blue eyes. Memories flashed through her mind. Teasing conversations at her desk when she was at the station. How he'd helped her fit in with her family. His smile, his touch, how he'd taken the time to tell her he loved her even thinking he might be going to his death.

"I love you," she said and swooped down to kiss him. At the last second, she remembered his injuries and barely brushed his lips with hers. "I refuse to let you go. I know you live in Santa Barbara, but we'll make it work."

He tucked her hair behind her ear and cupped her cheek. "I'm not going back there. I'm done with police work. I want to try something different."

"Like what?"

He started to smile, then grimaced and touched the corner of his mouth. "I'm not sure. I'll find something. So are you going to marry me or what?"

She kissed his palm. "I want a small wedding. Just family."

"Just family isn't a small wedding. Was that a yes?"

Pure joy filled her. "Yes. Always yes, Nick. I'll never say no to you again."

He raised one eyebrow. "That sounds like a good deal. Gives a man ideas."

She snuggled up to him. "Cheap talk for a man in your condition."

"I might surprise you."

"You already did. In the most wonderful way possible."

Epilogue

Two years later

Hannah turned the car into the long circular driveway in front of the Victorian house she and Nick were restoring.

"How are you feeling?" Travis asked for the fourth time that day.

She glared at him. "I'm fine. I've been fine. I'm going to be fine. It's just a baby, Travis." She stopped behind Kyle and Sandy's new minivan and turned off the engine.

Travis leaned over and kissed her cheek. "I know, but you're my sister and I worry about you."

"I handle communications. It's not as if I'm out on the streets catching criminals."

Travis winked. "No, you do that at home."

They got out of the car and headed for the house. Nick stood at the open front door, one-year-old Laura in his arms.

Hannah kissed him, then took her daughter. "How's my best girl? Are you excited about your party?"

Nick shook hands with Travis, then looped his arm around his wife. "I don't think she really understands what all the fuss is, but she's very excited about the birthday cake."

They walked inside. The sound of conversation and laughter filled the house. Most of the family was already there. Louise came over and touched her arm. "Hi, sweetie. How are you feeling?"

Hannah sighed. Telling everyone about her second pregnancy had obviously been a mistake. "I'm fine. Really."

Travis grinned. "Hey, I could have told you that. She's just pregnant, Louise. It's not some strange disease no one has ever heard of." He tickled little Laura and made her squeal. "It's not as if she hasn't done it before, either."

"I know, but I worry." Louise held out her arms and took the baby. "I'll take my granddaughter while you get changed."

"Thanks, Mom," Hannah said.

Nick followed Hannah up the stairs. "I'll come along to see if you need any help."

"More likely to watch," she flung over her shoulder.

He fondly swatted her behind. "That, too."

Once in their bedroom, she stripped off her khaki uniform and walked toward the closet. "How was your day?"

Nick sat on the edge of the bed. "Word is getting out. We're booked solid from Memorial Day through the middle of August."

"Great." She slipped on a loose cotton dress. Four months pregnant, she was starting to have trouble with her fitted clothes. The elastic waists would last another five or six weeks and then she was going to be back in maternity clothes.

She stepped into the bedroom. Nick smiled at her. Even after two years together, she was constantly surprised by how handsome he was. His blond good looks were a contrast to the dark-haired men in her family.

His gaze met hers. The love shining in his eyes warmed her to her toes. Two and a half years ago, if someone had told her how her life was going to turn out, she would have thought that person was crazy. She'd never expected to find a loving husband and a family. Yet here they were.

She walked to the bed and slipped onto his lap. "I love you, Nick."

He smoothed her long hair. "I love you more."

She kissed his nose. "Good. I like it that way."

They laughed as they started down the stairs.

"Oh, I forgot to tell you," he said. "Your mother is thinking of keeping the restaurant open for lunch now."

Nick and Louise had bought the Victorian house they'd admired two years ago, remodeled it and opened an inn. It had been successful from the beginning. Nick joked that the visiting in-laws were enough to keep it nearly fifty percent full all the time. Louise's restaurant was an integral part of the business. She offered breakfast and high tea.

"I think she would do well serving lunch. If it isn't too much for her."

He placed his hand on the small of her back. "She loves the work."

At the bottom of the stairs, they turned toward the living room. The entire family had turned out for Laura's first birthday party. Hannah took in the scene before her. Austin and Rebecca had their three boys nearby. Jill and Craig were with their three boys and two-year-old daughter. Travis held Elizabeth close. Mandy, their oldest, played with her younger sister. Holly and Jordan cuddled their eighteen-month-old, while Richard, Louise's husband, cradled Holly's newborn. Louise held Laura.

The little girl glanced up. "Mama!"

Hannah took her and held her. Nick settled his arm over Hannah's shoulders, completing the circle.

Hannah looked around the room, at this warm, wonderful Haynes family that had taken them in and made them their own. Together, they'd forged a miracle. A legacy of love strong enough to last through time.

* * * * *

IN CELEBRATION OF MOTHER'S DAY, JOIN
SILHOUETTE THIS MAY AS WE BRING YOU

a funny thing
HAPPENED ON THE WAY TO THE
Delivery Room

THESE THREE STORIES, CELEBRATING THE
LIGHTER SIDE OF MOTHERHOOD, ARE
WRITTEN BY YOUR FAVORITE AUTHORS:

KASEY MICHAELS
KATHLEEN EAGLE
EMILIE RICHARDS

When three couples make the trip to the delivery
room, they get more than their own bundles of
joy…they get the promise of love!

Available this May,
wherever Silhouette books are sold.

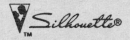

Silhouette®

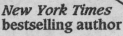

And the Winner Is...
You!

...when you pick up these great titles
from our new promotion at your
favorite retail outlet this June!

Diana Palmer
The Case of the Mesmerizing Boss

Betty Neels
The Convenient Wife

Annette Broadrick
Irresistible

Emma Darcy
A Wedding to Remember

Rachel Lee
Lost Warriors

Marie Ferrarella
Father Goose

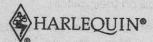 

This summer, the legend
continues in Jacobsville

*Diana
Palmer*

A LONG, TALL
TEXAN SUMMER

Three **BRAND-NEW** short stories

This summer, Silhouette brings readers a special
collection for Diana Palmer's LONG, TALL TEXANS
fans. Diana has rounded up three **BRAND-NEW**
stories of love Texas-style, all set in Jacobsville,
Texas. Featuring the men you've grown to love from
this wonderful town, this collection is a must-have
for all fans!

*They grow 'em tall in the saddle in Texas—and
they've got love and marriage on their minds!*

Don't miss this collection of original Long, Tall Texans
stories...available in June at your favorite retail outlet.

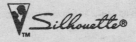